REVOLT
IN
APRIL

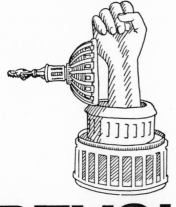

REVOLT IN APRIL

by Charles Mercer

The World Publishing Company
New York and Cleveland

Published by The World Publishing Company
Published simultaneously in Canada
by Nelson, Foster & Scott Ltd.
First printing—1971
Copyright © 1971 by Charles Mercer
All rights reserved
Library of Congress catalog card number: 78–142137
Printed in the United States of America

WORLD PUBLISHING
TIMES MIRROR

To Alma

as always

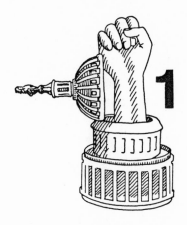

The legend of Joe McCurdy began with a very popular ballad that included these lines: "Joe McCurdy steps up and asks, Why give money to the Gov'ment? It don't know what money's for. Except to start another war. And then come back at you for more. So why give money to the Gov'ment?"

The fact it was largely stolen from Sir Alan Patrick Herbert went unnoticed, ballad-writing being a piratical profession. The important thing was that Joe McCurdy had been created. Next, his personality was shaped by stand-up comedians, to whom piracy is not unknown.

"After McCurdy got his doctor's bill he said that health is a blessing money cannot buy" (Izaak Walton). "McCurdy says the American people and President Porter have come to a mutual agreement on taxes. They are to complain all they want to about high taxes, and he is to tax them as much as he pleases" (Benjamin Franklin, who used a thought of Frederick the Great).

Many of the remarks attributed to McCurdy were not

especially witty, but they were timely. For all were concerned with the declining purchase power of the dollar and the growing belief that the government was powerless to do anything about it.

McCurdy sayings, like dirty jokes, thrived without benefit of publicity in the national press. They were exchanged in the everyday world of bars, bowling alleys, barber shops, beauty parlors, taxis, factories, offices, living rooms. Presumably the remarks flourished because they dealt with a basic human instinct: while dirty jokes were concerned with sex, McCurdy sayings involved that other powerful instinct —money.

In the days before matters took a turn for the worse, President William Paisley Porter himself acknowledged the legend of Joe McCurdy. Asked a difficult question about the federal budget at a White House news conference, the President replied, "You'd better ask Joe McCurdy about that." Then he laughed.

As a result of the President's remark, McCurdy's name was mentioned in news columns for the first time. The New York *Times* stated parenthetically in a report on the news conference: "For some time persons disturbed by taxation and inflation have attributed to a Joe McCurdy remarks critical of the government's taxation and anti-inflation programs. There is no indication that such a person exists."

Newsmen never have been content to let well enough alone. When they hear a voice, they must identify the speaker. A humorless hunger for fact was loosed upon the myth of Joe McCurdy. If the newsmen had left the subject of McCurdy alone, presumably he would have enjoyed a brief popularity and been forgotten. But an enterprising reporter for the *Long Island Press* located him in Canarsie and reported their interview in a front-page story. It seemed plausible that McCurdy should come from Canarsie, a community of numerous middle income families who were suffering grievously from the dollar squeeze. After the gentleman sobered up, however, he confessed he was not *the* Joseph McCurdy in question.

The hunt for Joe McCurdy became a journalistic pastime during that dreary winter. In every state of the union, newsmen who long ago had given up chasing flying saucers went after him in full cry. Though they expended columns of type on him, they never pinned him down. Then, near the end of March, *Time* magazine placed his imagined likeness on its cover as representing the theme of its lead story. While it dismissed McCurdy as a legend, it heard his voice as the loudest in the land. At the close of the article *Time* reported a recent remark in a St. Louis bar: "McCurdy says you can't drink beer from an empty glass. He says he's not going to jail. He's going to Washington."

Thus Joe McCurdy came to the White House on a bright Monday morning in April.

There was a strained air at the weekly staff planning conference. President Porter, who set the mood of those meetings, was unsmiling, preoccupied. Everyone realized something was wrong, but no one except Jonathan Hochstein knew what it was.

Hochstein arrived promptly, helped himself to a cup of coffee from the urn in a corner, and took his place at the long table. He felt all of his fifty-two years that morning, for he had slept less than four hours. Around eleven o'clock the previous evening a White House messenger had delivered to his Georgetown home a voluminous report which he had studied until three.

The planning of the Presidential schedule for the

coming week and the channeling of responsibilities were not enlivened by the usual wisecracks. Golden opportunities for irreverencies were passed up, as when the time scheduled for the President to greet the Mother of the Year and her six children was shifted so that he could meet with the spokesman for a birth control program in underdeveloped nations.

At five minutes to nine the President rose and said, "Jack, can you tear yourself away from the rest of the business? I want to see you." The staff members watched in uneasy silence as Hochstein followed him out.

When the two entered the reception room adjoining the Oval Office, President Porter finally spoke. "It's bound to leak."

Hochstein thought so too, but he said, "Let's hope not."

Senator Harold Garamond got to his feet when they appeared, and President Porter did a hesitant side-step that indicated he wished he could skip his appointment with the Senator just then. But he greeted him affably: "Harold, how are you? Come on in. Mind if Jack Hochstein joins us?"

The President's wife Alice, who had planned the redecoration of the spacious Oval Office, had made it seem bright and airy with pastel drapes, fresh flowers, and a collection of ceramic Boehm birds that gave an impression of sunlight even on the dreariest day. But there were strong reminders that President Porter was simply a tenant of the office and would never own it. The likenesses of fifteen eagles, from carpet to flag standards to ceiling, surveyed him indifferently. And above the mantel the true owner, Father George himself as rendered by Gilbert Stuart, gazed with grave, tight-lipped candor at the tenant, seeming to have just spoken his small Latin: *O tempora! O mores!* These and thou, too, shall pass.

When President Porter had sat down at the desk, Senator Garamond said, "Bill—Mr. President—I appreciate your fitting me in so quickly. But it is a serious emergency. I didn't get wind of the thing until Saturday, and——"

"Wind of what thing?" asked the President.

"I assume you know about it by this time. Bill, we've got a full-fledged tax revolt on our hands."

The President glanced at Hochstein. "I know. Where did you hear about it, Harold?"

"My legislative assistant picked it up from an assistant in Treasury. A pretty full rundown."

President Porter said to Hochstein, "So it will leak any hour now, and once it's public knowledge it will spread. Yes, Harold, the Secretary of the Treasury brought me the Internal Revenue report yesterday afternoon."

"In person?"

"In person." The President made a wry face. "When I was having a pleasant weekend up on the mountain. I sent it to Jack last night."

Senator Garamond sighed. "Bill, you know the bad slide we took in the last two Gallup Polls." He was being courteous; the President rather than the Party had taken the slide.

For longer than the President cared to remember— far back to the days when a younger William Porter and his wife Alice had been caught by a friendly photographer at Key West and now were framed beside a bold, porcelain eagle on the table behind his desk—the pollsters had been predicting his political demise. Yet it was William Paisley Porter who now sat in the Oval Office as President of the United States.

"I've been thinking about your problem," Senator Garamond continued. "The convention comes in August and——"

"There's a problem about my nomination for a second term?"

"Of course not, Bill. I'm thinking about your re-election. It looks certain now that Blake King will be running against you. I think, by the way, he learned about the tax revolt around the same time I did. I understand he's asking for floor time for a speech tomorrow. I have a hunch it will be about the revolt. And I'll bet he says that maybe these people who refuse to pay their taxes have a point. He's going to be a hero to an awful lot of folks."

The President said, "If Senator King says that on the floor of the Senate I would say he runs strangely. He would, in effect, be endorsing a mass violation of the laws of the United States. And I would hope that you, Harold, or some other friend of the Administration would point that out in a reply from the floor. We have done all we can to bring about tax reform."

"But the sad fact is," Senator Garamond replied, "nobody really gives a damn about tax reform. All they want is tax relief. Bill, you've run against plenty of heroes."

The Senator hesitated, for it was a touchy subject with William Porter. Many years previously he had barely made his way into the Senate after a bruising campaign in his midwestern state against a very popular opponent. Fewer years previously he had been defeated for the highest office by another hero type who had become a martyr following his assassination.

"And of course, Bill, you've run *with* a hero."

Again the Senator hesitated. Many wondered how much William Porter had enjoyed serving as Vice-President under a great war hero for two terms in what now seemed to have been the long ago. In fact, Porter's enemies, who were legion, had liked to point out, during his most recent race for the Presidency, that he had been a political bust for years except when riding the coattails of the great war hero.

"Bill, you have always run on your record."

"Yes, I have. And I will be in November's elections."

Senator Garamond leaned forward. "That's why I came to see you today. This revolt is composed of what Thomas Jefferson called the common man, the man Andrew Jackson called the bone and sinew of the country, the man you have called the silent majority and have done everything possible to help, the——"

"Excuse me, Senator." Hochstein leaned forward too. "The confidential report to us from Internal Revenue does not indicate that is wholly true. On the basis of the samplings that are possible at this time it appears that the tax-dodgers cut across all income levels."

Senator Garamond, who did not like to be interrupted in mid-rhetoric, frowned at Hochstein. "Then my point is all the more valid." He turned to the President. "Bill, it would be completely typical of your record if you went after these people with tooth and nail. On the other hand, it would be typical of a hero President to show leniency, to say in effect to these misguided souls, 'I see what you mean, folks. Your sense of frustration has led you to it. But slow down. Let's see what we can work out.' It's what Franklin Roosevelt would have done. It's what Blake King is going to start doing. Bill, I want to make just this one point. The only way you can win election to a second term is if you run as a hero. . . ."

After President Porter finally had eased Senator Garamond out the door he turned to Hochstein and asked, "What do you think of his idea?"

"Bullshit," said Hochstein.

The President paced back to his desk. "Harold may

have a point. He's just about the smartest politician I know."

"But he's not the President of the United States," Hochstein replied.

Sitting down and tipping his fingers together, the President said, "I imagine King has already leaked the story."

"I wouldn't be surprised, Mr. President. Wouldn't it be wise at this early phase for an anonymous spokesman in Internal Revenue to deny it? Otherwise, a lot of people who made their April fifteenth tax payments are going to decide they can't make their June fifteenth payments. The old safety-in-numbers game. The smart guys—and it happens that Senator Garamond's blood-and-sinews middle income group are not the smart guys—realize Internal Revenue simply is not equipped to handle the cases. As you know, they'll probably total over three hundred thousand."

President Porter felt his jaw, as if he had been slugged, while Hochstein waited vainly for the answer to his question.

At last Hochstein tried again: "I suppose most people will now start talking about that damn tax reform bill. It's probably what Blake will beat his gums about. But the so-called tax reform has been enacted and now is history. And I don't think that's at the heart of the present problem."

He waited for the President to ask him what he believed was at the heart of the problem. But President Porter simply gazed at President Washington, who possibly tightened his lips a bit upon his painful false teeth and gazed back at President Porter.

Made vaguely uneasy by the President's silence, Hochstein thought about what he would say if invited to express an opinion.

Gambit one, if asked about strategy: incredible though

it sounds, there's a growing recession at the same time there is continued inflation. The stock market is sick unto death. These are the causes of the tax revolt. We have given top economic priority to fighting inflation by sharply restricting government spending while the Federal Reserve Board curbs the growth of credit. But it has not worked. As you know, Mr. President, I personally have believed inflation could be stopped only if we could persuade both business and consumers that prosperity is not necessarily perpetual and price rises not inevitable. But we have not been able to persuade people. I've wondered if recession might not be the price of curbing inflation. And now we have both! I think it time we switch from anti-inflation to anti-recession policies, first by calling on the Federal Reserve to ease up on money.

Gambit two, if asked about tactics: we must pull twenty or thirty tax-dodgers out of the computers and throw the book at 'em. We must publicize what we're doing as an example to everybody else. . . .

President Porter lowered his gaze from the reliable old federal eagle of the seal on the ceiling and spoke at last:

"We won't deny anything from here—the White House. Somebody in Treasury is bound to do that. Treasury always denies everything. We're going to be in trouble if we move too quickly. Get your guys together, Jack, and give me all the options."

"By this afternoon?"

"Too fast," the President said. "Tomorrow morning. I want time to review the options before the afternoon Cabinet meeting. I may ask you to attend with me."

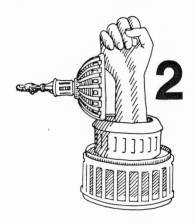

Later, when a magazine tried to recapitulate an "inside" account of the events that began to transpire in those April days, the story cut from the conference in the Oval Office to another part of the White House.

Meanwhile (the magazine reported), in the White House living quarters Alice Porter and her daughter Penny were being shown new evening gowns by the New York designer Antone Zinglinger. The report was not precisely accurate. At that hour Penny was taking a golfing lesson at the Burning Tree Club and Alice was talking on the telephone to her close friend Louise North.

"Then I'll pick you up about noon," she said, "and we'll go on to Helen's...."

A maid pushed a button which signaled the flawless functioning of a series of trivial events as the First Lady set out precisely on schedule, at five minutes before noon. Doors were opened and closed as she descended and stepped into warm sunlight which the burgeoning foliage diffused in mellow green. The limousine was waiting, and

Pete Harkness, her favorite agent, was holding the door open with a large hand.

"Good morning, Pete."

"Morning, Mrs. Porter." He bowed slightly. "This weather sure has brought the tourists out."

There were scores of them, straining at the iron bars along Pennsylvania Avenue. Penny had remarked that they always looked as if they were staring into the most fascinating zoo on earth.

"There she *is!*" A nasal voice from a border state came distinctly across the broad green lawn and the big central wheel of blood-red tulips.

The limousine encompassed Alice, insulating her from all but the loudest of noises, placing the world at a comfortable distance, leaving her without any sensations but those of stable temperature and motion. "A mobile sarcophagus" was Penny's description of a White House limousine.

The people in the crowd waved, smiled, made muted sounds, and Alice smiled and waved in reply.

Louise was waiting at the doorway of her Connecticut Avenue apartment house when the limousine pulled up and Pete swung out. As she came toward the car, Alice was struck by how much weight she had gained in recent months. It seemed incredible that long ago, in Greenleaf, Louise had been called the most beautiful girl in town. When she climbed into the limousine, she was actually panting.

"It's so hot," she said. "And only April!"

"But it's a lovely day," Alice replied.

"I called Helen after I talked to you," Louise said. "Fay will be there."

"Did you have any doubts about it?" Alice asked dryly.

Fay Stetson was one of those fringe people Helen had

picked up somewhere. To Alice's mind "fringe people" were those who had no connections with the federal government nor any definable vocation. She was a widow who lived in Georgetown and did not appear to have social ambitions. What mattered was that she was an excellent bridge player, good-natured and witty, who made the best fourth hand the three friends had yet found to join their frequent and enthusiastic games.

The driver took the Rock Creek Park route to Georgetown. Never had the city looked so beautiful. Drifts of white and yellow daffodils swept recklessly around pink flowering trees which consumed the sunlight in a fiery glow. They were approaching the Q Street Bridge when the limousine came close to an old jalopy in which two Negroes were riding. Plastered on its rear window were an American-flag decal and a sign which read:

ALL TAXES WE SPURN
ALL TAX FORMS WE BURN

"Look at that!" Alice exclaimed. "How awful!"

Soon they glided along a quiet street, turned into a close, and looked up at the walls and roofs of Helen's Camelot. Helen greeted them on the stone steps. Slender, with hair silvered, wearing bright green, she looked incredibly beautiful—incredibly because she once had seemed so plain.

"Fleet's in!" she cried while Pete Harkness grinned at her. "Pete, you want to case the joint for booby traps before we venture inside?"

Louise said, "Helen, that's downright macabre."

"I didn't think of it that way, Louise. But a guy from Sixteen hundred *did* case it this morning."

There were larger and more grandly appointed houses

in Washington than Helen's, but few more interesting. Its rooms were the despair of interior decorators, for they combined furnishings of many periods and places which had caught Helen's fancy. Yet the total effect gave one a sense of comfort, slight surprise, a variety of experience, like a stimulating conversation in an unexpected encounter. There were watercolors, charcoal sketches, and just one Matisse. There was the head of a moose which had been killed by a President of the United States in the long ago when Presidents fired rifles at wild animals. And on tables everywhere were signed photographs of Presidents and First Ladies, of Cabinet members, of the famous and forgotten who had enjoyed the hospitality of Helen's home. One, of a smiling Eleanor Roosevelt, was enscribed: "To Helen, who makes Washington still feel like home." On another, of a smiling Bill and Alice Porter, was written: "To Helen, with our deepest affection always."

Fay Stetson greeted them in the sun room. She was tall and well formed; her thin features and dyed hair guarded well the secret of her aging. Her voice had the husky timbre that often is a marination of gin and innumerable cigarettes. There was something about her—a manner of moving and speaking—that evoked a rather pleasing suggestion of sins gone but not forgotten. She ordered a dry martini straight up while the others chose whiskey sours.

Helen gave their orders to a maid, Janice Jones, who had worked for her for many years. After she had gone, Helen said, "Janice told me this morning she's leaving and going back to West Virginia. She's sick of Washington. And she says she didn't pay her income tax."

Alice stiffened and her tone was abrasive when she spoke: "Don't you withhold her taxes?"

"Of course. I'm a thorough employer. But she has

savings, and she decided not to pay the taxes on her interest. I guess she's put away enough. She says where she's going back in the hills Internal Revenue will never find her."

When Janice returned with their drinks, Alice, who had known her for a long time, said, "Janice, what's this I hear about your going to jail?"

Janice placed Alice's glass on a coaster, her expression serene. "I don't think I'll go to jail, Mrs. Porter. The jails can't hold *all* of us."

"But they'll hold *some* of you." Alice's tone had become abrasive again.

"But I mailed in my form. I just wrote on it I couldn't pay the amount I owed. That's not *evasion*."

"So now," Alice replied, "Internal Revenue will start adding percentages to the amount you owe."

"Let 'em, if you'll excuse me, Mrs. Porter." Janice was beginning to flush. "You can't get blood from a turnip." She finished serving them. "Mrs. Porter, I wish you wouldn't take this as something personal. I admire the President—and you. I voted for you."

"But how, Janice, is the government going to carry out its programs if people don't pay their taxes?"

Janice started to reply, but thought better of it. She began backing away, then fled.

Alice called after her, "How else can I take it but personally?"

"Impersonally, Alice." Helen's tone was sharp. "This is still the good old U. S. and A., the place where people can find the damnedest ways to express themselves."

"Nevertheless," Alice went on, "when you think what a wonderful country this is and all the freedom we have—"

"The other night," Helen cut in on her, "I was reading a translation of Juvenal's *Satires*, don't ask me why. And

I couldn't help but think what similarities there are between the Roman Empire as it began to decline and our country today. Old Juvenal has a lot of good lines. One, I remember, was about the government of Rome limiting the anxious longings of its people to two things only—bread, and spectator games."

"Now what does *that* mean?" Alice demanded.

"Maybe," said Fay, "it means we're becoming a nation of voyeurs. As my dear, departed Denton used to say, it never hurts to have a look."

On the previous occasions when they had played bridge, she had told some amusing stories about her dead husband, Denton Stetson—or, Dr. Denton as she liked to call him. Had she loved him or hated him?

"Mrs. Porter—" Though Alice had invited her to call her by first name, Fay insisted on addressing her as Mrs. Porter while calling the others Helen and Louise. She managed it graciously, however, giving the impression that she did it from respect. "Mrs. Porter, I don't think voyeurism presents much trouble to law and order. But I wish the government could try a little harder to curb violence here in the District. It's rough here on the Georgetown frontier. I guess it wasn't like this in the midwestern town all of you came from, Greenleaf."

"Scarcely," Helen said.

"A long time ago when I lived in Washington—before I married Denton—I knew a man from Greenleaf," Fay said. "He worked for your husband, Mrs. Porter. His name was Gene Schofield. Do you know whatever became of him?"

Helen's hand shook slightly as she put down her glass, and all looked at Fay curiously.

"We don't know," Alice said. "We only know it's good riddance."

"Yes," Helen said. "Well—"

"Let me try to remember how long ago that was," Fay said.

"A long time," Helen said. "Fay——"

"It has been exactly twenty-one years since we've heard from Gene." Alice spoke slowly, distinctly.

"Good heavens," Louise said, "that memory of yours, Alice. You never forget a single thing."

"Yes." Helen gave a mighty wrench to the conversation. "Fay, has Louise told you about her son Jim? About his being down in the Amazon country? I'm so proud of him. He's my godson, you know."

Alice frowned, as if she did not wish their conversation to turn in that direction. She said, "I remember years and years ago in Greenleaf . . ."

And they began going back in time, back to an age that seemed far more innocent. The Depression had not quite ended, nor the War quite begun.

Today you can drive from Attica, the state capital, to the town of Greenleaf in half an hour by the new interstate highway, but in the thirties it was a longer and more hazardous trip by narrow Route 48, which wound southwest. True, old 48 gives the traveler a more accurate impression of the countryside: the rich farmlands fall behind; the land heaves itself about a bit as one crosses many little rivers flowing toward the big river; the houses become unpretentious. By whatever route you come to Greenleaf, however, you don't feel you have arrived at a place of much consequence.

In 1939 its population was around four thousand, and today it totals only a couple of hundred more. Signs at its eastern and western approaches read: WELCOME TO GREEN

LEAF, HOME OF GREENLEAF COLLEGE. Recently the State Historical Society placed a marker at the eastern approach to town; it is a small plaque which even a sharp-eyed motorist might read only as: blur—GREENLEAF—BIRTHPLACE OF —blur—PORTER—blur—PRESIDENT OF—blur. . . .

Would William Paisley Porter, born of poor but respected parents in Greenleaf on July 12, 1913, ever have become President of the United States if, in the fall of 1939, a young man named Ben North had not been speeding back and forth between Attica and Greenleaf for many consecutive nights?

Women brought the two men together. The important woman to Ben North was Louise Speer, daughter of Greenleaf's most prominent physician. In the estimation of many, Louise was the most beautiful girl in town. When she caught Ben's eye she had been teaching second grade in the Grove Street Grammar School for two years.

Ben's father was Judge James Blaine North of the State Court of Appeals, and his mother had been one of the Paxtons who had made their money in farm mortgages; thus he might have been the most eligible bachelor in Greenleaf. Nothing was further from his intentions, however. For much of his life he had tried to stay as far from town as possible.

His wish had been abetted by Judge North, who had sent him east to preparatory school at Choate when Ben was fourteen. Then he had sent him to Yale for four more years. Next, to the Judge's delight, Ben was admitted to Harvard Law and did well there. Finally, after he had been accepted for a clerkship in a distinguished Manhattan firm, the Judge summoned him back to the Midwest by telegram for "consultation." Taking him to the Athenaeum Club in Attica for lunch and buying him two Gibsons, the Judge proceeded to explain why Ben was going to start his law apprenticeship with Martin, Gray, and Dunmore in Attica rather than on Broad Street in New York. Essentially it was because Judge North wanted him to. And Ben, being essentially a dutiful son even though he had found reasons to stay away from home for years, acquiesced without much protest.

He liked his father and looked forward to becoming friends with him. But a month after Ben went to work for Martin, Gray, and Dunmore, the Judge cheated him of friendship by dying of a heart attack. Though Ben found his mother difficult, he nonetheless drove down to Greenleaf occasionally to visit her.

In Greenleaf, the winters are cold, the summers hot. Yet between the extreme seasons there are golden days, especially in the fall. On a golden autumn Saturday afternoon Ben was driving slowly along Main Street on his way to his mother's house when he saw two young women strolling toward him. One was pretty, and the other struck him as stunningly beautiful. Surprisingly her name came to him instantly with the recollection of a leggy young blonde who had been pointed out to him in some summer past when he had been hurrying out of town. Louise Speer, Dr. Speer's daughter.

Stopping his car, he called, "Louise, how are you?"

The two girls halted and stared at him and his old Pierce Arrow. Louise spoke uncertainly. "All right. How are you—Ben?" So she at least knew who he was.

"Where are you bound?" he asked, as if they were old friends.

Louise continued to gaze at him. "This is my friend Alice Dawson—Ben North."

Alice's expression, like that of Louise, was unfathomable. "Nice to meet you," she said. "We're going to pick up Bill Porter." The name was vaguely familiar to Ben.

"And then we're going to the tryouts. Helen Davis has written a perfectly wonderful play. Some of us have gotten together and are going to present it in the high school auditorium. Proceeds go to the college alumni fund. It's truly a wonderful play."

"Perfectly wonderful," Louise echoed Alice. "It's called *The Courtship of Abraham Lincoln*."

Ben felt as if he had come upon the inhabitants of another planet who were doing strange things. Yet he could not break off his elementary observation of Louise. Could her Aphrodite features be transformed from their mid-America mask by passion? Her patulous blue eyes rather indicated to him that they could if she would. But would she? His gaze took in fine legs and breasts that her plain frock failed to disguise.

He said, "It sounds like an interesting play. Hop in and I'll take you to Bill and the tryouts." His tone was so commanding that they obeyed him.

As they rode toward the corner of Court and Water Streets Ben learned that Alice had come to town from a teacher's college in the northern part of the state and taught fourth grade in the Grove Street School.

At Court and Water a top-floor window of the old, three-story Petty Building was lettered w. p. porter, attorney at law. Though the name was vaguely familiar to Ben, the young man who approached the car was not at first. He was slender, dark-haired, of medium height. Though not handsome, his features caught and held one's attention, for they conveyed an intensity of thought or emotion. His ready smile made one know he would strive to please. Such an intense, mobile expression—sometimes called frank or honest—often caused people in those days in places like Greenleaf to remark that here was a young man who was "going places."

Suddenly Ben remembered. Bill Porter had been a year ahead of him in grammar school. A thin kid, bright and intense, either too slight or busy at other things to do much at games. Always working at all kinds of jobs. Very clean in the way of poor people who are proud. He and his devout Methodist family used to live in the southeast end of town. They had not been dirt-poor, Ben recalled; Bill's father had groped in the lower middle class, having bad luck in business, losing a bakery, a filling station—maybe something else too. Ben remembered his own father saying during that fateful luncheon at the Athenaeum Club, "A bright young man like Bill Porter would give his eye teeth to go to work for Martin, Gray, and Dunmore."

Bill, now the assistant town attorney besides having a private practice, greeted Ben warmly.

Louise said, "Ben, why don't you come along with us and try out for a part?"

Why not indeed?

More than a score of people gathered in the high school auditorium that Saturday afternoon. Helen Davis, the author of the play, addressed them from the stage. Louise said that although Helen was presently a secretary at the college, "She has great writing talent, she's really going places." Helen talked entertainingly about her play, which probably bore literary debt to Robert E. Sherwood's *Abe Lincoln in Illinois*, at that time a hit on Broadway.

The play concerned Lincoln's courtship of Mary Todd against the background of his feud with the politician James Shields, and it also involved the ghost of Ann Rutledge.

Helen would direct the play herself. It would be staged by Jim Carlton, a husky, serious-looking man who was sorting mimeographed copies of the play at one side of the stage while Helen spoke. Louise said that Jim had the

Chevrolet agency in Greenleaf and was a very hard worker.

"Let's read first for the role of Shields," Helen told them.

No one stirred, and Bill said, "I never could stand that man. I won't try for the part."

Ben never had heard of Shields.

"He was a real bumptious politician," Bill told him. "A quick-tempered Irish immigrant. He was governor of the Oregon Territory and—before they finally buried him —a U.S. Senator from Illinois, Minnesota, and Missouri. That role is not for me."

"I thought you wanted to be in the play," Alice said. "Do you plan to try out for Ann Rutledge's ghost?"

"I'm going to play Lincoln."

"You're not tall enough," Alice said.

"That doesn't matter. I *feel* like Lincoln."

Helen said from the stage, "Aren't there any volunteers?" She pointed to a thin young man with curly dark hair. "Gene? Gene Schofield, how about you?"

Gene grinned at her. "I want to be Lincoln."

"Everybody wants to be. All right, come up here and try for Lincoln."

Gene stumbled in haste as he climbed to the stage where Helen told him to take a copy of the play from Jim Carlton and turn to page twenty.

"Pretend, Gene, that I'm Mary Todd and you are young Mr. Lincoln come to break off our engagement. Sort of amble to me. Take your time and read over a couple of pages to yourself first."

But Eugene Schofield did not know how to amble. He was twenty-two years old that autumn, the editor of the town weekly newspaper, the *Tribune*, and he was in great haste to succeed in life. His voice was hasty, sharp as he read:

[21]

"Mary, there's been one almighty storm along the Sangamon."

"Mr. Lincoln, you came to discuss the weather?"

"The weather of a troubled soul, Miss Mary, the turbulence of a mind tossed . . ." He carried the reading through two pages, but he remained Gene Schofield, not Abraham Lincoln.

After Gene had finished, Helen said, "We might as well continue reading for the Lincoln role. Are there other volunteers?"

Bill mounted the stage. His voice, vibrant, compelled attention. When he said there had been a storm on the Sangamon, one imagined thunder and lightning. As he continued to read the lines, one gathered the impression of a complex man who was involved not only with Mary Todd but with some transcendental idea he had not yet revealed.

There was no question about his having won the role. Gene led the enthusiastic applause that followed his reading. They were the best of friends, and Gene seemed genuinely glad that Bill had won the role. He appeared most happy to settle for the role of Shields.

Louise prevailed on Ben to try for the role of Mary Todd's father. Colonel Todd, as conceived by Helen, was a caricature of a nineteenth-century Southern gentleman. Ben, finding fun in his hamming, was pleased when he won the part over other contestants.

Alice received the role of Mary Todd, Louise that of the ghost of Ann Rutledge.

There were other parts in the play, but the principal players and doers were Bill and Alice, Ben and Louise, Gene, Helen, and Jim. These were the people who went to Spooner's Diner that evening and began to develop relationships that would assume curious patterns long after their play had been forgotten. . . .

The Courtship of Abraham Lincoln was a great success. It played to full houses on Friday and Saturday night early in December, probably because Jim Carlton and Gene Schofield had run the most intensive ticket-selling campaign ever seen in Greenleaf, and it raised nearly seven hundred dollars for the college.

After the Saturday night performance Louise gave a party for all of the cast and stagehands at her home. As time passed and Helen and Jim failed to appear, consternation grew. Gene, greatly perturbed, finally went in search of them. When he returned around two o'clock without having found a trace, he was convinced they had met with a serious accident.

On Sunday afternoon Ben and Louise, Bill and Alice and Gene were drawn together by their wonder and concern over what had happened to Helen and Jim. If the two had been like some people they knew, they would have imagined hanky-panky. But with Helen and Jim it was unthinkable.

Ben left for Attica that night, still wondering what had become of them. On Monday evening Louise phoned him at his apartment. She sounded breathless.

"Ben, do you know what they did? They went off and got married!"

The agenda for the meeting of the President's Cabinet had been set a week in advance. But by Tuesday afternoon the race of events in that April time of trial made the agenda seem outdated.

On Tuesday morning the New York *Times* and the Washington *Post* carried lead stories about a tax revolt. Both quoted informed sources and carried a denial by an anonymous Treasury spokesman that such a revolt existed. By late morning, however, the Administration's case appeared to be weakening; both the Associated Press and United Press International had dropped attribution to the *Times* and the *Post* and in new leads were quoting informed sources of their own.

Senator Blake King made matters worse for the Administration by obtaining floor time for his speech on Tuesday noon, thus giving a fresh lead to the afternoon newspapers and providing new fodder for the evening television newscasts. King, an eloquent speaker, played to a packed Senate press gallery. He saw the revolt as aimed at his favorite targets: "Preposterous Administration defense spending, military fat-catting. . . . The so-called tax reforms were really no reforms at all. They did not help any of us common men. . . ." Both friend and foe agreed that King was running strong. His frequent denials that he had any interest in the Presidency had begun to make him the leading contender for his party's nomination.

Meanwhile, as *Newsweek* would report in its next issue, White House administrative assistant Jonathan Hochstein was working quietly behind the scenes. "Hochstein, brilliant former Wall Street lawyer and professor at Harvard Law, is one of the most respected of Porter advisers—perhaps because he always keeps his cool."

Actually, however, Hochstein was upset.

There certainly were scenes, but behind them he found little with which to work except a dribble of information from Internal Revenue. There was no one he could try to influence. There was no situation he could hope to change. His job, with the aid of his two young assistants, was to analyze. Though he wished fervently to be a decision-maker, he had learned long ago that the decisions of a Presidential adviser were mainly confined to such matters as whether to put a fresh blade in his razor of a morning. President Porter, a strong-minded man who usually kept his own counsel until the final moment, made all of the important decisions.

As often happens in politics, love, and war, the thing everyone was talking about was not really germane to the issue at stake. Everyone was talking about the inadequacies of the so-called tax reform bill which had been enacted into law. Yet that fact was irrelevant to the situation the government faced. Hochstein emphasized that in the final draft of his situation report, which he completed after eleven o'clock on Monday evening when everyone but the bored early-morning stenographer had gone home. He could only suggest. He could not lecture. He could not be Ralph Waldo Emerson or a *Life* editorial writer trying to set the world straight with a midnight essay. Just the facts —and the options open to the President on the basis of the facts.

There were plenty of options—and facts available to support every one of them. Significant fact: this was not a hard-core revolt by Thomas Jefferson's and Blake King's common man, perhaps because most common men had their taxes withheld at the source of income. Option one: ignore the whole thing at present and pretend it does not exist. Option two: declare publicly that the dear common man of the silent majority is innocent of tax-dodging. The sinful dodger, fellow solid citizens, is not you but the disaffected American—the hippie, the yippie, the plunger, the protestor. . . .

President Porter, like Hochstein, had been a good lawyer. Once, in fact, he had pleased Hochstein by remarking in praise of something he had done: "Jack, what a good lawyer needs is a very good lawyer." So it would be foolish to submit an incomplete brief to him. The summary, therefore, could not ignore a fact that would be apparent to the President long before he reached the conclusion of the report: this appeared to be an authentic rebellion that cut across lines of political affiliation, of race, of economic or social status, and expressed a desperate dissatisfaction with the present nature of American government and life. These people felt that the only means of protest left them was to refuse to pay their taxes.

At this juncture in the summary Hochstein wished he could seize writer's license and express his personal opinion on how things had come to such a pass. How he felt that much of the dissatisfaction stemmed from the slow and tortuous methods whereby the President had tried to withdraw the nation from the idiotic war in Asia. How he felt the Administration had not paid sufficient attention to many important areas of American society. Such opinions, however, were simply good reasons for doing what sometimes had tempted him: throw in the towel and return to his New York law practice. Under the ground rules of a situation report they could not be expressed because they involved decisions already made and thus were irrelevant to a decision yet to be reached.

The ground rules did provide, nevertheless, that in conclusion the author of a situation report could offer a personal opinion on the wisest method of dealing with the problem under scrutiny. Hochstein offered his opinion bluntly and briefly. Since the dam had busted long ago and far up the river, it was pointless now to think of repairing it; the only thing to do was to try to build the levee higher down here—but fast. Give 'em hell, Mr. President. Make an example of thirty or forty tax-dodgers from a variety of social groups by throwing the book at them and convincing everybody else that Uncle Samuel always gets his buck. . . .

When Hochstein arrived at his row house in Georgetown he composed himself for sleep by turning on a recording of Scriabin's "Divine Poem" with Yevgeny Svetlanov and the USSR Symphony. In the kitchen he ate a peanut butter and jelly sandwich and drank a big glass of milk while the gorgeous, enigmatic music poured through the empty little house like a splendid sunset. Then he went to sleep.

Six hours later when he awakened to Tuesday, Scriabin's music had left him. Instead, his mind hummed with the ballad of Joe McCurdy. It was annoying. Yet was it significant? As he began to shave, frowning at the reflection of his broad, sagging, undistinguished face with customary morning dislike, a word popped at him as if suddenly written on the mirror. Conspiracy. A dirty word. But every lawyer knew conspiracy was as prevalent a human tendency as adultery.

When Hochstein reached his office, he pulled his situation report back from the Presidential route box and had his secretary retype the last page. To his closing personal opinion he added one thought: the Internal Revenue Service should make every effort to determine whether anyone in these United States named Joseph McCurdy was a tax delinquent. Then he sent the report on its way to the President.

Just before noon the President's personal secretary, Liz Hatch, phoned and said the President expected him to attend the Cabinet meeting at two o'clock.

Hochstein had never attended a Cabinet meeting. Indeed, the Cabinet met infrequently, for President Porter had found—like other Presidents before him—that as a body it served no useful function. In the extraordinary proliferation of government it was simply a collection of department heads, each representing his own interests. If long ago the Cabinet actually had been a body that advised a President, it had become a group of executives who consented to whatever the boss wanted to do.

So this proposal of the President's to bring the tax revolt up for Cabinet discussion was something new. Perhaps it indicated the President was seeking all possible opinions on how to deal with the crucial situation. Or did it mean the President intended to *tell* them how he would cope with it, knowing he would have their rubber-stamp consent?

When Hochstein entered the Cabinet Room he had the uneasy feeling of being an interloper at a gathering of

Christian elders. So many dark gray suits. Even the portraits on the walls were of Protestant saints—the General, Roosevelt the First, Professor Woodrow, all heroes to Methodist Porter and none vastly admired by Rabbi Hochstein. What was he doing here behind the President's chair? It was a question the Vice-President seemed to ask as he fixed Hochstein with a brooding gaze.

The Vice-President did not like him. The Attorney General respected but did not like him. The Secretary of Defense tolerated but did not like him. The Secretary of the Treasury outright detested him. These men did not like him because he often opposed viewpoints they and, generally, President Porter held dear. And *that* was why he was here as a counselor to a President who liked the idea, though he had not achieved the fact, of a balanced administration.

Hochstein had thought the President might take up first the crucial matter of the tax rebellion, but that was not his style. He led the Cabinet through the agenda, and it was past three o'clock before he said:

"Gentlemen, a new matter has come up since our last meeting that I'd like to discuss." Then, without glancing at his notes on a yellow ruled pad, he presented succinctly and accurately the facts and options as Hochstein had set them forth in his report. "In summary," the President said, "the general options as laid out by Mr. Hochstein are: ignore; mollify; prosecute. It is Mr. Hochstein's personal opinion that the government should prosecute—and swiftly."

The Attorney General's deadpan, of which a curved pipe was an almost permanent feature, took in Hochstein, expressing his approval only with a quick puff-puff-puff of smoke. The Vice-President rinsed a bit of the starch out of his thick neck and actually nodded.

The Secretary of Health, Education, and Welfare, a good friend of Hochstein's, asked, "Mr. President, for those of us who have paid our taxes, could prosecution be explained?"

"That's why we have an Attorney General," said the President.

"Mr. President," said the Attorney General, "I defer to Mr. Hochstein, who initiated the idea and has vast experience in the intricacies of the tax laws."

Hochstein flashed him a friendly grin. "Counsel is putting me on. I was chasing ambulances. Well, we all know that IRS charges twelve percent a year as interest on the underpayment of taxes. Also, IRS can impose criminal penalties if it determines that the failure to pay full taxes is willful. And this is the area that concerns us, I believe. The really artful tax-dodgers go to great pains to cover up their resources—switching money into bank accounts under phony names and all that sort of thing. Investigation of such cases takes a tremendous amount of time and effort and manpower. Most of our good citizens don't realize that it's basically an honors system, that Internal Revenue can't hope to keep up with all of them."

"Chiefly," interrupted the Secretary of the Treasury, "because Internal Revenue personnel has been cut too drastically for budgetary reasons."

Hochstein, ignoring him, continued: "Let me run over the steps that constitute *action* when somebody sends a Poor Peter letter with his return. There's the bill in the mail—with interest on it. And then another bill. Maybe a third. Next a letter from the collections officer. And then another letter from him. Then personal contact. If Poor Peter is still ducking, the collections officer can now get a lien on the guy's bank or brokerage account, he can put a lock on his door. And finally we come to *levy*."

Hochstein took a memorandum slip from a pocket.

"Scarcely anybody understands the difference between lien and levy. When I hold this piece of paper in my hand, that is lien. I'm saying, 'World, beware, this is mine.' But then I *take it*"—he folded the slip and put it back in his pocket—"that is *levy*. When I recommend fast action to the President, I mean fast *levies*—and thorough publicity of the levies as an example to others. Some of you may remember what Internal Revenue did when the Amish people decided it was against their principles to pay taxes. The government stepped in, levied their horses, and sold them. It wasn't long before the Amish decided that paying taxes was *not* against their principles.

"Now, as most of you probably know, these steps usually take weeks, months, sometimes years. But in this situation the process must be compressed into days. On thirty or forty judiciously scattered cases around the country I would recommend we be at the stage of levy by next week. If a guy owns a candy store, for example, *seize it*— and publicize the seizure in every way we can. If a family must be turned into the street, do it—and let the newsmen take all the pictures they want. The point is, *these people are breaking the law*."

He settled back to indicate he had finished while the Attorney General came close to smiling and went puff-puff-puff on his pipe. How strange to find allies in the enemy camp.

President Porter said, "Mr. Hochstein made one other recommendation I did not mention. He suggested that Internal Revenue make every effort to locate any person actually named Joseph McCurdy who refused to pay taxes."

The Secretary of Health, Education, and Welfare shot Hochstein a glance that said, *You're kidding!*

"Can you try to do that?" the President asked the Treasury Secretary.

"It would help," the Secretary replied, "if we could have McCurdy's Social Security number." Then, realizing the silliness of his statement, the Secretary grimaced and said, "Skip that remark." His hands displayed a tremulo that made Hochstein think how deeply this crazy revolt was cutting into the government.

The Attorney General spoke. "Mr. Hochstein has an interesting thought. He is concerned about a conspiracy. It's an area that should be thoroughly investigated."

"I suppose so." Oddly, the President did not sound impressed. It was especially odd since over the years no one in government had been more deeply concerned about conspiracy than he. The Attorney General took his pipe from his teeth and rapped it sharply in an ashtray.

Opinion moved clockwise around the long table. It was overwhelmingly in favor of swift prosecution. There were only two demurrers.

The Secretary of Health, Education, and Welfare: "It's April of an election year in a country that is deeply disturbed and fractured. I fear what might happen if the news media cut loose on people being evicted from their homes and businesses. I think it might have precisely the reverse effect to that intended. I am against fast prosecution. I recommend going slow and exploring more fully various ways in which the government might mollify the— why not call them truants?"

The Secretary of State: "By drawing swift and dramatic attention to the situation I'm afraid we might make it seem even worse than it is. I advocate waiting while thinking and exploring further."

After the clock-hand of opinion had returned to President Porter, he said, "Thank you, gentlemen." And the meeting was adjourned.

So it was to be another of those situations in which no one knew the direction of the President's thinking. Those whose advice he followed most often saw it as Hochstein did. And yet— As Hochstein left the Cabinet Room he heard the Attorney General rap-rap-rapping his pipe in an ashtray.

It was almost five o'clock when Liz Hatch phoned him. "Mr. Hochstein, Mr. Porter hopes you can attend the dinner for General Bridge this evening. Cocktails too, you know. He asked me to tell you he knows it's awfully short notice, but he'd like to talk with you afterward."

Hochstein uttered a moaning sound after he hung up. He should be flattered that the President wanted to confer with him rather than with the Attorney General or someone else of greater importance. But he felt beyond the age of flattery.

It was almost ten o'clock before the President led Hochstein upstairs to the Lincoln Room, a favored Presidential lair. Sitting down beside a table where the Great Emancipator supposedly had composed his thoughts, he said, "Jack, what makes a President remembered as great?"

Hochstein, taken aback, curbed a facetious reply: He goes out and gets himself assassinated. Realizing the President was deadly serious, however, he seemed to think swiftly on several planes at once. Dear God, Senator Garamond had gotten to him with that hero twaddle yesterday. When a pragmatic, capable man began worrying about the verdict of history it could be fatal, for he started trying to use other sets of values as bases for his judgments. Let them not unhinge this rather undistinguished Administration with intimations of great distinction. Anyway, the age of greatness seemed dead; it was the age of facile expertise.

But Hochstein must say something, and so he replied, "Circumstance. I think it's sheer circumstance that makes a President remembered as great." He did not really believe it.

President Porter began to talk about his idol Theodore

Roosevelt. Hochstein, who thought the first Roosevelt must have been an egotistical bore, scarcely listened.

This altogether human wish of William Porter's to be a great President was not something new. Hochstein had seen evidence of it many times. Often, in spontaneous remarks to some group, the President would express a rather wistful wish to speak *memorable* words—and then would go on about baseball or the number of times he had been here or done something similar there. The press knew his predilection for figures as "the numbers game," but Hochstein analyzed it more deeply. He saw President Porter as a basically shy man who did not enjoy crowds or strangers, who disliked making public utterances, who sometimes seemed to say almost anything in order to get it over with.

"Jack, I've never forgotten something you said four years ago."

At the Party's nominating convention, Hochstein, having decided the nation could be served best by Porter in the White House, had interested fellow volunteers with a line that had come not quite off the top of his head: "The country's on the verge of a nervous breakdown. It must have Porter's stability."

The President went on, "Has a government or people ever been destroyed by what you call a nervous breakdown?"

"Lots of them," Hochstein replied. "In fact, nearly all of 'em. That is, by my definition. I'm not sure how psychiatrists put it, but I think a nervous breakdown is a combination of an overreaction and an underreaction. A great strain—and an irresponsible retreat from strain. It's happened to every European nation time and again. But it hasn't quite happened here yet, though we came close in the 1930's. We're a beautifully resilient people and we have a beautifully resilient form of government—so far. I think we must hold some kind of historical track record. But this tax revolt has me worried. By my definition it's classical breakdown."

"Yet we've offered every possible form of stability," the President said. "I used to talk a lot about crisis and the good effects on a man's or a nation's soul in surviving it. But my thinking has changed. A nation can't go on indefinitely living from crisis to crisis without tearing itself to shreds. And this nation has had too many crises in recent years. The underlying philosophy of our Administration has been to shift the focus from crisis management to crisis prevention." He made a wry face. "And so now we're trying to manage another crisis."

"The buck, the buck!" Hochstein said. "The dollar ain't what it used to be, and never will be. Man cares more about the buck than about his balls."

He realized he was not being helpful. His function was to argue and to *think*.

The President said, "I can't forget Harold Garamond yesterday—his thought about a great President showing understanding—clemency—compromise."

Hochstein stifled a groan at the thought of *greatness* again. He said, "Mr. President, I hope you *won't*. It would be weakness rather than greatness. We are what we are, and we must remain so—conservatives."

The President frowned. "I don't know why you always insist on calling us conservatives."

Because, goddamnit, we *are*, Hochstein thought.

The President was revealing a paradox that often perplexed Hochstein. Though William Porter's excellent intellect usually questioned the hackneyed, his emotions seemed generally receptive to it. Thus, while avowing social and political awareness of the new society, he was forever invoking the old society's laws and orders. Thus,

[35]

too, while a thorough conservative, he did not like to be called one. From this paradox stemmed the observations of the President-watchers, who liked to talk about there being two Porters: an old and a new; a personal Porter who was quite different from a public Porter. The paradox revealed a President who wished to be *everything*. Sometimes he seemed like the brightest boy in school who could not get over the fact he had failed to be captain of the football team.

Their conversation continued in a vein that began to remind Hochstein of a rambling college freshman bull session. He realized there was something President Porter wanted to say, but for some reason could not bring himself to express. Never had he heard him go on like this; always the President had a direction in a conversation. For the first time in his years of White House service he believed that President Porter himself did not know what he was going to do.

Rather than coming to a conclusion, their conversation died away in a mood of mutual despondency. A hall clock boomed eleven as he said good night and went down the stairs. On the first floor he came upon Helen and Louise and offered them a ride home.

When Louise entered her apartment, she poured a bourbon and sat down, trying to calm herself. It was no fun being a divorcée, a fifth wheel at every social occasion.

She found herself gazing at a photograph of her son Jim taken just before he entered Harvard. Jim, whom they had named after Jim Carlton, was truly handsome—and then he had gone and spoiled it by growing a beard! Louise really didn't understand him. He had had the best of educations, but what career had he chosen? *Birds!* Such a good boy, but such a problem, or at least creating problems where none need have existed. Fortunately, to Louise's and Ben's way of thinking, a ruptured eardrum that he had suffered from scuba diving had kept him out of military service in the foolish Asiatic war.

But other things, as Louise saw them, had not gone as fortunately for him. Take his relationship with Penny Porter. Jim had been a junior at Harvard when Penny entered Wellesley. She had fallen head over heels in love with him. She was a pretty, bright, pleasant child, and Jim had been kind to her. But why had he kept saying he never could fall in love with her? Why had he not just given it time? Their marriage could have been an ideal one.

Alice and Bill always had liked Jim; they might even have learned to tolerate his beard. But why had he found it necessary, when Bill ran for the Presidency last time, to announce to Penny that he was against Bill and for what's his name? It just about killed Penny, who had fierce loyalty to her father.

At the very end of the campaign, when that big rally was held for Bill in Madison Square Garden, Louise had had to admit that she sympathized with Jim over what happened. The Party had been so worried about there being some kind of demonstration against Bill at the Garden that they wouldn't let in any hippie types, even anyone with a beard. When Jim showed up with Penny and some of her friends, the guards had cut him out. He and Penny had thought at first it was because the Party people believed it would be bad publicity for Penny to be seen with a bearded escort. Later Ben had learned the guards had turned back *everybody* who wore a beard. Jim had been half angry and half amused when the guards shoved him out of Penny's party. He had yelled, "Neither Jesus Christ nor Abraham Lincoln could get into this goddamn Party affair!" And then he had gotten into a fight with a police-man. . . .

Louise poured herself a last drink and wished she could find something pleasant to think about. *Everything started so well, but it all ended so badly.*

Louise had been seeking a husband for two years before she decided on Ben. Prospects in Greenleaf were not bright. Until Jim Carlton married Helen it had not occurred to Louise that he would make an excellent husband. And she had not recognized Bill's sterling qualities either until, too late, he had assigned his emotions to Alice. All that were left in town seemed to be horny young men who barely made a living. Gene Schofield was one. Gene had a bad habit of making all-out passes at women. Louise had had to put him in his place long ago, and Alice and Helen had done the same. Once Gene was put in his place, he became a docile friend.

Louise, like Alice and Helen, never discussed sex. But she thought a lot about it. She believed that Ben, like Gene, was horny—and that Bill and Jim were not. She dreaded marriage to a horny man until she convinced herself that Ben would not think of making a pass at any woman but her.

He was an insistent lover who sometimes excited her.

She never let him go too far, but she told herself she had to let him go as far as she did lest she lose him forever. Gradually, by holding back and at the same time holding out to him the promise of some really tremendous future sexual experience, she wore down his young stud's resistance to marriage. In February he asked her to marry him, and the wedding was held in the Greenleaf Episcopal Church in June.

It was the grandest wedding of the year. Alice was maid of honor and Helen a bridesmaid. Bill, Jim, and Gene were ushers, but somewhat to Louise's consternation, Ben insisted on his best man being Vince Braden, a friend since Yale who clerked with him at Martin, Gray, and Dunmore. It had never occurred to her that Ben had close friends besides those in Greenleaf.

As a wedding trip Louise and Ben went to New York, where they stayed at the Plaza. Louise did her best to fulfill Ben's expectation of that really tremendous sexual experience, but secretly she felt the sexual act must be somewhat like golf: only long practice could bring about its perfection.

After they returned to Attica Louise was lonely. Ben, striving to become an associate in the firm, worked long hours—usually into the evening and often all day on Saturday. As a result, Louise fell into the habit of driving to Greenleaf at least once a week and often spending the night. She enjoyed visiting with her parents and Ben's mother, but she missed Alice, who had taken a summer job as a hostess on a Great Lakes cruise ship plying out of Cleveland.

To her disappointment, Helen had little time for her. She was writing a novel on a new portable typewriter which Jim had bought her. She would not tell anyone except Jim what her novel was about, but she did let drop some confessions that struck Louise as odd:

"The typewriter Jim gave me means more to me than

every stick of furniture in the house. . . . It's better not to talk about what you're writing, or you'll begin to think it's crazy. . . . Well, yes, Jim knows. In fact, I read my day's writing to him nearly every evening. Maybe more knowledgeable critics will comment on my work someday, but I'll never know a kinder, more enthusiastic critic than dear Jim. . . ."

Louise felt that Helen somehow did not display a *healthy* attitude for a recent bride. Imagine bothering Jim that way every evening. Suppose Ben came home every evening and talked about the cases he was working on!

Early in September when Alice reported by postcard that she was back in town, Louise drove down and picked her up after school.

"I couldn't take it for more than one cruise," Alice told her. "Uck! All those slimy men always grabbing at you. I tried to find a job in Cleveland, but I couldn't land anything interesting. So I went home. There was no place else to go. Pa has sold the farm and they've moved to town. It was so dull. So now it's September, and I've traded that dull town for this one."

Although Bill proposed marriage to Alice incessantly and monotonously, she kept turning him down.

"I *like* you, Bill," she told him in the presence of anyone. "But I'm not ready to settle down—not in Greenleaf. I want to travel, and it doesn't look to me as if you're going to travel far from Greenleaf."

That September evening Louise took Alice to an inn near Centerville where they could have beer on a pleasant terrace before dinner.

Alice took a sip of her beer and said, "I'm marrying Bill in November."

"Grand!" cried Louise. "Why did you wait till now to tell me?"

"Because I didn't know till now myself. Bill doesn't

know it either, but he'll be very pleased when I tell him."

Louise gaped at her.

"I was thinking about it today," Alice continued measuredly, "when I heard there's a little house on Water Street that can be rented furnished for forty a month beginning in November. And that's the sort of information—of *fact*, that determines Bill's and my marriage."

Louise never had heard Alice—or Bill—cry poor. But it was true that both were as poor as church mice despite their persistent hard work.

"So," Alice said, "I see you a blushing bride. And I see Helen a blushing bride. And I ask myself why shouldn't I be a blushing bride too?"

"You—*love* Bill, don't you, Alice?"

"Do you love Ben?"

"Of course I do."

"Of course I love Bill. And so we're going to be married and live happily ever after on Water Street and never see the rising sunlight kiss the minarets of Marrakesh." Her tone, at first matter-of-fact, became dry. "I wonder if there are any minarets in Marrakesh. . . ."

Alice and Bill were married on the first Saturday afternoon in November. Louise and Ben stood up with them in a simple ceremony in the First Methodist Church. Then Mr. and Mrs. William Porter took a two-day trip someplace, Louise never learned where. By Tuesday they were back at work and living in the little house on Water Street.

Louise's birthday was in early December. For reasons convenient to everyone, the date set to celebrate her twenty-sixth was Sunday, December 7, 1941.

All were at the Carltons' by one o'clock that rainy Sunday afternoon. They had not been together long when

Bill and Gene began carrying on about communism menacing the good American life. The way they talked you would have thought a battalion of communists was fighting its way up Court Street at the very moment.

Gene, ever seeking agreement with his opinions, asked Jim, "Don't you think that's right?"

"I guess so," Jim replied. "But why don't you guys pick on some menace your own size? I mean one you can do something about. Like the one Alice was talking about the other day. Here in our land of milk and honey, right here in our own town, young Dr. Sprague estimates that nearly twenty percent of our school kids suffer to some degree from malnutrition. Why not let's do something about that menace? Why, for instance, don't we start a program of free and nourishing school lunches?"

Gene, whose father had been a Methodist preacher, always espoused morality in the columns of the *Chronicle*. While he pondered what might be immoral about free school lunches, Bill spoke.

"You have a good idea, Jim. I'd be for it. There's only one thing wrong with it."

"What's that?"

"You could never get it passed. The majority of people in town would be against it. They'd call it socialistic."

Ben asked, "Do you know the voters that well?"

"I do."

Louise said, "Bill, you should go into politics."

"Never." Bill's tone carried great conviction. "That life is not for me. Appointive office is all right. I was glad to be raised to town attorney last month when Joe Zinkand stepped down. But no politics. All I want to be is a good lawyer."

"We were talking about free school lunches," Jim said. "You say you favor them, Bill. Yet you say there's no point

[43]

in fighting for them because you think the majority of voters would be against them. Maybe you should give some second thoughts to entering politics after all."

Suddenly there was a high-pitched wailing sound, as if the volunteer fire department siren was stuck again. They looked out and saw that the next-door neighbor, old Mr. Breeme, had come outside and was standing in the rain, head tilted back, uttering the strange sound. Jim rushed to the porch, and through the open doorway those inside heard Mr. Breeme's strangled cry:

"Jesus Christ, *turn on your radio!*"

They listened, stunned, to the news of the Japanese attack on Pearl Harbor. War, until now at a comfortable and discussable distance, had come to Greenleaf. . . .

Jim went to Attica the next day and enlisted in the Marines. Three months later Ben joined the Navy. To Louise's distress he did not seek a commission in the legal branch, but began training to become a deck officer.

Louise came home to stay until she could join him, and before long she found Greenleaf the boring place that Alice said it always had been. Helen went to Washington with the hope of following Jim, but after he shipped into the Pacific she wrote that she liked life in the capital and intended to remain there.

On a golden October day they learned of Jim's death on Guadalcanal. Two days later Bill enlisted in the Army. For another month Gene went about with a furtive manner and a sheepish expression, then turned himself in to the draft board; he was to spend the next three years as a private first class working a mimeograph machine at Fort Sheridan, always on the verge, he claimed, of being sent off to combat.

Ben had two weeks' leave before assignment to San Diego, where he promised he would find a place for Louise to live. But then he was reassigned to San Francisco, and she arrived there just one day before he sailed out the Golden Gate aboard a destroyer. For the first time in her life Louise did not want to go home to Greenleaf. She found a small apartment on Telegraph Hill, took a job as a librarian, and discovered with surprise that she enjoyed living alone in a strange city.

Alice joined her there the following August after saying good-bye to Bill, a second lieutenant fresh from Judge Advocate General's School, who had inside information that he was sailing from Newport News for Europe. For weeks Alice and Louise puzzled over his confusing letters in which he described being in someplace unlike any in Europe they had ever read about. At last a lenient censor permitted him a line of explanation: "Damn it, I'm in the Aleutians! You can sail from Newport News to the Aleutians. There's water all the way." He was to spend the rest of the war there. Ever after he was to explain, "Well, somebody had to be in the Aleutians."

In later years Louise and Alice were fond of describing the rigors of being war-widow roommates in San Francisco. Actually they enjoyed it immensely. Although neither ever would admit it, possibly they had the happiest time of their lives there.

To Louise the war seemed to end as suddenly as it had begun. Suddenly Ben was back, a destroyer commander and veteran of countless dangers and battles, beribboned, sun-bronzed, handsome. Oh, he looked grand!

And then there was nothing to do but go home.

One evening Ben came home from the office and asked, "Do you think I should run for Congress?"

Louise, who was pregnant and feeling terrible, replied, "Oh, I don't think so. It must be a dog's life."

He said, "It's the running rather than the winning

that's a dog's life. All that crap you have to say. All that crap you have to eat."

Nevertheless, he mulled the question for a few days. Louise was alarmed when she realized he was seriously considering the matter. Dreading the prospect of being a candidate's wife, she tried to dissuade him in every way she could.

"Some people think I should run," he told her. "Or *somebody* should run. A youngish war-veteran type. The Party hasn't had a man in office from this district since 1932. That was old Tom Applegate from Greenleaf. Remember him?"

Louise had not realized that the area of Attica where they lived was in the same Congressional district as Greenleaf, and Ben explained how the district had been gerrymandered long ago.

The next day he made a surprising announcement: "I don't want to be a Congressman. But I know who would make a very good one. Bill."

Louise was delighted. "He *would!* He's such a hard worker, so conscientious. And Alice is so bored with Greenleaf she'd do almost anything to get out of there." Then she had second thoughts. "But suppose he should win?"

"Well, Louise, that's the point of his running."

"But I'd miss Alice so if she went off to Washington."

Ben's fondness for Bill, which had grown with time, pleased Louise. He saw Bill as a man of integrity and intelligence, greatly talented in the law, who had not had a fair break. "If we lived in one of those idealistic socialist states that don't actually exist," he told Louise, "Bill would be farther ahead in the profession than I am. I was lucky in having doors opened to me. Bill didn't have the same luck. And he deserves it." Ben had directed to him in Greenleaf every case that he could. He had frequently urged the partners to bring him into the firm in Attica. But it appeared that a long time would elapse before it would be expedient for the firm to hire Bill.

"I can't think of a better man for public office," Ben said.

Thus it happened that William Paisley Porter became the Congressional candidate of his Party from the eighth district after being unopposed in the primary. . . .

The law partners let Ben devote much of his time and energy to Bill's campaign. And Louise had not realized what an extraordinary amount of time and energy was devoted to a race for elective office in the United States of America.

Bill's opponent, the incumbent Congressman for twelve years, was a regular whose record seemed to assure him the vote of just about everyone who could totter to the polls. This worthy opponent, Emil Lansberg, appeared to have only one thing working against him: though of military age, he had not served in the recent war.

At the first campaign strategy conference, held in the Norths' apartment, Louise served coffee and cake to sixteen people. To her surprise, Bill and Alice brought Gene with them. After all the political professionals had had their say, Gene spoke up:

"I want to offer something against Lansberg. I learned it through my work on the *Tribune*. The former chairman of his draft board is sore at him because of a post office appointment. So he gave me this information. During the war Lansberg had seventeen draft deferments."

Ben said, "But Gene, those were automatic deferments because of his office."

"What difference does that make, Ben? They were *deferments*. And Mr. and Mrs. Zilch, who had a son killed or wounded or just losing time while serving, equate them with sin."

A couple of old pols suddenly looked interested.

[47]

"My idea is this," Gene continued. "The American Legion is holding its state convention here next month. Let's get Bill on the program. Let him make his kick-off speech there and bring out this fact about Lansberg."

Bill said, "I don't want to conduct a smear campaign."

"Bill," said an old pol, "you don't want to conduct a smear campaign until once you have been smeared. *Then* you will have become a politician."

Gene took a sheaf of papers from a briefcase. "I tried a first draft for Bill's Legion speech. I—uh—mimeographed copies of it, and wish all of you would take a couple of minutes to read it over."

"I don't want to conduct a smear campaign," Bill repeated.

No one paid any attention to him as each scanned the speech which Gene distributed.

Finally the campaign chairman said, "This is a damn good speech. I like this part here, Bill, where you say, 'When I was fighting in the Pacific, there may have been an atheist or two in foxholes. But there certainly weren't any Congressmen.' This speech will make headlines and sock 'em right in the old Ingersoll. . . ."

It did indeed. Events proceeded smoothly, with occasional harrowing moments. For example, just before the Legion parade was to begin, Ben, who was not a Legionnaire, rushed to the apartment. Gene came with him. Frantically they rummaged through closets and drawers until they found what they were hunting: Ben's service ribbons.

"Your Silver Star is the best for Bill to wear." Gene sounded breathless. "And loan him your Pacific campaign ribbon with all the battle stars. Hey, Ben, loan me your Purple Heart. I can't march wearing only my damn Good Conduct Ribbon."

Then they hurried away like boys going out to play.

Though Emil Lansberg was a seasoned politician, he seemed uncertain how to reply to Bill's speech. Finally he cited the fact that Bill had sat out the war on a safe Aleutian island doing paper work in an office. Somehow this brought on Lansberg the wrath of the Legion, which accused him of waging a smear campaign.

No one ever had run a harder race in the eighth district than Bill. He was on the go seventeen and eighteen hours a day, and Alice went with him constantly. They were an attractive couple, a different-looking breed from the political hacks to whom the voters were accustomed. Bill's speeches, largely combining creations by Gene and Ben, were also a refreshing change from weary old promises.

It was no wonder he won by a handsome majority. And it was natural he should take Gene to Washington as his legislative assistant.

Louise never did understand why such a fuss was raised about the Butler case. Bill's role in it brought him to national attention, though one of the unresolved debates of mid-century was whether it earned him more enemies than friends.

The case, as she followed it in the Attica *Chronicle*, seemed simple to Louise. Jerome Butler was a highly placed government official whom an odd-acting man named Roland Whittier accused, along with several others, of having been a member of a communist spy ring before the war. Whittier made his accusations before a House committee of which Bill was a freshman member. Butler denied the accusations, vehemently and scornfully. But Bill did not believe him. With Gene's aid, he pursued the investigation remorselessly in the hope of having Butler indicted.

At the height of the controversy Ben had to go to Washington on business; Louise went with him, and they stayed with the Porters in the house they had bought in the District northwest. Bill was greatly worked up over the Butler case; Alice said he even had developed insomnia because of it.

The first evening after dinner he asked Ben to go over parts of a transcript of the hearings with him line by line, explaining his reactions in detail. He kept asking, "Do you see what I mean?" and Ben kept nodding. At last Ben said, "You're a good lawyer, Bill."

"Then you agree that he's guilty."

"No," Ben replied slowly. "I——"

"Ben!" exclaimed Louise, who felt that if Bill said Butler was guilty then he was absolutely guilty. "How can you say that?"

Ben, ignoring her, said to Bill, "I merely agree that his case looks weak on the points you have brought out."

Bill looked angry. "It seems clear to me, in light of all the testimony we've heard, that we're dealing here with a far-reaching communist conspiracy against the government of the United States. How far does it go? Isn't it possible that our most vital secrets have been tapped by the Soviets?"

"It's possible," Ben replied mildly. "But it doesn't seem very probable to me. I've read carefully all the transcripts you've sent me. And I appreciate your sending them along. It looks to me as if there was some kind of conspiracy before the war. But it was at a time when the political climate was quite different than now. And it strikes me as a sort of half-baked affair that never penetrated far into significant areas. It was undertaken by second- and third-raters who never enlisted the help of any but second- and third-raters in government."

"Ben North!" Alice spoke sharply. "You sound like

some of the Ivy League snobs we've heard froth off at Helen's." Then she added quickly, "Well, I don't exactly mean that, but——"

"Of course not." Bill spoke as quickly. "Who's more loyal than you, Ben? But I think some of us have to think about who is more *disloyal*. I don't care how hard some of the writers take off on me—and they've been taking off very hard—I'll stake my political career on this thing."

Ben leaned back and folded his hands. "May I ask a question? Are you going at the thing as hard as you are because you truly believe you're exposing a dangerous conspiracy that exists today? Or are you doing it because you think it's good for your political career?"

"I think I've already answered the question," Bill replied. "Of course I believe we're dealing with a corrupt and dangerous situation."

"Then more power to you. Because I'm not at all sure you're on a politically expedient course. You have almost total support back home in the eighth district. But you're making mortal enemies in a lot of other places. . . ."

The Butler case dragged on interminably. A federal grand jury indicted him on two counts of perjury, he finally was brought to trial, found guilty, and sentenced to prison. Hundreds of thousands of acrimonious words were written about the principals in the case by some who believed Butler innocent and others who thought him guilty.

Louise and Ben stopped discussing the case. She did not ask whether he believed Butler innocent or guilty, and he never told her what he thought.

One day Bill came back to Attica from Washington and told Ben, "I want to run for the Senate."

Ben said, "The next Senator is going to be Governor David B. Caldwell, who doesn't happen to be a member of our party. As you know, he announced as soon as old Tyler said he wouldn't run again—and Caldwell is as good as in."

"I want to run against him," Bill said. "Gene thinks we can make it."

"Nobody in his right mind would want to run against Dave Caldwell."

"*I* do, Ben. *Tell* them. And then let me talk to them."

The four were sitting on the edge of the Norths' swimming pool, dangling their legs in the water on a hot Saturday afternoon in June. Alice, who was three months pregnant, was wearing a sunsuit. Little Jim and a young neighbor friend were paddling at the shallow end of the pool. It was so peaceful there in the sweet odor of honeysuckle while sunlight dappled the water that Louise wondered how Bill could bear to spoil it with talk of politics.

"You're not ready for the Senate yet," Ben said. "You're just beginning to find your way around the House."

"Is that what they say?"

They, of course, were the leaders of the Party's state political organization. While Ben had declined office in the organization, he was highly regarded by its leaders who often sought his opinion. He had an admirable gift of offering sensible advice without sounding like a prig. It was one reason why he had become a partner in the firm while relatively young. Louise had heard people say he was destined for the judiciary, though Ben never mentioned such an ambition himself. She hoped the talk proved to be true, for then he would not have so many pressing duties. As it was, the more money he made and the more prominent he became, the more time he spent away from the handsome house he had bought them in the Glenview section of Attica.

[52]

Bill persisted: "Why is Dave Caldwell invincible? Is he really smart?"

"No, he's really stupid. But since when was intelligence a prerequisite to success in politics? Look at Warren G. Harding—and maybe it will give you good insight into David B. Caldwell. The guys he's hired to form what he calls his kitchen cabinet are secretly amused by his obtuseness. His favorite line with them is 'Keep me informed, boys.' So they inform him, but he doesn't really take it in. But look at him. Handsome. That prematurely white hair. A colonel in the war. A genuine combat colonel, though I wonder what his exec thought of him. That beautiful wife of his who used to be an actress. All that money. The hearty, friendly manner that is really a kind of condescension. Voters eat that up, you know, once they're convinced the runner is a bit better than they. Well, Dave has convinced 'em. And people will fall into the classical American pattern of voting for their betters. Again, remember all that money he has himself and can raise easily. It takes a lot of money to run for the Senate. Why bother, Bill?"

But Bill was determined to be bothered, and Gene acted as a gadfly. Alice, too, was eager for him to run. Reluctantly at first, but then with wholehearted effort, Ben gathered support for him and found men who would contribute money.

Bill fought the uphill battle with untiring strength. He had one basic theme that he drummed incessantly through remote hamlets and the streets of cities: clean up the mess in Washington which had been caused by Caldwell's party. Turn the communists out of government. Bill Porter could do it. *He* had already begun.

Caldwell, in turn, scorned him as a mastiff might a feist. He flattered the voters as being his peers, his comrades in arms, who had enjoyed increased prosperity and benefits under the rule of his party. Though a majority of newspaper managements in the state favored Porter, a majority of reporters preferred Caldwell. Bill, feeling their hostility, began to show flashes of hostility himself.

Ben warned him against it, saying that one cause of the reporters' antagonism was the fact that he repeated the same idea so often that it was almost impossible to report fresh stories about his campaign. Bill tried to broaden the scope of the campaign, but then something happened.

Stories began to circulate that Caldwell's wife had been a member of "pink" organizations, that she was friendly with communists, that she might be a communist herself. Asked about the rumor at a news conference, Bill replied:

"I know nothing about it. I'm not conducting a smear campaign. I won't stoop to personalities."

Reporter: "Do you believe the story?"

Porter: "I don't know anything about it."

Reporter: "Do you disavow it?"

Porter: "How can I disavow a story I never started?"

Reporter: "With your excellent security contacts in Washington, couldn't you check on Mrs. Caldwell's record?"

Porter: "I think it's up to my opponent to explain his wife's record. I am not conducting a smear campaign."

Caldwell, furious, leaped for the bait before his advisers could explain the hook to him. He lashed out at William Porter in defense of his wife; he lashed too hard. Many believed that one who struck so fiercely possessed some secret worthy of defense. Others believed that Bill had instigated the story, and the more he denied it the more they were convinced.

Ben was disgusted as the campaign sank into a brawl. He suspected Gene of having started the story about Grace

Caldwell and asked him if he had had anything to do with it.

Gene neither affirmed nor denied. He simply grinned and said, "Well, Ben, I don't think you understand street-level politics. Not everything can be settled at a board of directors meeting."

"You son of a bitch," Ben replied, "you mean I don't understand gutter-level politics."

Thereafter they tried to avoid each other.

It was the closest senatorial race in the state in more than fifty years, but Bill emerged the happy victor. Ben was not at all happy about it, however, and Louise thought he might have no more to do with politics.

Yet Ben did not lose interest in politics. He was, in fact, more concerned than ever with Bill's career after Bill won the Senate seat. As he told Louise:

"Bill is as honest as any man I've ever known. But he's also one of the most ambitious. And he doesn't fully realize yet how much money it takes for a career in politics. It's a shame he and Alice are so poor. He told me during the race that they have a twenty-thousand mortgage on their house in Washington. I wanted to take it over at an easier rate, but he wouldn't let me. He told me, 'Anyone who investigates wrongdoing, as I do, has to make sure his record is spotlessly clean. You know and I know that I'd pay back the principal and interest to the last cent. But if word got out, who else would know? I'd be accused of corruption, and you'd be accused of buying a pipeline for some of your clients.' Bill was right, of course. But because he can't afford much travel I'm afraid of his getting out of touch with affairs in the state. And at present there are lots of things here that need his close attention."

From Ben's concern grew his idea for a carefully administered fund which would aid Bill in his political activities. Ben's partners and several Party leaders thought it an ideal plan, ethical as well as legal, far superior to the usual quiet arrangements whereby politicians received juggled accounts to carry on their activities.

There was nothing secret about the Porter Political Fund. Ben was its sole trustee and administered all of its monies. Gifts were solicited only from individuals, with each gift limited to five hundred dollars; corporations were not allowed to contribute. Ben made payments to William Porter upon receipt of bills or vouchers involving only political speaking and mailing schedules. Not one cent went for Bill's personal use, and the fund enabled him to carry on political activities without the usual subterfuges and payroll padding by which many, perhaps most, Congressmen hoodwinked the taxpayers. Once a year a certified public accounting firm in Attica conducted an audit of the fund. Ben sent a report of the audit to each contributor. In the first year he collected and disbursed about seventy-five hundred dollars. The next year the amount totaled around eight thousand.

In Bill's second year in the Senate he fired Gene as his legislative assistant. When he returned to Attica briefly for a speaking engagement, he was rather incoherent about the firing.

"I don't know what came over Gene. I really don't understand it. Ever since the last race he's been drinking heavily. I kept telling him, 'Gene, take it easy, take it easy.' But the trouble wasn't drinking alone. I guess that was only a symptom of something else. I no longer trusted him. He was shirking his duties. And then he showed up at our house one evening. He'd been drinking and blew his stack. He told me off. Said he was sick and tired of hunting for

[56]

communists under every sofa cushion. Crazy stuff like that. A complete reversal from everything we've always believed in. So I told him he was through."

Ben, thinking it good riddance, asked, "Where is he now?"

"I don't know. He just disappeared."

Louise thought it good riddance too, and Alice agreed with her. Before long they forgot Gene in the thrust of other events.

A strong element within the Party sought and obtained the agreement of a great war hero to run for the Presidency. The General was, in fact, an international hero, one of the renowned men of the century. Another Party element, more conservative, favored another candidate, a midlands senator who indicated that as President he would lead the country away from its international role. These two elements clashed at the national convention.

Bill was there as chairman of his state delegation. Ben was one of his floor managers. Alice and Louise went too, for it promised to be an exciting event.

Ben strongly favored the General, as did about half of his state delegation. But whom did Bill favor? To Ben's growing consternation he could not tell. Or, at least, Bill would not tell him. At one moment he had something good to say about the General. At the next he had something equally good to say about the General's adversary.

An old pol said, "Bill's playing his cards close to his vest."

"I hope," Ben replied, "he doesn't play 'em so close that he can't see them himself."

One midnight when they emerged from a long session in a hotel room, Ben cornered Bill in a corridor recess and said, "Look, tell me, *who* are you for?"

A strange expression came to Bill's face. Ben, thinking

at first he was looking at someone down the corridor, glanced swiftly over a shoulder. But then he realized Bill's expression was that of someone gazing into the future; it was the expression of Norman Rockwell's Boy Scouts.

Bill said, "I'll let you know in plenty of time, Ben. And then we must *all* be together on it."

So might have spoken Richard to some impertinent hostler whose only function was to saddle the King's horse.

Ben slammed shut the hotel room door, awakening Louise. He swore and said, "If you must fight battles, for God's sake bear the risks of them."

She heard what he said, but she didn't know what he meant. Even when he explained, she did not understand.

The next day Bill, with the help of Ben and many others, swung his state delegation solidly behind the General. It was done precisely at a strategic time. Later, following his nomination, the General summoned Bill to his hotel suite and thanked him personally; he detained him there for a long time and commended his record in Congress.

When Ben, highly pleased, told a reporter about Bill's lengthy interview, the reporter smirked and said, "The General says that to all the girls."

But the General did not. For, several hectic hours later, he announced that his choice for running mate was Senator William Paisley Porter.

As Ben and Louise started on the drive back to Attica, she said, "I'll never forget them standing up there in front of the convention—Bill and Alice, and the General and his wife." She had said it a dozen times.

And Ben replied as always, "Neither will I."

But then Louise said something new: "Looking at them I couldn't help but think, Ben, that you could have been standing there as the General's running mate."

"No, Louise, I could not."

"But——"

"I know. Bill ran first when I could have run. But there all similarity ends—and never forget it. If I had run and won, I wouldn't have handled those investigations the way he did. And if I hadn't done that, I'd have been just another green Congressman. And so I wouldn't have become a Senator. I take back what I said the other night about Bill. He's run all the risks of his battles. Nobody else can take credit because he really has done it on his own, he's made the decisions all the way through. I'm glad for him. And there's no envy or malice when I say Bill *needed* what's happened to him. I did not. That doesn't mean I'm a better man. It merely means I'm a different man. If I somehow had gotten into the House, I wouldn't have done anything memorable or maybe even have lasted very long. Because a part of me always would have been outside myself looking on and saying, 'Don't make an ass of yourself, the hell with it.' But one man's weakness can be another man's strength. So old man North is going to devote his full energies to the practice of law."

"Aren't you going to help in the campaign?"

"I suppose I'll tote some folding chairs. But what of importance can I really do? The General—and Bill—can't possibly lose."

He proved a poor prophet. . . .

A couple of weeks later he came home early from the office one hot afternoon and announced he was going to jump in the pool and stay there. Jim was delighted. They played in the water while Louise sunned herself on the patio and read magazines. She was immersed in a smashing good love story when a shadow fell across her and she looked up, startled, to see a tall, thin man standing beside her chair. Beyond him was another man, short and stout. Later she conjured something Hitchcockianly sinister about their sudden presence, but at the time she thought they were the men who had promised to come and check the eaves.

They were reporters, and they wanted to speak to Ben. He had been trying jackknifes off the board and doing badly; when Louise called him, he muscled out of the pool and came to them, rubbing his face with a towel. After the men had introduced themselves, Ben said, "I don't like to sound chicken, but could I see your credentials?"

Satisfied they were who they claimed to be, a reporter for a West Coast newspaper and a writer for a magazine, he invited them to sit down.

"Mr. North," one of the men said, "is there something called a William Porter Fund that supplements Senator Porter's salary?"

"There's a Willam Porter Fund, but your phrase about it supplementing his salary sounds sort of mendacious to me. He doesn't receive a cent from it personally, and the fund is in no way secret. Hundreds of people in the state know about it."

Then, slowly and thoroughly, he described the workings of the fund while the men made notes. He answered all of their questions and gave them the name and telephone number of the head of the accounting firm which audited the fund.

After they had gone, Louise asked, "Do you think you should have told them so much?"

"Of course," Ben replied. "What is there to hide? The whole plan is perfectly aboveboard. If I'd been evasive, they'd figure there was something dead up the creek."

But the story which appeared the next day made it seem there was something very dead up the creek. It sounded as if a cabal of rich men was paying William Porter to do its bidding in the United States Senate. It was the sort of story that every enemy of William Porter took delight in repeating, the kind that both the credulous and cynical found believable. The story spread with the speed of electric impulses.

Reporters for the wire services were the first to check with Ben; they were followed by inquiries from what seemed to be nearly every newspaper, radio, and television station in the country besides many foreign journalists. Though Ben had offered the gold of truth, the journalists believed he shammed with dross. Was the story that had been published true or false? Well, part was true and part false. In his honest effort to separate truth from falsehood, fact from innuendo, Ben fractured the patience and credulousness of his impatient, incredulous questioners.

Within hours he was at bay. He left his office, had his telephone disconnected, and, peering from behind a curtain of his house like a hunted criminal, saw that a vigilante band of journalists had him surrounded. After dark he slipped across his back yard to a neighboring house and asked a friend to drive him to the airport.

Somehow, Bill seemed to be the last to realize the fate in store for him. Perhaps it was simply a matter of poor communications, of telegraph operators who left their keys too soon in the tank towns of an eastern state. In any event, Vice-Presidential candidate William Paisley Porter and his wife had been blissfully chugging along in their campaign train, playing to large and enthusiastic audiences from the rear observation platform, when, from a siding in the shadow of a plant which stank of sulfurous chemicals, the candidate heard boos and glimpsed a crudely lettered sign that read PORTER TELL THE TRUTH FOR A CHANGE.

Others besides him saw and wondered. A couple of hours later at another stop the AP general desk finally got an urgent message through to its correspondent aboard the train. Bill Porter called a news conference at seven that evening and gave substantially the same account of the fund as Ben; for further details he suggested that their offices check with Ben in Attica, not realizing that the journalistic tribe already had hounded Ben out of town and started him on a curious, impulsive journey.

Bill, taking a Methodist satisfaction in the truth setting him free of blame, remained calm and cheerful until around ten that evening. Then the Chairman of the National Committee and his chief adviser, an unsuccessful former Presidential candidate, finally reached him. Bill talked with them from a stationmaster's office near his sided train, and when he returned to his compartment he was badly shaken.

Ben found him there about six o'clock the next morning after a night-long journey by plane and auto that ended with his scraping a shin when he stumbled over a railroad track. Bill, wearing a faded robe, stuck his head out of his compartment as Ben argued loudly with a train guard. A sleepy reporter was approaching, and Bill plucked him inside. The air-conditioning had failed and there was a sour smell in the compartment. Bill's unshaven face looked puffy, his eyes were red-rimmed, his hair tousled. Slamming shut the door and locking it, he demanded:

"What did you tell them?"

"The truth. They've distorted it. They don't want to believe it."

"Nobody wants to believe it." Bill's voice was hoarse. "They got me on the phone last night. The Chairman said the General is in a towering rage. That's what he said. 'The General is in a towering rage.' And he said, 'If you can't immediately set your house in order, then withdraw from the race.' *Set your house in order!* I tried to explain to him it *is*. But——"

[62]

"Sit down." Ben sank wearily onto a chair. "Here's my idea. Break off your schedule today——"

"It's already canceled. The Chairman said I'm not to make any more appearances till they've decided on the next move."

Ben stared at him, then said, "I've brought everything with me in this briefcase. All the records, all the——"

"Give it to me." Bill extended a hand.

"Wait a minute, Bill. Get shaved and dressed and let's get off this train. We'll rent a room in town and work together on a full, careful statement that——"

"Give me the records, Ben." Bill rested his right hand on the briefcase.

"Well, naturally, that's why I brought them. But——"

"Ben"—Bill's gaze avoided his—"I have to go this alone. The Chairman—the General—everybody says——"

"I understand that, but I'm trying to help you."

"Ben"—Bill's gaze finally met his fleetingly—"they— they say I have to disassociate myself from you. They said, 'Get North entirely out of the picture.' That's what they said."

Ben felt a burning behind his eyes that might have been tears he had forgotten how to shed. He did not remember saying anything else. When he left the train he did not have his briefcase. . . .

He wished urgently to get home to Attica and tell Louise all that had happened. Instead, acting again on impulse, he went to Washington and finally gained admittance to the Chairman's office. The Chairman put it bluntly:

"Mr. North, I'm sure you had the best of intentions when you started that fund. But now all of us feel the best way you can serve the Party cause is to go underground and stay there till the elections are over. Frankly, I don't know whether Porter will remain on the ticket. There's a strong move to dump him, and the General is inclined to go along with it. He can't afford to have his name and reputation tarnished with——"

"Please," Ben interrupted. "What tarnish is there? That's why I came to see you. Do you and the others have a clear understanding yourselves of what——"

"It doesn't matter what we understand," the Chairman said. "It's what the *public* understands, and right now Bill Porter threatens to drag down the whole ticket with——"

Ben continued to argue until the Chairman dismissed him. It was, he knew, not simply dismissal but banishment.

When he reached home and told Louise what had happened, she listened sympathetically. But then she said, "Wouldn't it be terrible if this thing should ruin Bill's political career."

Later that night Alice telephoned Louise. She had come back to the Porters' apartment in Attica while Bill had gone someplace in order to prepare for a television and radio appearance in which he would explain his situation to the American people. Would Louise come over and stay with her?

"Why of course!" Louise replied. "I'll be over in a few minutes. Ben will stay with Jim till it's over."

She did not return until the following midnight after Bill had talked to a nationwide audience from an Attica television station. Ben watched alone in the living room with pained fascination as Bill, joined at the close by Alice and little Penny, made an extraordinary emotional appeal to the voters.

When Louise came home her eyes were red and her voice shrill. "I was right there in the studio with them. Wasn't he wonderful! Wasn't *she* wonderful! Afterwards we had a good cry."

"I don't know how he did it," Ben said. "I couldn't have if my life depended on it."

"Then you couldn't be Vice-President of the United States," Louise replied. "Bill *will* be."

And in November he was.

Ben did not see or hear from him after that early morning on the railroad siding. But he hoped, as inauguration approached, that his banishment would end.

At last Louise received a phone call one evening from Alice in Washington. She came from the phone looking both puzzled and pleased.

"Alice wants me to attend the inauguration. But I guess I won't go because she didn't mention your coming too. I can understand in a way. Can't you? You know, give it a little more time for things to—die down a bit more."

Ben opened a newspaper and spoke from behind its pages. "Yes, I understand. Go, Louise. You've never been to an inauguration."

So she went.

After Hochstein left Louise at her apartment house that Tuesday night he sped toward Georgetown with Helen.

"Mrs. North doesn't like me," he said. "I don't know why."

"You mean you're such a lovable person and all? Come, Hochy, you're supposed to have the hide of a rhinoceros and be very bright besides. Louise doesn't dislike you personally. She's the same toward everyone in government who's close to Bill. They all remind her of an unpleasant fact about her life."

"I hadn't thought of that," Hochstein said. "I mean the fact her husband fell from grace."

"Bill couldn't do anything else."

"Why not? You mean he didn't *want* to do anything else for fear the name of North would remind the public of that long-past painful incident he wants to forget. You're always so defensive of the President, Helen."

Was he rebuking her? Yet his own loyalty to the President was beyond question. Hochstein's enemies said many things about him, one of the less cruel being some doggerel that began, "Jack be nimble, Jack be quick . . ." Although Hochstein could be both nimble and quick in the political arena, he had strong convictions, was totally honest, and never hesitated to present his boss with an unpleasant fact or a different viewpoint.

The close of Helen's house was lighted like a stage. The Jaguar, crossing the electronic eye, signaled the night watchman, Dave McKenna, who limped from the service doorway, pistol loose in his holster. The elaborate precautions of life in the nation's capital, though sensible, always struck Helen as absurd if one believed in historical "progress": castle, keep, and peasantry run wild so late in the twentieth century!

"Come in, Hochy, and I'll pour you a drink."

As he began to fix her a light vermouth and soda, he said, "I can't get over you people from Greenleaf."

"What about us?"

"The way you've stuck together instead of spinning off in all directions as most people do. Personally, I know scarcely anybody today I knew twenty-five years ago."

"Some of us have spun off," Helen said. "And some stuck together—more loosely than it might appear. Shared memories, I guess."

Hochstein poured himself brandy and sat down. "You people must see things about the President that no one else can. You must remember a bright, sensitive boy whom the world has hurt deeply in his honest effort to shape it into his own sincere likeness. All those dirty political wars. And his skin is really as thin as tissue paper. Why did he want to bother with it?"

She pondered his remark, seeing deeply into him. Behind the political strategist, the thinker, the lawyer, behind the Ivy League patina, the bold navigator who had flown more than one hundred B-24 missions over Europe in World War Two, the gay bachelor chaser of beautiful *shkotzim* girls, behind all these there was this fifty-two-year-old Jewish kid who had graduated from Erasmus High, whose father had run a candy store, whose true roots still were in New York, who had a great feel for cynicism and loving.

The chiming of the front door bell interrupted her musing, and Dave McKenna shuffled in, holding his old felt hat before him like a tray. "Sorry, Mrs. Carlton, forgot to give you this. The only message tonight that asked you to call." He took a slip of paper from his hat, and she read his careful Spencerian hand:

Please call Mr. North at home until midnight 212-883-5595.

It was just ten minutes before twelve, and she said to Hochstein, "I don't know why, but I have to call my lawyer in New York."

"Sounds impressive," Hochstein replied. "I never thought about it before, but I'll bet your lawyer is Ben North of Burton, North, McGinnis, and Mosely."

"I'll bet you're right," Helen said, lifting the receiver and beginning to dial.

Hochstein wished he could listen to her conversation, but, rising and taking his brandy with him, he strolled to the far end of the room and gazed at some first editions of William Faulkner which were embraced by carved ebony children's arms mounted as bookends.

He was intensely curious about Helen Carlton. People liked to say of her home, "This is the house that books built," but Hochstein knew that was for the birds. No author lived and entertained so grandly unless his name was spelled Harold Robbins or something similar. People also remarked that "Helen invested wisely." Had she bought IBM or Xerox when they were selling for 15? There was another story that she had done well in real estate. And there were the usual stories that circulated about any very wealthy widow who had not received her money from a deceased husband: how she had slept discreetly with a Texas oil billionaire, a member of British royalty, a renowned and wealthy governor—the identity of the sleeper depending on the gossiper of the moment. Hochstein did not believe any of it.

At the other end of the room Helen was making no effort to keep her voice lowered. "Well yes, Ben, I can take the shuttle up tomorrow morning. But don't you just want to use your own judgment which I'll follow anyway? . . . Well, all right. . . . What time? . . . No kidding! About taxes? . . . Ben, that's priceless. Of course you can take me to lunch. . . . See you then."

Hanging up, Helen called, "Hochy, since when have you been devoted to the works of Faulkner?"

He ambled back at her.

She said, "I had an appointment with Ben on Thursday, he found out late this afternoon he has to be in court. You know him, don't you?"

"I've met him in a business way a couple of times. You have a good lawyer, Helen. They say the best about him: he loves to go to court."

"He's been awfully good to me. Anyway, I'm going up there tomorrow. He's seeing me at noon right after— Hochy, guess what! There *is* a Joe McCurdy! And he has a tax problem! He has an appointment with Ben about it."

Hochstein took a step forward, and then a step backward. He must have cracked his deadpan, for Helen said:

"Why do you look so shocked? Why shouldn't there be a man named Joseph P. McCurdy with tax problems?"

"Joseph P.?" asked Hochstein.

"Well, that's what Ben said. He brought home a copy of his schedule so he could figure where to fit me in. And he laughed and remarked about my following Joe McCurdy —Joseph P. McCurdy."

"Is the guy a regular client of North's?"

"How should I know?"

"Well, you don't just come in off the street and get North to give you an hour of his expensive time."

Joseph P. McCurdy, a man with tax problems, consulting at eleven tomorrow morning with the senior partner of the President's former New York law firm! If coincidence, it had an extraordinarily long and twisted arm.

"Hochy, you act upset. You're doing a kind of minuet there with your feet."

"Am I?" Hochstein brought his heels together and gulped some brandy.

Helen smiled at him. "And now your nostrils are twitching. Do you smell something?"

"Conspiracy." He could not resist saying it. "One of the most familiar odors of the legal profession. I have a keen nose for it."

"What on earth are you talking about? There's been too much conspiracy talk in Washington for too many years."

"Maybe so. But remember the song Ariel sang in Gonzalo's ear:

'While you here do snoring lie,
Open-eyed conspiracy
    His time doth take
If of life you keep a care

[70]

> Shake off slumber, and beware:
> Awake, awake!' "

He grinned. "Shakespeare. *The Tempest.* Act Two, Scene One."

Helen applauded. "Bravo, Hochy, bravo. I didn't know you had it in you. I thought all you could quote were old federal statutes. Well, you were telling me this tax revolt is a really serious situation that poses a threat to Bill's second term and you feel there is some kind of conspiracy behind it."

"I never said anything of the sort, and you know it. I said there is no revolt to speak of, the President is certain to win a second term, and the only conspiracy is something you imagine. What time did you say your appointment is with North?"

"I didn't say, but it's at noon."

"And Joseph P. McCurdy's appointment is at?"

"Mmm—eleven o'clock. Hochy, let's talk about the tax revolt. I know it's serious. As serious as the stock market situation. What is Bill going to do about it? Did he give you any clues when you talked about it at the White House tonight?"

He stared at her silently, and she grimaced.

He said, "As I remember, North's office is on Pine Street."

She sighed. "Yes."

After Hochstein had gone, Helen strolled through the labyrinth of rooms, turning out lights and leaving others burning, angling some pictures differently, putting in a drawer a jeweled dagger which was a gift from a Moroccan prince. So many *things,* and everyone always saying how precious they were to her. No one knew that in the early hours of nearly every morning she felt they were an insupportable burden.

Climbing the short flight of stairs to her apartment, she passed into the large writing room and locked the door behind her. Originally, spacious windows had afforded the writing room pleasant views of the garden, but she had had the windows sealed and now books lined the walls from floor to ceiling around the room. Except for the doorways to the stairs at one end of the room and to her bedroom and bath at the other, there was only one large break in the rows of books.

A painting framed there and kept perpetually lighted was the only picture in the room. It was a portrait of Jim Carlton, done by Paul Sagorin from photographs. Jim wore a white short-sleeved shirt, open at the throat, such as he used to wear on summer evenings in Greenleaf, and Sagorin had captured that special expression of his, that hint of a smile as when he had been about to say something but then had thought better of it. You would think that Sagorin (who had not yet become famous) had known him well, for wherever she went went in the room Jim's gaze was upon her. No doubt it was a very romantic painting, yet it had some rare quality Helen never could define. But after all, she never had been able to define precisely the rare quality of Jim Carlton. . . .

She still found it hard to believe they had been married.

In her teens Helen had made up her mind no one ever would ask her to marry. Convinced she was bright, she was equally certain she was very plain. It took her a long time to discover that boys failed to pursue her not because she was bright or plain but because she had a mordant wit: they thought she was laughing at them. But by that time she had immersed herself in a satisfactory world of writing stories in which she could make herself beautiful, stupid, and not at all witty.

Until three days before the play was to open in the high school auditorium, she had found Jim Carlton simply the most interesting man in Greenleaf. *He grows on you* was the way she thought of him during the weeks of rehearsal. Accustomed to doing everything for herself, she was surprised to learn how helpful a man could be.

Then, on that Tuesday evening after nearly everyone had left, she had been struggling futilely with a piece of scenery when Jim came out of the shadows and said, "Here." However, instead of taking hold of the canvas frame, he wrapped his arms about her, kissed her deeply on the lips, and said, "I love you, Helen."

She was so astonished that she had actually felt faint. Her mind signaled alarming messages such as befuddled the beautiful heroines she had ceased to create because magazine editors had found them incredible.

Jim said, "Will you marry me?"

And she, with unimpeachable honesty, replied, "I think I'm going to be sick."

But she had recovered herself and soon decided that marrying Jim would be the most exciting experience in the world. In her practical way she then asked, "When?"

He looked her up and down and said, "We can get a license in Centerville tomorrow and have a justice of the peace I know there perform the ceremony Saturday midnight after the last show."

So it was done. They stayed until Monday morning at the Merwin Hotel in Attica, and by that time they had discovered that loving was as natural as breathing to both. . . .

Now, after gazing at his portrait for a time, she went into her bedroom. She struggled constantly against the sleeping pill habit, but she knew she would not sleep tonight unless she took one.

Recently a column in the Washington *Post* reported that Helen Carlton had turned down an offer from a New York publisher for her memoirs. The item quoted Helen as saying, "Many of my memories are in the public domain. The rest are too private to be of concern to anyone. . . ."

After Jim enlisted in the Marines, she had only two weekends with him before he was shipped overseas. He phoned her in April, 1942, saying he had come to Quantico from a Southern training camp and would have a pass for the entire next weekend. Indeed she would meet him in Washington! Luck was with her. The very next day she was able to sublet their house, furnished, to the man who had taken over Jim's Chevrolet agency. She crammed all the essentials into two suitcases and, of course, took her portable typewriter.

Jim was waiting for her in the lobby of the Willard Hotel on Friday evening when she trudged in with her luggage. At first she did not recognize him. There stood a lean, handsome Marine sergeant wearing a smart uniform and high, polished boots such as she had never seen before. . . .

Around nine o'clock they started out of the hotel to go to O'Donnell's Restaurant. A pudgy colonel started toward the revolving door onto Pennsylvania Avenue at the same time as they. Jim hung back respectfully. But the colonel grinned, tossed him a salute, and said, "After you, Sergeant."

As they crossed Fourteenth Street Helen asked, "What was that all about? Aren't you supposed to salute *him*?"

It was the only time she heard Jim speak with frank pride about anything he had done. "This get-up I'm wearing means I've been accepted by Red Mike Edson's Raiders. That's an elite unit. Not bad for an old guy of thirty-two."

If he was dismayed by her decision to leave Greenleaf and find herself a job in Washington, he did not show it. He warned her he did not know how long he would be at Quantico or anyplace else. She said she realized that but would take her chances.

She saw him on one other weekend before he was sent to the West Coast and then into the Pacific.

Helen's life in Washington in 1942 was like that of thousands of other young women. War had transformed the nation's capital from a quiet, provincial city into a frenetic complex whose chief industry seemed to be clattering typewriters turning out triplicates of everything. The search for competent workers consumed bureaucrats like a quest for gold.

Helen went to work in the Navy Department's Bureau of Ships, far down Constitution Avenue, for what to her was the fabulous salary of $52.50 a week. In the 1700 block of N Street Northwest, where handsome old houses were surrendering themselves to roomers, she found a tiny two-room apartment with ceilings fifteen feet high. Not much but its history commended it: the two little rooms once had composed half the dining room when the house had been inhabited by Assistant Secretary of the Navy Theodore Roosevelt, and the bath and kitchenette represented the transformation of a butler's pantry. Yet the historical fact enchanted Helen as much as if she had found a habitable villa in the Roman Forum.

Six mornings a week she walked down Connecticut Avenue to her job because she believed the exercise healthful. Often she ate dinner at a small cafeteria named the Vesuvius on Connecticut just below Dupont Circle. Her job was dull, her fellow workers and bosses uninteresting; she had no friends and lived unto herself.

In these respects her life was as barren as that of thousands of other government workers, many of whom quit and went home from loneliness and boredom. However, Helen found life interesting despite the routine. She had fallen in love with Washington, and she hoped that when Jim returned from service he would not want to go back to Greenleaf. Though nothing important happened in that drowsy spring and humid summer, Helen lived with the constant expectation that it soon would.

Perhaps her sense of expectation came from the fact that she was writing another novel—her third—in every spare moment when she was not out exploring the city. Was expectation the unquenchable fire that characterized a writer, and was writing simply its only possible fuel? Each of the two novels she had finished in Greenleaf had been returned by a dozen publishers. Though she had not yet published anything, she seemed incapable of discouragement. She thought of herself as a writer, and she was convinced she was creating her best work to date—a novel about several women who had come to Washington as wartime government workers and lived together in a rooming house.

On Sunday, August 9, Helen went out early to buy the *Post*. She had intended to go to a People's Drugstore for breakfast, but she didn't get there. Headlines proclaimed that the Marines had landed on a Pacific island named Guadalcanal. Recalling Jim's censored letters, she knew instinctively where he was. She hurried home and turned on her radio, and thereafter she bought every available newspaper and listened to the radio constantly. A letter from Jim early in September was unsatisfactory in its blandness. She knew more about the situation on Guadalcanal from reading and listening than Jim ever would admit to her. The Marines, fighting heavy Japanese odds, endured torrential rains and subsisted on damp rice and dehydrated potatoes. Sometimes a single sentence in a correspondent's report would keep her awake for hours in torment: "The night was vivid with flares, shellfire, obscenity, raucous challenges, and the screams of dying men."

September 17 was a day of heavy rain in Washington. Helen, arriving home about six o'clock, groped for her mailbox in the dimly lighted vestibule. A man moved slowly out of the shadows, and she stepped back in alarm.

"Mrs. Carlton?"

Making out his features, she saw that he was really a boy. On the shoulders of his wet Navy raincoat were an ensign's gold bars.

"You are Mrs. Carlton?"

She must have said yes, for he held something out to her, and then, incredibly, she saw that his eyes were filled with tears.

"I'm sorry," he gasped, and fled.

The telegram regretted to inform her that Master Sergeant James Carlton had been killed in action on September 10.

She walked for what seemed to be hours, lowering her tear-hot face in the cooling rain. At last she found herself coming around Dupont Circle from the north. She could not bear the thought of going back to her apartment; just then the image of her typewriter waiting with a blank sheet of paper rolled in seemed the greatest mockery of her empty life. Supposedly she must try to eat something.

She turned into the Vesuvius. It was only eight fifteen, and the small cafeteria still was crowded. She went through the line and took something, then found a vacant table. Looking down at her chicken pot pie, she breathed deeply with a resolution not to cry again.

"Is this seat taken?" a man asked. "I don't mean to intrude, but there's no other place."

It happened all the time at the Vesuvius that strangers shared the same table. Helen glanced up at an aging man she had seen there several times previously; his white hair and benign face somehow made her think of a judge.

He made no move to begin unloading his tray until she said, "No, it's—vacant." Perhaps it was the word "vacant" that made her start to cry again. "I'm sorry," she said at last, while he, frowning, finished arranging his dishes on the table opposite her. "I—I just got some bad news."

He sat down and swallowed a spoonful of soup. "Tell me about it."

She did. And when she looked up at him again she saw that his bright blue eyes were dimmed by tears.

His name was John Quincy, his wife of forty years had died in February, and he was alone in the world. Maryland used to be his home, but now he lived in an apartment house on the Circle and found this a convenient spot to take his meals.

For a long time that was all she learned about him. Whenever they saw each other at the Vesuvius at dinnertime they sat together. Their conversation was impersonal, but Helen found that she enjoyed Mr. Quincy's companionship at dinner.

The letters that came from Greenleaf after she told their friends of Jim's death were like messages from another planet. She was uncertain what to do, but she was determined not to go back there.

On a bright November morning her boss, a retired naval captain, came panting from the chief's office, cast her a look of stark amazement, and told her to follow him. What had gone wrong? The Admiral rose from his desk, took her by the hand, and told her effusively how proud he was to have her "in my crew." But what could have gone so right?

A lieutenant stepped forward and read some gibberish that told the tale. Helen understood it only slowly. Jim had been awarded the Congressional Medal of Honor posthumously for heroism on Bloody Ridge in Guadalcanal, where he had died at a machine gun while covering the redeployment of his company and enabling it to . . . She wept for the first time in days. Now, just as she was beginning to cope with the grim fact, Jim had brought it all back. He had gone from her forever not as a result of a chance bullet, which she was beginning to accept, but through a calculated act of courage that had meant almost certain death.

The young officer had more to tell. Tomorrow afternoon at the White House President Roosevelt would present her with the medal and the citation. A car and escort would call for her at her apartment. . . .

The next afternoon Helen, as in a trance, rode to the White House with a friendly, gray-haired Marine brigadier. The man who took her hand and smiled up at her from his wheelchair looked and sounded precisely like the President, whom Helen had seen in photographs and newsreels.

It was done, with the deep feeling of a ceremony of death or marriage, and then the President took her hand again and said, "Of such stuff as your husband, thank God, our country is made."

A tall woman stepped to Helen, hand extended, and said, "Mrs. Carlton, I'm Eleanor Roosevelt. Won't you please come up for tea?"

Perhaps the President knew Helen was at the breaking point, for he smiled and said, "Tea? Tea! If Mrs. Carlton doesn't want a good stiff drink, then that's really something to tell to the Marines."

A half-dozen people gathered upstairs in Mrs. Roosevelt's living room. All offered Helen the deference due a hero's widow, but Mrs. Roosevelt treated her like an old friend. She realized she was revealing more about herself to the First Lady than she had to anyone in a long time. Only then did she know how lonely she had been.

"How wonderful you're a writer," Mrs. Roosevelt said. "Don't let the Bureau of Ships sink your writing."

"But I haven't published anything yet," Helen replied quickly. "I'm just—trying."

"I know lots of writers who should keep *trying*—and have not published anything yet." Mrs. Roosevelt turned to a tall, dark man who had been introduced as Nathan Stone. "Do you agree, Nathan?"

He did, and Mrs. Roosevelt told Helen he was the editor-in-chief of Parker's, the well-known New York publishing house. Helen felt in greater awe of him than she had even of the President. Her awe must have showed, for Parker, a kindly man, tried to put her at ease.

"I'm down here on a fishing expedition, Mrs. Carlton. If the government is going to ration our paper, then we'll have to ration what we publish—and try to make every book the *best*. So far I've had only one good nibble. A juvenile writer. We're trimming our course and going to emphasize books for younger readers for a while. Why bother with junky novels at a time like this? In the past three days, I've come across not just one but *two* junky novels by writers who have studied *Grand Hotel* and have written almost identical stories about people coming to work in Washington in wartime."

Helen felt she was dying, almost as painfully as she

[80]

had died when she heard about Jim. They must have sensed it by her expression, for Mrs. Roosevelt said quickly, "Why, Nathan, maybe Mrs. Carlton—" And he, as quickly, said, "Of course such a theme can be—"

Helen breathed again. She said, "I've abandoned fiction—adult fiction. I'm trying biography—uh, for young people."

"Really?" Stone gazed at her intently. "What are you writing now?"

She uttered a nervous sound. "It's a strange coincidence. I'm—almost embarrassed to mention it. But I'm working on a biography of President Franklin Roosevelt."

Helen quit her job and wrote a forty-thousand-word biography of the President in twenty-two days. She sent a copy to Mrs. Roosevelt, who invited her to lunch and gave her deeper insight into a few episodes in the President's life. After revising the manuscript quickly, Helen mailed it to Nathan Stone.

That evening when she went to the Vesuvius for the first time in more than a month, Mr. Quincy brought his tray to her table.

"Well, Mrs. Carlton, I thought you'd given up the old Vesuvius for more fashionable places."

She did not tell him she had been eating out of cans. She did not tell him anything for fear of bragging—which, she believed, always brought bad luck. She simply said, "I've been working overtime."

As she rose to leave, Mr. Quincy said, "You haven't told me about the great thing that happened. I saw your picture in the paper. It's an honor to be acquainted with the wife of such a brave man. Why didn't you mention it, Mrs. Carlton?"

[81]

"It would have sounded like bragging."

Mr. Quincy smiled. "I like that. I don't believe in bragging either. Good evening, Mrs. Carlton."

A telegram of acceptance came from Nathan Stone. It was followed by a contract and a check for fifteen hundred as an advance against royalties. Then the new juvenile editor of Parker's, Adele Shackford, came to Washington and took Helen to lunch. By the time they parted, Helen had agreed to write four more biographies of famous American Presidents.

Obtaining working space in the Congressional Library, she discovered that she was a highly proficient hack. She could write a forty-thousand-word biography of any President in three weeks. Adele Shackford insisted, however, that Helen was not a hack, that she treated her subjects objectively, entertainingly, never worshipfully.

Possibly in an effort to justify Adele's praise, Helen invented the Burke family—two young sisters and a brother whose father was a heroic airplane pilot. When the Burkes breathed life in *Say, Pilgrims!* on Parker's juvenile list Helen did not visualize that their adventures would continue through twenty novels which would sell more than one million copies. . . .

One bright afternoon in September, 1943, Helen left the Congressional Library early to catch a trolley downtown and shop for furnishings for her new apartment on Sixteenth Street above Scott Circle. While waiting on a safety island, she saw Mr. Quincy come from the House Office Building. Glimpsing her, he waved, and crossed over.

"Mrs. Carlton, I haven't seen you in weeks. Where are you bound?"

"Woodward's. You're looking fit, Mr. Quincy."

"I feel terrible. Just been to see my Congressman about a stupid zoning law in Maryland. It's death on taxes. I'll give you a lift. I'm parked over in that no-parking area." She walked with him. "So you're a writer! All I ever learn about you I read in the papers. Read in the *Star* about your autographing party at Brentano's and Mrs. Roosevelt being there. I'm not a great admirer of our President, but I bought a copy. Liked it. It doesn't read like a children's book."

"They tell me," Helen said, "that's the secret of successful books for children."

"What are you doing with all your money?"

"Putting it in the bank—what's left."

"Do you like money, Mrs. Carlton?"

Helen glanced at him in surprise. "I work hard to make and save it. As a matter of fact, I guess I'm crazy about money."

"An honest answer. What would you do if you had a lot of it?"

"I'd travel. But mainly I guess I'd just like to *have* it. I grew up poor."

"Honest again. If you'd like to ride out to Maryland with me I'll show you how you can make a lot of money."

The idea appealed to her sense of adventure—and greed.

Following a side road out of Silver Spring, they passed into an area of untilled farmland. Mr. Quincy said he owned the land on both sides of the road, about two thousand acres of it.

"So you're in real estate." Helen was disappointed in him. "And you want to sell me a lot."

"I am *not* in real estate." He sounded indignant. "I spent forty years making a dishonest living as a lawyer. Why should I want to compound the crime and spend my last days dealing in anything so thoroughly reprehensible as real estate? I've been hanging onto this property for years, paying the taxes, watching Washington creep out to me. All the big District dealers are pestering me. Their offers keep going up, but I won't sell till the taxes put me on my back—a position I expect to assume before long. In twenty years, maybe less, this land will be worth forty thousand and more an acre. But I won't be here in twenty years. Even if I were, the taxes would long since have strangled me. I don't have that kind of money. Would you like a cold beer and then some supper?"

Mr. Quincy made his proposition over beer. He invited her to become his "partner" in an effort to keep the land from the big dealers as long as possible. For each two thousand she contributed toward taxes in their joint effort she would receive title to one acre of choice future building sites. It sounded dangerous, yet fascinating.

"But why me, Mr. Quincy?"

"I like your style. My wife had a style like yours. I have no living relatives, not even a close friend left. There are just names and faces around any more. Before you do anything you must get yourself a good, honest lawyer. There are still a few in the District. I'm my own lawyer. Have your lawyer investigate me and my land and my proposition thoroughly. If I think he's cheating you, I'll let you know. As I said, Mrs. Carlton, I like your style. It's always struck me, looking on from a distance, that writers have more of a gambler's nerve and true grit than any other species. But I never really knew a writer till I met you. And now I see my hunch was right."

Mrs. Roosevelt, ever fascinated by any endeavor requiring nerve, offered Helen an excellent lawyer. By the end of the year she held title to twelve of Mr. Quincy's acres. And after two more years she owned thirty-four acres of empty land.

In those years Helen was a fabulously prolific writer who worked nine and ten hours a day six days a week. In addition to the books published in her own name, she wrote juvenile fiction and nonfiction under pseudonyms for two publishing houses besides Parker's.

She never took her books seriously. Secretly she was ashamed of her work because its facileness showed she had quit the creative ordeal that had marked her beginnings as a writer in Greenleaf. Occasionally she thought she might try to write a good book for mature readers, but as time passed she knew she never would.

Many of her friends were eloquent apologists for what she was doing. Soon after Bill began to run for Congress Ben came to Washington on business and brought Louise with him. Helen, learning of their visit, asked them to stay in her apartment.

Louise praised her books lavishly. "And you're obviously making a good living at it. It's such clean work when you see all the filth that's published these days. . . ."

Ben did not say anything until—finally: "The important thing, Helen, are you *enjoying* what you write?"

Right then she made up her mind about a matter she had been pondering for some time. She always had liked and respected Ben; he impressed her as being more like Jim than any man she knew. An opportunity to broach the subject came the next morning when she served him breakfast at seven o'clock. He, like Helen, was an early riser, while Louise always slept late.

She told him about her agreement with John Quincy. Her lawyer had died a few months previously and she was dissatisfied with the way another member of the firm was handling her affairs. Would Ben serve as her lawyer?

He was frankly amazed. Before he agreed he pointed out that he practiced far away in Attica and had no knowledge of real estate matters in the Washington area. But Helen had made up her mind—an act that never gave her any trouble.

He said, "You've driven a strange, hard bargain with yourself, Helen. Aren't you afraid this straining for a big pot of money at some future time may affect your writing?"

"No, because my writing goals have become simple and predictable." She told him about that afternoon at the White House. "I made a compromise. I'm honest enough with myself to know I've gone about it like launching a career of prostitution. I do it solely for money, with facility but without much pleasure. I've read that whores often come to their profession after a simpleminded act of infidelity to someone or some ideal they cherish. Well, I went through a creative ideal I cherished—two and one-half novels and forty short stories rejected. And I've sometimes thought that I bring to my career the techniques learned in an act of love."

Ben seemed at a loss. "But all for money?"

"Then call it ambition. That lower-middle-class disease. Bill Porter has it—and so does Alice. I wasn't surprised to hear he's trying for a career in politics. He's insatiably ambitious, but brings no deep convictions to politics. I can say that about him because I can say the same of myself and what I'm doing. Have you ever thought to what an extent compromise characterizes our American society? We've developed it into a simple reflex, sort of like a gull's wings in a shifting wind. Compromise has become such a reflex that people rarely do what they wish or say what they mean, and after a while they naturally don't know what they want or can even remember what they once thought."

Helen, fearing that she would become downright misanthropic, had for some time been trying to make amends with charitable gestures toward her fellows. In seeking to discipline her feeling, she hit upon an especially masochistic course: she became a friendly and attentive hostess.

In her smiling effort she learned to accept a depressing fact of life: almost everybody in the world will come to your home, drink your liquor, eat your food, smoke your tobacco, and go away with a word of perfunctory gratitude but no thought of reciprocation. For the innumerable grabbers and hustlers of the earth it always was a pleasing vindication of their grabbing and hustling.

When Bill came to Congress, Helen invited Alice and him and Gene to dinner. She also invited four others; a Congressman and his wife, and a well-placed official in Interior and his wife, taking care to inform each couple that the other would be present, and thereby kindling in each the warm prospect of extracting some future favor. There was no trick in getting these grabbers and hustlers to her dinner table. (As she had heard people who worked on Constitution Avenue say: "It never hurts to have friends on the Hill." And as she had heard people from the Hill say: "It never hurts to have friends on Constitution Avenue.")

That evening the Congressman and the Interior official, hearty types both, began their encounter with the splash and bellow of walruses, letting off their competitive strain without breaking anything of consequence. Meanwhile Bill, Alice, and Gene sat on the sidelines as watchfully as penguins.

At first Helen felt sorry for them. Bill's and Gene's shoes were too narrow, their lapels too wide; Alice's dress was not quite right in some indescribable way. Their manner was tense, their few remarks strained.

But then Alice discovered that the women were much like herself and she entered into the traditional talk: children, hired help, shopping, real estate covenants. Helen, who had become adept at carrying on a lucid conversation with women while managing to hear what the men were saying, saw that Bill and Gene had begun to play the Congressional game. Bill played rookie to the veteran Congressman—respectful, attentive, eager to learn, until his manner won the veteran's accolade:

"You'll fit right *in*, Bill! Don't worry. Any questions, you drop 'round an' ask *me*."

Gene, in turn, played loyal squire to his Sir William, letting it be known that while the master was new in this particular field, he had wielded a keen blade in other engagements. And then, to show that he was a man among men, Gene lowered his voice and told a raunchy story that sent the older men into fits of phlegmy laughter.

To Helen it was pretty grim. But Alice, Bill, and Gene, lingering after the others had left, raved about a wonderful evening and heaped gratitude on her for having introduced them to such important people. Their thanks merely made her feel guilty over pretending to find satisfaction in an occasion she had detested.

Gene, staying on after Alice and Bill, increased her sense of guilt with a remark:

"I thought you were against us. Bill did too. Jim having been a New Dealer, you know. But tonight proved we were wrong."

They were right, however. She never had voted for their Party—and thought she never would.

After another drink Gene became sentimental about Jim, times past in Greenleaf, and then about himself and his climb to the nation's capital. He made Helen uncomfortable. When he began to talk about her being attractive, she eased him out the door.

Gene seemed to imagine that she entertained a lot because she hoped to capture a man. Yet nothing was further from her intentions. The thought of anything more than passing male companionship was distasteful to her.

[88]

She had loved Jim, and he had loved her, and the notion of trying to repeat that profound emotion seemed as foolish as it would be to try to conquer Mount Everest a second time.

Nevertheless, Gene continued to display fitful gallantry toward her. For reasons she could not fully analyze he was attractive to women; he was not handsome or graceful, nor was he an entertaining conversationalist. Perhaps, however, most women liked the thing about him that Helen did not: he had a restless, driving energy that seemed undirected and often took the form of a bumbling curiosity. Intensive questioning was his notion of conversation, and Helen observed how many women were therefore flattered by his attentiveness. She heard a couple of women say he was "sexy," but she thought he simply seemed far younger than his years.

In any event, he sometimes took her to parties where she met people she would not have otherwise—Southern Congressmen, agents and minor officials from the Justice Department, itinerant majors and colonels from the Pentagon. They were a loud, hard-drinking, freewheeling bunch, and their women sounded like the destruction of piano wires. Gene liked them—and they liked him. Party lines made no difference, for Gene was in the thick of the fight against the goddamn Commies. Among members of the Texas delegation, where he was a favorite, he took on the accent of the Panhandle with an ease that left Helen aghast. She would see him two or three times within a few days, and then she would not hear from him for a couple of months.

Sometimes she wondered why he always turned up again. The telephone would ring and he would say, "Dahling, how's my gal? Helen, I've *missed* you. Why don't you ever invite me to your exclusive little parties? Listen, a character from Oklahoma is giving a wing-ding at the Mayflower Saturday night...."

Usually she would accept because it was something to do, it was a glimpse of an American way of life that was baffling, a little frightening—and later would make her solitary life on Sixteenth Street seem all the more serene by comparison. Gene would drink too much and tell the most extraordinary lies and paw at her on the taxi ride home, where almost invariably she shut the door in his face.

Four times he asked her to marry him. The third time was on the night after a grand jury had indicted Jerome Butler for perjury. Helen had invited five people to dinner that evening—Adele Shackford, who had come down from New York on business for Parker's; an Associated Press reporter and his wife with whom Helen had become friends; and a young couple from the State Department with whom she was equally friendly.

The conversation was chiefly about the Butler case and the news of his indictment that afternoon. All of the guests, convinced he was innocent, were indignant. Helen expressed herself honestly: she was not certain whether he was innocent or guilty. They jumped on her civilly, for at least she was not one of the uncivilized who thought Butler guilty, and they worked hard to convert her.

Adele was emotional. "Helen, if there's one thing convinces me Butler is innocent it's the fact your friend Porter thinks he's guilty. I can't *stand* Porter."

"Who can?" asked the man from State.

"Helen can," said the AP reporter gloomily. "We met him and his wife here at cocktails a couple of months ago."

"My God!"

"What can't all of you stand about him?" asked Helen.

"His narrow-mindedness," said State. "His instinct for persecution. You can see it in his angry manner. My God, he'd say or do *anything* to further himself. He reminds me of what H. L. Mencken said about FDR. If he thought cannibalism would help his cause he'd start fattening up missionaries in the White House back yard. . . ."

After dinner they finally were talking about something else in the living room when the doorman buzzed from downstairs and said that Mr. Schofield was on his way up. Helen felt panicked, but before she could prepare the others, the apartment door bell rang insistently.

"Helen, pal gal—" Gene pushed in. His tie was askew, there was lipstick on his shirt collar, and his brow was beaded with alcoholic sweat. He paused uncertainly, blinking at the guests.

Breathing deeply, Helen introduced him.

"Schofield?" asked State. "Not the House investigator who——"

"Yes!" Gene beamed at him. "I just came from a little party up on the Hill to celebrate the indictment. Isn't it great!"

"It's murder," said AP.

"Right!" Gene grinned. "And the Butler did it."

"According to the script that you and Porter and that maniac Whittier wrote, he did it," said State. "But then you guys are the greatest fiction writers I've ever heard of. . . ."

Once Gene realized he had stumbled upon enemies, he defended the actions of the investigating committee valiantly. Yet to Helen there was something pathetic about his defensiveness. She felt sorry for him because he was outnumbered. And her friends argued with such pious superiority that she wondered who really was the inquisitor and who the victim of the rack. After they had decided they had punished the poor devil sufficiently they departed with the sanctimonious air of having done justice.

Gene sprawled in a chair, looking utterly spent. "Please," he said, "just one more drink."

She served it to him.

"Thank yaw." He mimicked broadly an accent that did not really apply to the man from State. "Deucedly decent of you, old gel." Then, in an equally exaggerated nasal accent of Greenleaf: "You hunt with the hounds and run with the hare."

She was silent.

"Why can't I get along with people like them?" His voice rose plaintively and he looked close to tears. "Why do those Ivy League bastards always act so goddamn superior?"

Helen explained that the couple from State had attended the University of California and the AP reporter was a graduate of Vanderbilt.

He leaned toward her. "Helen, please marry me."

"Come off it, Gene." Her tone rose in exasperation. "We've been through that before. I don't love you and I'm not going to marry anybody."

"I don't love myself. I wish I was somebody else. You're the only one who broke clean from Greenleaf. I *hate* that place. Bill didn't break from it. Neither did Alice or Louise. They never will. You could teach me how to stop being such a lousy son of a bitch if you'd marry me."

She did not know what to say to him.

Suddenly he got unsteadily to his feet and poured the remnants of his drink over a potted pothos plant. "Maybe that's a start. Does this stuff kill plants?"

"I don't know. Time will tell."

He left without another word and closed the door quietly behind him.

A long time passed before she saw or heard from him again. She went to Europe and lived and worked in a village in Provence for six happy months. When she returned to Washington, Bill was in the Senate. After a time she invited Alice and him to dinner, deciding not to include Gene.

When she inquired about Gene, Alice stated her disapproval of him plainly.

"His reputation has become simply awful." No one could look more grimly disapproving than Alice when she chose. "I've told Bill he has to look out for his own reputation—by association. I mean he simply can't afford to have a legislative assistant who carries on as Gene does with women and liquor. . . ."

But when he appeared one evening, as Helen had known he inevitably would, he was sober, subdued in manner, totally different from the Gene Alice had described. Helen felt there was a subtle but profound change in him.

He took her to dinner and a concert, and when he brought her home he declined a nightcap. He was talking thoughtfully about a legislative program that interested her when he suddenly asked a strange question:

"Helen, do you think Butler was really guilty?"

Surprised, she said, "Well—I don't know, I'm really not sure."

"Neither am I," he said measuredly.

She was astonished.

"I've been doing a lot of thinking lately, Helen. You remember how I used to carry on about intellectuals, people I thought were snubbing me—enemies of the government and all. Well, I don't feel that way any more. I think I've been too eager to go places—to get ahead. And the way I was trying to do it was by trampling people I called enemies. But I realize something now. I'm my only enemy...."

She saw Gene several times in the next few weeks, and on each occasion she enjoyed him thoroughly. They might yet become the closest of friends.

But she was totally unprepared for what happened on a Friday evening after he brought her home from a movie. He prowled restlessly about the living room, deeply disturbed about something.

At last he said, "Helen, I've reached a crisis. I have to make a new start."

"A crisis over what?"

"I can't tell you just yet. Eventually I will. But I need help. Will you help me?"

"Of course, Gene. What can I do?"

"Don't give me an answer yet. Just do one thing. Will you consider whether in time you'll be willing to marry me?"

She locked her hands together tightly. "Gene, I want to do anything I can to help you. But there's no sense in building false hopes. I like you, but I don't love you. I'll never marry you."

He stared at her blankly for a long time. Then he said, "Good-bye," and left.

Helen Carlton never saw Gene Schofield again.

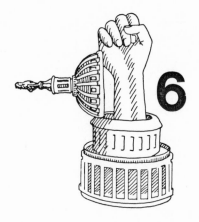

Around half-past ten on Wednesday morning Ben North called in a bright young associate, Chris Marlowe, and asked him, "What am I doing with this file on Joseph P. McCurdy?" He was half kidding.

"You agreed to see him, Mr. North," Marlowe said. "At least he *claims* you did. He says J. P. Westcott talked to you about him."

Westcott, a client of Burton, North, McGinnis, and Mosely, was the president of a company which manufactured, among other products, something called MUST. He had phoned Ben a week previously and asked the firm to take the case of McCurdy. "A hell of a nice guy," Ben remembered him as saying. "He's the guy whose campaign put MUST across. Now he's got a raw tax deal. . . ." Ben had agreed that the firm would look into his case, but he did not recall saying he would handle it personally.

"I thought you were taking care of him," Ben told Marlowe. "But his name showed up on my appointment calendar for eleven today. What's the story on him?"

Marlowe made a gesture that expressed apology. "I sent you a memo about him last Friday, Mr. North. I guess Miss Thomas short-stopped it and put him on your calendar. McCurdy came to see me on Friday. That's when he insisted on seeing you. He's a very persistent character. He kept waving the name of J. P. Westcott in my face. He doesn't really have a case at all. He——"

Miss Thomas, who had been signaling Ben to no avail, opened the door and spoke raspingly: "Mr. North, Mr. Ducasse in Chicago has been waiting on the phone."

"Okay, okay. I'll look it over, Chris, and get you in here. . . ."

But Ducasse was not on the phone. Ben, waiting for him, chose to blame all the difficulties of the day on the efficient Miss Thomas. His gaze took in a memorandum under the firm's old letterhead of Burton, North, McGinnis, Mosely, Hammond and Porter. Porter had left for the Presidency, Hammond had gone into government too, and Burton had been lying half dead of a stroke for nearly three years. Which left McGinnis, who was opposed to nearly everything North favored, and Mosely, who favored everything North proposed as long as it did not affect him. Which left North. And which meant Miss Thomas was not altogether to blame for the vagaries of a business day.

It was well after eleven before Ben had squared away matters with Ducasse, and Miss Thomas had announced in her most forceful manner that McCurdy and Marlowe were waiting. Only then did he have a chance to glance at McCurdy's file. What he scanned he found incredible before he signaled Miss Thomas to bring 'em on.

There was something of Falstaff about McCurdy. Large, bearded, rumpled, he exuded a hearty manner and a trace of last night's wine and garlic. His booming voice bore a hint of the Hoosier, but his thick beard, wild thatch of black hair, and theatrical-sized rimmed glasses indicated he was a dropout of middle America.

"Sit down! Sit down!" Ben boomed back at him. Then, to disguise his consternation at the man and his problem, he perched his reading glasses on his nose and resumed scanning Marlowe's brief report.

Marlowe, knowing that the normal efficiency of office operations had somehow come unhinged, looked embarrassed. He did a little two-step around McCurdy, as if he had brought a huge unruly sheep dog into the senior partner's office.

Ben decided it was one of those occasions when he should act tough. Frowning over his glasses at McCurdy and slapping Marlowe's report with the back of a hand, he demanded, "What is this? What the hell do you expect us to do for you, Mr. McCurdy?"

McCurdy grinned, the tip of his tongue slipped out of his hairy face, and he seemed to pant with delight. But he did not say anything, and Marlowe, thinking better of saying something, closed his eyes.

"So last year you had a gross of $50,486 and estimate your gross this year at $45,000. You say you can't make your tax payments because you're broke. And the federal, state, and city governments have not taken any action against you yet. What do you want from us?"

"Advice." McCurdy, still grinning, spoke softly. "Your services as defense attorney when they start to prosecute me."

"We don't handle cases like yours," Ben replied. "I'll refer you to a firm that does."

"J.P. will be sorry to hear that," McCurdy said. "J. P. Westcott, that is. Will you refer him to another firm too?"

Ben contained his anger at the ineffectual blackmail and frowned at Marlowe's report. "When you come to tax court, Mr. McCurdy, as you eventually will, can you suggest a defense?"

"Broke," said McCurdy. "Taxed out of existence by a government that treats its people as a tiresome nuisance. A victim of this omnipotent superstate that uses its great machinery for manipulating private lives and destroying those who resist manipulation."

Ben looked at him with a kind of dread. He said, "Go on," as if urging a robot to a further predictable act.

"We angry victims cover the whole spectrum, Mr. North. We include the blacks, the low-income whites, the students, the tax-ridden, the price-gouged, the traffic-jammed, the war-weary."

Ben groped in a pocket for his cigarettes. "You forget the pollution-choked."

"Yes, the pollution-choked."

"And you forget to give credit for your lines to Russell Baker, who published them in the New York *Times* several years ago."

McCurdy showed surprise. "Did he? Maybe he got them from me. It doesn't matter. The one free thing left to exchange is ideas. But how did you recognize Baker's remarks from so long ago?"

"Because I was impressed by them. I came close to quoting them—though I didn't—in the summary of a case I was pleading in Appeals. If I had quoted them, I'd have given credit to Mr. Baker."

McCurdy cast him a look that said, *Well, good for you*, and Ben retreated from his position of moral superiority by lighting a cigarette.

"I see you list your occupation as free-lance advertising writer. I thought copywriters were always on the payrolls of specific agencies."

"Some of us aren't. I was with Street, Blazer, Kaufman

till three years ago. Then I realized I'm talented enough to be my own man. I do more than write copy. I plan programs, I show art directors how they're all wet. I have a knack for convincing people they want junk they can't afford and don't need."

"In other words, you have contempt for your job."

McCurdy shrugged. "I'm forty-four. Too old to do anything except enjoy life. But it's bastardly hard to enjoy life on fifty grand a year in New York. Would you believe me?"

Grudgingly Ben did believe him. Mentally he ticked off the figures that had brought this plight on McCurdy: $50,000 gross, $2,200 deductible, $47,800 taxable. Federal tax of $16,000 plus surtax plus state and municipal taxes. No real estate or mortgage deductions.

McCurdy picked up the sad story, such as was known to everyone in the upper income brackets, and carried it on at length. He had a wife and two children, all prisoners of Manhattan. Of course they had looked around at houses in Westchester and Connecticut, but the whole awful commuting routine with its fringe deficits had repelled them back to Manhattan. There, of course, the kids had to attend private schools because the public schools were unthinkable even to a bleeding heart like McCurdy. Cost: $2,500. Summer camp for them: $2,000. If you lived in Manhattan, you had to get out in order to survive. Thus a vacation for Mommy and Daddy: $2,000 more. Everyone said you didn't need a car in the city, but you certainly did. You had to get out, cursing your way through the traffic of the Long Island Expressway in the smog of a Saturday morning toward the expectation of something you never could find. Monthly garage rent: $100 plus tips. An annual food bill of $5,400? God, try to buy it cheaper for a family of four. Even on Murray Hill was it absolutely necessary to pay an annual rent of $7,800? "I *like* Murray Hill," said McCurdy. "And when I used to meet taxes they allowed me one room of the six deductible because I *work* there."

The prosaic rather than the unusual is essentially the province of the law, and McCurdy's story was so commonplace in Ben's experience that he began to sympathize with him. Indeed, it would be easy to try to describe his own problems in living on a gross income more than three times that of McCurdy's: alimony to a first wife, bills from Lord & Taylor for a second, aid to a son, upkeep of a cooperatively owned apartment on upper Fifth Avenue, a place on Long Island, the sloop, three clubs. . . . The money he had inherited from his parents had come to seem a mere pittance to which it had been necessary for him to add a slavish labor in order to live with the eternal hope of a little relaxation.

Realizing he was wool-gathering and wasting time with a client he did not want to serve, he switched to another track: "Did the fact you have the same name as the legendary Joe McCurdy have anything to do with your decision not to pay your taxes?"

McCurdy began to grin and pant again. At last he said, "That's no legendary character, Mr. North. That's me."

Marlowe made an agitated movement, and Ben, snubbing out his cigarette with care, wondered if McCurdy was insane.

He said, "Please try to explain that remark."

"As everybody knows, Cy Benson wrote 'The Ballad of Joe McCurdy.' I helped him with some lines. He's a friend of mine. We fooled around with it just for the hell of it over lunch. We and some other guys sometimes eat lunch together at a place on Second Avenue. Nobody was more surprised than we were when the ballad caught on. All of us know people in television and show business. I do a lot of TV commercials and last year I wrote bits of the Spencer Worth Show—the one that went only thirteen weeks. It was easy to keep feeding the myth of Joe Mc-Curdy. It was fun—and it had a point."

"Then there is nothing spontaneous about that—thing."

McCurdy, obviously enjoying himself, stretched out his thick legs and lighted a cigarette.

"The only spontaneous thing I know of, Mr. North, is the wish to live and let live and be happy. Everything is predictable if you feed it and let it grow—everything from hair to babies. But I'd call this thing both spontaneous and predictable. Everybody has been yakking for years about the revolt of the kids. They haven't seen anything yet. Wait till they see the revolt of the middle-aged and old. This thing that's just getting under way with those of us who find we can't pay taxes. Or should I say we find it's not *worth* paying taxes to Russell Baker's omnipotent superstate."

Ben, groping for a sense of the responsible in so much irresponsible nonsense, said, "In legal terms you may be describing a conspiracy."

"Then are they going to indict Russell Baker and a hundred other writers who have written similar things?"

"If they refuse to pay their taxes—yes."

"Just about everything is a conspiracy," McCurdy said, "and everybody is judged guilty by the superstate. The black man who conspires with his fellows to try to improve his lot, the youngster who conspires with his fellow young life-lovers to protest the insane death awaiting all of us in the arms race, the . . ."

Ben stopped listening because the sense in McCurdy's nonsense had no place in the practice of the law until reduced to specifics. Then he found himself listening again as McCurdy began to be precise.

"I know a guy fifty-eight years old who has been earning fifty to sixty thousand a year for a long time and hating every minute of it. Last December he said the hell with it and he and his wife took what they had and moved to Nova Scotia—and he's never coming back to pay his taxes if they ever can find him. I heard of a guy who did the same thing—but he chose Switzerland. I heard of another retired guy living on about ten thousand a year who has taken to the desert north of Tucson. His attitude is 'Try to find me, and then see what you can get. . . .' "

It was almost noon, and Helen Carlton must be waiting. The day would run its inexorable course, and Joseph P. McCurdy had no significant place in it. Ben thought of various ways whereby he would manage never to see him again.

"Mr. McCurdy," he finally interrupted him, "there are specific means by which the government will prosecute each case you mention. Slow, maybe—but inevitable. And it will prosecute you."

"When?" McCurdy sounded eager.

"In its own good time. I presume Mr. Marlowe has outlined the steps to you."

"Yes." Marlowe, recognizing that the senior partner was dismissing McCurdy, got to his feet. "I've explained that fully, Mr. North."

But McCurdy made no move to rise. So Ben pressed the button which would signal Miss Thomas to clear the decks.

She opened the door and said, "Mr. North, your son has been waiting for some time."

Ben got to his feet, pleased by the usually unimaginative Miss Thomas' sudden display of imagination; Jim was several thousand miles distant in South America.

"Your son?" McCurdy got to his feet too.

Ben herded Marlowe and him into the outer office, and then stopped dead. There stood Jim!

He almost dashed at him. Jim, grinning, grasped his hand and bent a bit to lay his cheek against his father's, for he was six feet three. Ben stepped back to admire his altogether handsome son, who was twenty-four this spring. Jim had not changed, apart from the fact his lean face was deeply tanned. By his mother's standards he still needed a haircut and his sideburns were too long; his moustache, too, defied his mother's wishes. He wore a turtleneck sweater under a corduroy jacket.

"Jim, I thought you still were somewhere in the Amazon country."

"I caught a tramp back from Belém. Landed in Brooklyn last night and went to the Y."

"The YMCA? What are you doing there? Why didn't you phone?"

"The Y is cheap and comfortable enough and they really guard the valuable stuff I brought back."

"But good Lord the Y!" Ben became aware that McCurdy stood beaming at Jim. "Mr. McCurdy—Mr. Marlowe—my son Jim."

"It's good to meet you." McCurdy clutched Jim's hand and would not let it go. "What were you doing in South America?"

"He's a naturalist," Ben said. "An ornithologist. Jim, have you phoned your mother?"

"Not yet, Pop. I have to go down to Washington today or tomorrow."

"Well, I'll phone Rita. I'll take you to lunch. We'll go to the Hunt. You have to wear a shirt and tie there, but I have 'em in my closet crash kit. Let's see, the shirt has French cuffs so you'll need links." He turned to Marlowe. "Chris—"

Marlowe said, "I have a lunch date, Mr. North. But I know that Boughton is working through the lunch hour and——"

"Take mine," McCurdy said, and began to unfasten his cuff links. "I'll get 'em back from your father sometime."

"Mr. North," said Miss Thomas, "Mrs. Carlton is on the phone. She's calling from La Guardia. Her shuttle flight was delayed an hour by smog and——"

"Aunt Helen!" Jim exclaimed. "Thanks, Mr. Mc-Curdy, I'll make sure you get them back."

Ben, who had forgotten about Helen, said to Miss Thomas, "Tell her Jim just came home and we'll meet her at the Hunt Club for lunch. Give her the address." He turned to McCurdy, from whom he wanted no favors. "Thanks, Mr. McCurdy, but——"

"See you." McCurdy, grinning and waving, left for the reception room, and Marlowe followed him. . . .

The Hunt, like most downtown Manhattan eating clubs, had its special ambiance. It affected a Georgian atmosphere; a genuine Copley on a wall, lots of pewter and paintings of red-coated huntsmen. Ben did not like it much or go there often; usually he had coffee and a sandwich at his desk. But that Wednesday he wished he could dawdle away the afternoon with Jim at the Hunt.

"A Scotch while we wait for Helen?"

Jim shrugged. "I guess so."

One of the surprising things about Jim was his indifference to food, drink, and sleep. He could eat practically nothing, or anything. He could drink anything, or absolutely nothing. He could sleep anyplace for brief or long periods as they fitted into his essential plans. Ben had decided it was a result of a basic trait in his character: he detested routine and lived by inspiration.

It had been the best of trips, Jim said. "Thanks for it, Pop."

"Unlike Queen Isabella, I didn't have to hock the crown jewels. Now that you're back, would you like to help me get the sloop out? We could do a shakedown up to the Cape. I mean just the two of us."

Ben meant they would not take along his wife Rita. Jim did not dislike Rita; rather, like a bottle of Scotch at breakfast, she did not fit into his scheme of things. Probably the feeling was characteristic of many sons whose fathers divorced and married again.

"You'd better not count on me, Pop. I have to see the people at the *National Geographic*. I have some things to check at the Smithsonian. Guess I'll find a pad in Washington for a while and get the magazine articles in final shape. How's everything with you?"

"Okay. The old machine lumbers on."

"And how's Rita?"

"Fine. She'll want to see you. Plan dinner with us tonight. Your room is as you left it. Use it till you're ready to go to Washington." Ben put the invitation forcefully, hoping Jim would accept with good grace. He did it for the sake of Rita, who, like many second wives, imagined that the child of the first wife did not like her. She would not understand, as Ben himself did fully, that Jim simply was indifferent to her—which, even more than dislike, was a source of dismay to a beautiful, proud young woman like Rita. "Well, here comes Helen on the run."

Tears came to Helen's eyes as she embraced and kissed Jim. She carried on about being late and fussed with gloves and bag while gazing at him in a rapt maternal way. Sometimes it troubled Ben that Helen had designated her adored godchild as the principal heir to her considerable fortune. Fortunately Jim did not know it. By the time he came into his inheritance it was to be hoped he would be so deeply immersed in his naturalist's profession that the money would work for good rather than ill.

Jim talked enthusiastically about his adventures in the Abuña country on the vague borderlands of Brazil, Peru, and Bolivia. He transported them into a land of uncivilized Indians, dangerous reptiles, unmapped jungles, treacherous rivers. The strange birds which he had sketched and photographed in his months-long travels sounded like the tamest creatures of that nether world. A year previously he had gone to the Amazon country as a member of a Museum of Natural History expedition. But this time he had done it on his own with the help of guides and hired hands who had joined and left him like shadows. He had had a small grant from the National Geographic Society; Ben had de frayed the rest of his expenses.

"Now"—Jim spoke slowly—"I want to get started on the next one."

"What will that be?" asked Helen.

"It will sound real crazy to you."

"I doubt it."

"It will take a few years to do. I want to write a book— not just for ornithologists. There's a stream of life—I mean bird life—that rises in the interior of Alaska and flows southeast across Canada to New England and joins another stream coming down from due north. It's a fascinating southeasterly stream—Hudsonian curlews, fox sparrows, savannah sparrows, Canadian warblers, Wilson's warblers, juncos. Anyway, I want to follow its course, coming and going, between Alaska and Florida over a few migratory seasons. I want to try some banding. It involves a lot of travel of all sorts—canoe and so forth. But what I want to study and write about is not just migratory habits. There's a tremendous variety of country between the ends of the journey. I want to deal with the relationships between men and birds along the way. It's a subject that never has been developed in the way I visualize it."

"It's fascinating," Helen said. "A possible title might be 'The Stream of Life.'"

"Not bad. Anyway, I want to talk to some people in Washington about a grant."

"How much do you hope to get?" asked Helen.

"Fifteen hundred, a couple of thousand. Then——"

"Not enough," Helen said. "Count on me for ten thousand as a start."

Jim stared at her. "Don't be crazy. You can't just——"

"Yes, I can, Jim. I've never given you anything except some books and cameras and stuff. You have a perfectly wonderful subject and you have to *expedite* it. I don't know a thing about birds except what you've told me. But from you I get the impression they're rather more interesting and intelligent than man. They don't wage mass wars and invent things to torture each other with. So count me in."

"But——"

"When are you coming down to Washington?"

Jim hesitated.

"You must stay at my place."

Ben, vividly recalling himself when young, pitied Jim. *Stay with me. Be mine.* Since it was the illness of the aging to be possessive, it must be the health of the young to resist being possessed.

"I'd love to, Aunt Helen, but——"

"I know. I forgot about your mother."

"I don't want to stay with her. I *can't* and get any work done."

Ben said, "When I was your age and everybody wanted a piece of me, I learned to be crafty. Here's what I suggest. After lunch Helen and I have to go back to the office and talk. I'll phone Rita. Both of you come to dinner. Pick up your traps at the Y and bring them to the apartment. Sort out what's essential to you in Washington and leave the rest of the stuff at the apartment. Then both of you fly down and you spend the night at Helen's house. Tomorrow get your own place. *Then* call your mother."

Jim looked relieved and Helen, smiling, said, "That's a deal, Ben. A nice division of interests. You should have been a judge."

"I used to want to be. But then I took comfort in a remark Thurman Arnold made after he quit the bench and returned to private practice. He said, 'I decided I'd rather talk to damn fools than listen to them.' "

Which somehow reminded Helen of Joseph P. McCurdy. "So he really exists?"

"Yes."

"Am I violating counsel to ask what his tax problem is?"

"Yes, you are. But I can tell you he's a nut. Tomorrow he'll receive a letter stating we cannot represent him. And his patron can like it or lump it and go elsewhere. McCurdy's motive seems transparent to me. Through us he hopes somehow to embarrass the President of the United States. It won't work."

Jim said, "To me that makes him a good nut."

Ben looked at him impassively.

"He struck me as a pleasant guy," Jim said.

Joe McCurdy swung along Pine Street, glancing up occasionally at the soot-brown sky, gasping for oxygen through multiple microns of sulfur and nitrogen dioxide, carbon monoxide, and hydrocarbons, wondering in what dreadful way his life finally would end. At Nassau Street

[108]

he plunged backward from the path of a turning taxi, and suddenly was certain that he was being followed.

At first it was an excruciating idea. Not in years had he felt someone was tailing him, and he believed he had cured himself of his paranoia. Yet here it was again, an instinct as sure as the scent of fox piss to a wise old Welsh hound. Crossing Nassau Street, he rested a foot on a low ledge, pretended to pick at something on his worn-out loafer, and cased the way he had come.

There were two of them. One was the guy who had come down from the law offices in the same elevator with McCurdy. Now another had joined him. They pretended to be young clerks out for a dollar lunch. But they were Feds! McCurdy knew it by their durable shoes, their unobtrusive Bond suits, their thirtyish ages, their so forgettable faces. When they passed him without a glance, he was amazed, for even the sharpest Fed found it impossible to pass the target without a glance.

He trudged on, relieved and yet disappointed too. It was his hope—indeed, his fervent plan—to be prosecuted. But how—in fact, why—had they picked up his trail at North's office? Well, he had been mistaken. The Feds had melted into the noonday throng; probably they were on a lunch break from another job.

When McCurdy started into the Wall Street subway station to take a Lexington Avenue train uptown, he took another look back. Here came Fed number two. McCurdy hurried down the steps, his heart knocking. Seeing a vacant telephone booth and remembering he had promised to phone his wife Hank, he stepped in and groped for a dime.

The Fed passed, barely glancing at him, and stepped into another vacant phone booth. Now there was no question about it.

Each Wednesday for several weeks Hannah McCurdy

had been giving her time to the cause of raising funds for relief of the starving Bokankos who were hapless victims of a Congo civil war begun in jest. McCurdy dialed the number with a trembling forefinger, and Hank answered in a businesslike manner.

"Hank!"

"Darling!" She whispered the word. "What happened?"

"It's going to work. I can't go into details now. I'm in the subway. The Feds are tailing me."

"No!"

"Yes!"

"How wonderful! I can't wait to hear about it. I'll come home early. You'll be there?"

"Yes, after lunch."

"Oh, take care, love!" She seemed to croon the words. "You're so brave."

"No, I'm an awful coward." But her tone gave him courage. "Got to go, love."

The Fed came through the turnstile a moment after McCurdy and pretended to absorb himself in a copy of the *Post* bulldog edition. Its front-page headline read:

TAX REVOLT
IS SPREADING

Earlier McCurdy had scanned the story that began: "Despite vigorous Administration denials, there are numerous indications that the tax revolt has spread widely throughout the nation. . . ." As usually was true of news stories that had negative leads and cited "indications," there was not much substance to the report. But it was the sort of situation the dear old *Post* enjoyed thoroughly; Max Lerner, in his inside column, had couched the revolt in a position of moral loftiness with historical analogies to the

New England tax revolts of the late eighteenth century. Yes, most of the good guys were chewing on it with relish after a long spell of having little to grind but their teeth.

When McCurdy stepped on an express, the Fed sat down a half car distant from him. McCurdy, his thoughts reeling with the bucketing train, tried to imagine why the federal government was paying him such close attention at this stage of events.

At Fourteenth Street he crossed the platform to an uptown local—and lo, agent number one was sitting down the aisle from him. They were giving him the duet treatment, which was something special. Leaving the train at Thirty-fourth Street, he climbed into the murk where Park Avenue squeezed its way past the grimy old armory. There was a loud explosion, and McCurdy jumped as if creased by a bullet. It was only the backfire of a passing truck, but he dredged a cigarette from a pack to quiet his pulsing nerves. He had lighted the cigarette and begun choking and coughing before he remembered he had resolved upon leaving North's office to quit smoking (as he did in nearly every waking hour). Dragging on his cigarette and blaming the burning in his chest on the damnable hydrocarbons from the damnable traffic, he made his way south and east toward Second Avenue. He did not bother to look back, for he knew he still was being followed.

In a less frenetic century the site of Campbell's Bar and Grill would have been on the sylvan shore of Kips Bay, but the bay had long since been choked with rubble and rubbish, and Campbell's plied its trade in a concrete wasteland of dingy tenements and pretentiously ugly apartments. Its ambiance was purposefully seedy, for Campbell had limited ambition and wished to preserve his establishment as a quiet shelter for gentlemen seeking refuge from family, home, and business.

Tom Mahoney was tending a scantly populated bar

when McCurdy came in. Cy Benson was there with Dr. Sam Steen and Hugh Scribner. All stared at McCurdy as he stepped heavily up to them and climbed onto a stool beside Sam.

"I've been tailed all the way from Pine Street," he told Tom calmly. "In a minute a guy will come in and sit there at the end of the bar. He's wearing a gray Bond suit, plain tie, glasses, about thirty. He'll order a beer and pretend to read the *Post* while he listens. When he leaves, another will take his place."

"You using another name?" asked Tom.

"Of course not. Did Christ change his name on the way to Calvary?"

"No," said Sam, who practiced analysis just off Park Avenue, "but I imagine he felt a strange ecstasy as he lugged his cross up the hill."

"Bloody Mary?" Tom asked McCurdy.

"The bloodiest."

Cy looked at him in the mirror. "Do you think North tipped them off?"

"Of course not," McCurdy replied. "His ethics are unimpeachable. That's why I got him to represent me. Here he comes!"

"FBI?" asked Cy.

"T-man, I think. Don't think Justice is involved yet."

Hugh said, "Tom, turn on the tape."

Tom flicked a switch on the audio panel behind him and there were a few fading notes of "The Stars and Stripes Forever" as the undistinguished man came in, sat down at the end of the bar, opened his *Post*, and said, "Draft, please."

Tom served McCurdy his Bloody Mary, then gassed a draft for the Fed as a voice on audio said:

"This is Billy Hoover again, back with Ed Graham of

the Attorney General's office for a little more conversation. You were saying, Mr. Graham, that there really *is* a Joe McCurdy."

GRAHAM: Of course there is. We in the Justice Department know who he is. But, if you understand what I mean, we can't exactly put a handle on him. He's operating with the same methods of some of our best politicians. Like President Porter himself. The Attorney General told us at a conference the other day—and I quote him—"McCurdy is working with amorphous public emotions, dumped on the bare ground like so much raw concrete, which he has busily scraped into the mold of a tax revolt."

HOOVER: Where do the tax protestors come from?

GRAHAM: From every element of the nation's life, Mr. Hoover. All the people who feel they are being treated as a nuisance by a supergovernment interested only in its own aggrandizement. . . .

The Fed, who had put aside his *Post* and was leaning forward intently, asked, "What station is that?"

Tom put a finger to his lips, and Sam said, "Quiet!"

GRAHAM: . . . The middle-aged middle classes who feel the blacks are getting more attention than they. But then we find that the blacks are joining the tax protest in just as large numbers because *they* feel they are getting less than the whites. . . .

"What station?" demanded the Fed.

"Mister, you from New York?" Hugh asked him.

"Yes, Forest Hills."

Tom regarded him with astonishment. "And you haven't heard of the *underground* station?"

[113]

GRAHAM: . . . and those who feel there's too much military spending won't pay their taxes. And those who feel the government is wasting money on the space program to the detriment of badly needed housing won't pay their taxes. . . .

The Fed leaned far over the bar, trying to see the audio dials.

"Right now," Tom told him, "it's coming in at just above eleven hundred. Just below WNEW."

HOOVER: Behind this vast tax revolt, Mr. Graham, there seems to be something very ominous: the ill-health of the economy. What are your views on that?

GRAHAM: Mr. Hoover, many of us in the federal government are nearly at our wits' end. We are beginning to feel that we must make a drastic cut of billions of dollars in our military spending.

HOOVER: Yes. But before we go into that, we'll interrupt with a little music.

The strings and horns of a country band playing "The Ballad of Joe McCurdy" rollicked forth and a hillbilly voice began to sing the familar words:

> Joe McCurdy came today
> After weeks of work at little pay.
> He puts his dollar on the bar,
> But the man says it won't go far.
> Chorus dirge: No, no, Joe!
>   It won't go, Joe!

"It's fading," Cy said.

Tom tuned the dials, and they heard the voice of William B. Williams on WNEW. "Gone again," Tom said.

"What's today's lunch special?" asked McCurdy.

"It's Wednesday, isn't it?" Tom replied.

"Bring me a martini to the table before the lamb stew," Cy said.

"Make it four," said Sam.

After Tom had brought them martinis, the Fed eased to their table and said, "Excuse me, gentlemen, I don't mean to intrude."

They cast him looks that said *Then don't*.

"But I thought I knew this town, and I never before heard of the *underground* station. What's the story on it?"

Hugh said, "Yesterday morning about half-past eight I caught it around nine hundred."

"Last week when I was in Rochester," said Sam, "a bellhop tipped me off on the megacycle and I caught it around nine in the evening."

"They move around the country," McCurdy said. "Surprised you haven't heard about it."

"But the FCC must be investigating."

Sam shrugged. "As I understand it, the Administration has the FCC so busy investigating *legitimate* news media that it doesn't have time to investigate the *illegitimate*."

"If you miss the programs," Cy said, "you can buy tapes of 'em."

"Where?"

"All over. Anyplace on Forty-second Street. Ask the guy who sells you pot."

McCurdy, watching the Fed back away, wished he could see through his face into the interior being. It was getting increasingly difficult to remember, let alone read, almost anybody's face these days. How did mothers recognize their children, or wives their husbands? Faces were becoming like mercury in tubes, reflecting nothing but the emotional temperature of the moment.

"Joe"—Sam jogged his elbow—"I said God bless."

"God bless." McCurdy raised his martini.

"What are the depths of your thoughts?"

"Faces. So many closed-in, forgettable faces. North's is the same. A lifetime devoted to noble pursuit of the law. But his face just a mask. Met his son, who has a noble, open countenance. He told me the son watches birds. The father watches the law. Is there a moral?"

"Probably," said Hugh. "But you're more masked than anyone. All you guys with beards are."

"A beard is just common decency," McCurdy said. "Men wear pants to cover their peckers, don't they? Since the current fashion is to hide your thoughts, why not do a good job of it and wear a beard?"

"Tell us about North," Cy said. "Will he represent you?"

"Now he thinks not, but he will."

"Because what's his name—Westcott—will put the boots to him?"

"No. North doesn't give in to pressure like that—and because he doesn't, Westcott wouldn't quit him as a client. He'll represent me for another reason."

"What is it?"

"I can't tell you yet."

"The Christian epic," Sam said. "Our Redeemer would not let His disciples in on absolutely everything. Just hints, parables, rare insights. Joe, at the rate you're going, you'll have me believing in your resurrection."

"How did you know the Feds were tailing you?" asked Hugh.

"How do we know the Feds are?" said Sam. "Did the guy flash a badge and say he was a T-man? We have only Joe's persuasive word for it."

"We know," McCurdy said, "because you'll observe

the first just left and now the second has taken his place at the bar."

"Oh, Christ!" Sam touched a hand to his forehead. "Excuse me, I mean, oh, McCurdy! So help me, I'm going to have another martini. The lamb stew is lousy here, but the company's immortal. . . ."

After lunch Sam climbed Murray Hill with McCurdy. It really is no hill at all that slants up from Third Avenue to Park, but McCurdy began to puff as he plodded along.

"I'm really disappointed in you," he told Sam. "I thought sure I could count on you to renege on the April payment."

"Cowardice," Sam replied. "I cheat the government out of thousands every year. All sorts of expense dodges and stuff. But I just couldn't bring myself not to pay 'em anything. I'm an awful coward, Joe."

"So am I," McCurdy said. "But it's good to be a coward. Then when you do something brave your ecstasy is really wonderful."

They paused in front of the apartment house where McCurdy lived and Sam said, "Ecstasy, eroticy. At our ages it's mostly the martinis."

"Here comes the Fed up the other side of the street. Will you grant me, Sam, that the individual is the same as the one who sat down first at the bar?"

"I grant you," Sam replied, "but the last I knew this was a public street. Let's stand here a minute and see what he does."

"Want to come up to my apartment?"

"No, I have a patient at two thirty."

"So you're afraid of guilt by association. I'll bet you don't have a patient on a Wednesday afternoon. No doctor —not even an analyst—has office hours on Wednesday afternoons."

"I have a patient." Sam watched the Fed passing on the other side of the street. "I'm treating her for frigidity."

"How do you treat a female for frigidity?"

"First I undress her. Then I sit across the room from her and tickle her clitoris with a long ostrich feather. Never fails. There goes your Fed, Joe. Straight up the street. What's happened to your theory?"

"You've forgotten about Fed number two."

"Where is he?"

"I don't know. But I can feel him watching me."

Sam moaned and walked on while McCurdy turned into his apartment house. Charles, the day doorman, greeted him effusively.

"Charles," said McCurdy, "in a minute or so a guy will come in here and say, 'Wasn't that Joseph P. McCurdy just came in?' I'm not sure what he'll say next. Maybe he'll say he has a message for me and ask what apartment I live in."

"They're *after* you!" Charles exclaimed.

"Yes."

"We're all with you, Mr. McCurdy."

"You're all with me," McCurdy replied, "but your taxes were withheld by the management. You just didn't declare your tips."

"Want me to throw him off?"

"No. Tell him that's right. I'm Joseph P. from Twenty-four B. Give me a buzz after he's gone, Charles."

When McCurdy let himself into his apartment on the twenty-fourth floor, he knew that Hank was home. He knew by the smell of her—a fragrant scent that always reminded him of things like ripe lemons and melons and hot raspberry pie.

"Yoo hoo," he called, "it's me."

"Yoo hoo, darling!" she cried. "I'm in the bedroom."

Like Venus, Hannah McCurdy did not appear to age with time. Stripped now to pantyhose, she looked to McCurdy as when he first had seen her in the buff two decades past. She was an inch taller than he and wonderfully proportioned, with fair skin prone to blush. The generosity—indeed, the bounty—of nature extended to her face and tumble of jet hair. Hellenic, for sure, her features were: large dark eyes, wide lips, a nose and chin that somehow defied all matronly convention.

Stepping to him with a bankbook in hand, she smothered him in an embrace. He nibbled her neck and, over her shoulder, gazed at the reflection of her marvelous back in the mirror. Her badge of courage seemed to glow in the afternoon light: a strawberry mark just abaft her left kidney, the unhealed result of a policeman's kick when she had been demonstrating against war in Bryant Park a year previously.

He brushed some of her hair out of his eyes and said, "On the way home I had a fantasy about you."

"What was it, dear?"

"I thought what I'd do if you ever turned frigid. First I'd undress you and put you on the bed. Then I'd sit on the dresser and tickle your clitoris with a long ostrich feather."

She squeezed him harder and squealed with delight. "Oh Mac! You're so *original!* But you don't have to worry about *that.* Maybe it's a sign you're in a creative mood. Are you going to write at your book this afternoon? I'm going to make beef Stroganoff for dinner."

"I can think of more creative things to do." His hands reassured themselves that her vital places were all there. "The kids won't be home for at least an hour."

"Yes!" she exclaimed. "But first tell me about it all. No, *first,* before you do, I want to tell you I put twenty-three dollars in the savings account this morning on my way to Congo Aid."

"Wonderful, Hank! Terrific! How much does that make it now?"

"Seventeen hundred and forty-six. And seventy-four cents. It soon will be enough to——" The intercom clamored in the hall. "Oh, damn, who can that be?"

"Charles."

Charles spoke shrilly when McCurdy answered: "It was *him*, Mr. McCurdy. I know it was. He asked what apartment you lived in, and I told him."

"Good work, Charles. What happened then?"

"He went away."

"Thank you, Charles. Keep up the good work." McCurdy hung up and faced Hank, who had followed him. "They've traced me. Internal Revenue has me clear in their sights now."

"Oh, Mac!" Hank's eyes grew moist as her arms wound about him again. "You're so wonderful! Now tell me everything that happened."

Helen Carlton and Jim North boarded the last Eastern shuttle flight at five minutes before twelve that night at La Guardia. As they went along the aisle, Helen saw Fay Stetson seated alone next to a window.

"Fay! What are you doing in New York?"

Fay cast her a droll look. "Why does anybody come to New York? I was trying to find out what's happening to the *money!*" She looked at Jim. "Then again, some of us come to New York to find a handsome young man."

Helen introduced Jim, and they took the seats beside Fay's. Since the air-conditioning was not functioning adequately, Jim pulled off his jacket.

They had been airborne for several minutes when Fay leaned across Helen and spoke to Jim. "What interesting cuff links. Aren't those red herring on black onyx?"

"You've got me." Jim looked at one. "I hadn't noticed what they are. I meant to leave them with Pop, but forgot about it."

"That red on the black," Fay said. "That's a red herring. See the herringbone design? Where did you get them, Jim?"

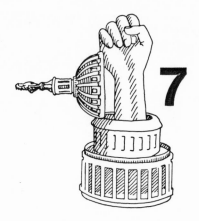

7

Hochstein, waking very early in the warm spring dawn, had a strange and frightening sense of imminent disaster. Maybe it was the result of a dream, but the feeling was strong enough to impel him swiftly through the morning rituals and take him to his White House office before seven o'clock.

Both the Washington *Post* and the New York *Times* carried front-page stories stating that today the Administration was expected to reveal its plans for dealing with the tax revolt. It was news to Hochstein, and he doubted it was true. Though this was only Thursday, it seemed to him President Porter had been delaying the decision for a month or more. When would he make up his mind?

Hochstein had begun shoveling through the accumulation in his basket when a messenger came in with a sealed envelope from Treasury stamped Confidential. Opening it, he read:

McCurdy Joseph P., 35 East 36th Street, New York, N. Y. 10016. Social Security Number . . .

After finishing the report, he dictated an immediate action memorandum to Justice, requesting an urgent, complete check on *McCurdy, Joseph P.*

One of his assistants, young Gabriel Gaines, looked into his office about half-past seven and said, "You're early, Hochy. Anything up?"

"Insomnia. Gabby, you've been fooling around with some FCC stuff. Have you heard of any underground radio stations?"

"No."

"Neither, I think, has anybody except a naïve Treasury agent. I want a volunteer to try some of the record shops when they open and see if he can buy recordings of a kooky thing that pretends to be interviews with government officials that are—uh—anti-Administration."

Gaines took off his glasses and held them up to the light, as if taking a sun-fix. "Hochy, that's interesting. The other night some neighbor friends of ours . . ."

Gaines was back from his home with the tape before half-past eight. Sonbren in international affairs had a player which he claimed was essential to his duties, though Hochstein suspected him of secretly enjoying classical music during office hours. The three listened attentively to a few notes of "Yankee Doodle" and then a voice—

"Friends, this is Billy Hoover—"

Gaines, ever helpful, said, "You get the symbolism, Hochy."

"That's not symbolism," said Hochstein, "that's caricature. I never heard about these tapes. How can I get so out of touch with life? Sonbren, start it over again. . . ."

HOOVER: Our guest today is Cyril Anjou, assistant director of the Space Administration Center in Houston. Mr. Anjou, as we all know, you are in charge of the Mars project. Your goal, I understand, is Americans on Mars by 1984. Why 1984? Does it have anything to do with the work by George Orwell?

ANJOU: Senator Orwell?

HOOVER: Senator?

ANJOU: Excuse me, I don't at the moment recall whether he's from North or South Carolina, but I do want to say this: Senator George Orwell has been most helpful to us in our Mars work. . . .

Hochstein was enjoying the recordings thoroughly when Sonbren's secretary looked in and said the President wanted to see him.

Was the President ready to make a decision? His schedule for the day was listed as open, which usually meant he would be occupied by something of vital importance.

Hochstein scampered up the winding stairs of the Executive Office Building, hurried past the graffiti of political cartoons in the outer chamber and into the President's private office.

"Jack, any new developments on our problem?"

He sat down slowly. "Well—there *is* a Joseph P. McCurdy. . . ." After he had recounted what he knew, the President said:

"I suppose you're having McCurdy checked."

"Yes. I sent an urgent to Justice."

·"And what do you expect to learn?"

Hochstein did not like the aspect of his character he was about to display. "That McCurdy has a criminal record. That he might—uh—be subversive. That he and some cronies conspired to urge and coerce others—I refer to Section B, Paragraph twenty-eight of the law as amended in 1971—to default payment of their lawful taxes. I recommend that he be brought to swift trial under *criminal*, not civil provisions. And thus all who have not paid their taxes —or are considering not paying them in the future—will see they are the dupes of a criminal, possibly a *subversive* conspiracy."

"But what if McCurdy is neither a criminal nor a communist agent? What if he is simply engaging in a form of protest?"

"Mr. President, if the current trend continues, the projected loss in tax revenues will approach three billion this year." Which, Hochstein knew the President realized, was another way of his saying that something *would* be hung on McCurdy because it *must* be in an effort to shame or frighten others into paying up.

"Would you argue, Jack, that McCurdy is responsible for the decision of numerous people not to pay their taxes?"

"No, sir. I'm only seeking a feasible way of prevailing on citizens to obey the law."

President Porter looked at him for a time, then began to talk of other matters, thereby convincing Hochstein that he would not come to a decision that day.

Though Hochstein was absorbed by the problems of the tax revolt, he had other long-standing commitments. That day he had a date at half-past twelve in Warrenton with a leader of the opposition who seemed bent on compromise on legislation of vital importance to President Porter. Hochstein dared not break the luncheon date. He was there on time after driving fast through the warm Virginia countryside.

The powerful gentleman did a powerful amount of talking. It was four o'clock in the afternoon before Hochstein could take his leave and find a public pay phone from where he called Gabriel Gaines.

"Gabby, anything new on Subject A?"

"Plenty. The Governor of New York has blown his stack and opened Pandora's lid. He's issued a statement that New York tax returns are off twenty percent and the state faces an overwhelming deficit. And Senator Blake King is at it again. He demands that the President *explain* what is happening. Both these are late developments. Hochy, I'm beginning to get a feeling of total unreality."

"Well, son, how do you think old Grampa Hochstein feels? So what other good news do you have?"

"The New York *Post* carries a story that there *is* a Joe McCurdy."

"That's a serious leak. It has to be plugged."

On the other hand, why try to plug a leak when the whole dam was busting? Hochstein suddenly was surfeited with the uncontrollably bizarre events of these days and the jargon whereby man tried futilely to cope with them. Language no longer was adequate to the problems. When the problems became indescribable, future history might be written in mathematical symbols. Or had the mood of hysteria infected his thinking too?

"Do me a favor, Gabby, and check my calls and basket for anything important."

When Gaines came on again he said, "Mrs. Carlton called. She said it was essential, underlined, that you call her as soon as possible."

It was unlike Helen to act so determined in her social messages.

"And a secret report just came for you from Justice."

"Open it."

In a moment Gaines said, "It's a report on McCurdy. . . . He has no fingerprints."

"You mean none on file with the Bureau."

"Yes. . . . He took out a passport to go to Brazil in 1959 and has kept it renewed since. Born in Los Angeles.

He's forty-four. Filed a photostat copy of his birth certificate with the State Department. This is interesting. The Los Angeles Bureau reports that the BVS there has no record of the original certificate. But of course records often get fouled up. He has a son, Peter, twelve, and a daughter, Patricia, fourteen. His wife's name is Hannah and——"

"I know about that from Treasury."

"About her arrest record?"

"No kidding! What about it?"

"Apparently the New York Police Department has her on their famous misdemeanors list. She's been arrested four times for kicking up a row at antiwar demonstrations."

"Oh that. I understand the wives and children of some of our most distinguished citizens are on that list. What else?"

"My God, Hochy, the Bureau must have had its entire force working on McCurdy all day long. Did you request fingerprints and a wiretap?"

Hochstein grimaced, remembering how often in practicing law he had protested wiretaps as a violation of civil liberties. He told Gaines, "What I did was make an urgent request for a complete check as fast as possible."

"Well, they sure got the message. The Director himself is obviously het up about it. You know he has a nose for such things."

Hochstein grimaced again, for he often had protested some of the Director's methods. What strange fellows climbed into bed together in a tax revolt!

"They've got everything on McCurdy," Gaines said. "Pictures. Advertising stuff he's written. Reports from friends and enemies. His wife went to Vassar and her grandparents on her mother's side were Jewish."

"Jesus," Hochstein said wryly, "she sure sounds real subversive."

"Last year," Gaines continued, "McCurdy was arrested in Litchfield, Connecticut, for driving past a stop sign and arguing with a cop. Back in 1969 he joined in the Washington peace march. The McCurdys are Unitarians. The kids——"

"Gabby, stop putting me on. Tell me something significant."

"I'm getting there," Gaines said. "I'm just reading along. . . . Well, here, McCurdy got his Social Security card when he was twenty-two years old. But before that there's *nothing* on him. No records of schooling, military service——"

"You said he has a Los Angeles birth certificate."

"But they insist that doesn't check out. Hey, this is interesting, they can't *get* his fingerprints."

"What d'you mean?"

"I mean they've been trying all day, and the usual places where these fingerprint experts know to find and transpose 'em—well, the prints aren't there. I remember when I was a lawyer in Justice—when these print experts can't *find* 'em, they get *frantic*."

Hochstein touched a hand to his forehead. "Yes, Gabby, yes. So they have not yet succeeded in getting Mc-Curdy's fingerprints. Is there anything else?"

"The tap isn't working. McCurdy has an unlisted phone, and they're plugged into it all right. But he hasn't made any calls out and every time somebody calls him, he answers and says, 'This is Joe McCurdy. I warn you that this telephone is being tapped.' Nearly everybody has hung up without saying a word—everybody except the reporters, who get his number from the ad agency where he arranged to have it made available to the press. He confirms the story in the *Post* to them and gives each some quote. Apparently he was out early this morning and that's when he must have talked to the *Post*. When the agents put onto the case got there he was coming home by taxi. Hasn't been out of his apartment since. Neither, apparently, has his family. The Bureau reports, and I quote, 'Investigation is greatly impeded by the large number of reporters and photographers on the scene.' And just one other thing. It requests the White House to let it know immediately of any fresh information available to us. Think of anything, Hochy?"

"Not at the moment." Hochstein hung up.

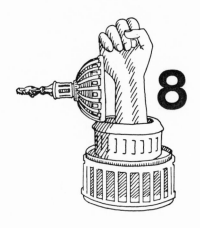

Helen, having awakened early on Thursday, took a cardboard box to the sun room where Janice Jones had coffee ready and a place set for Jim North. When she opened the box, which was crammed with old snapshots and photographs, she was unprepared for the montage of memories that came to her. Despite her urgent wish to find a photo of a specific face, she dawdled over the pictures—and one thought led to another.

John Quincy frowned sternly across the hood of a vintage Oldsmobile. On the back of the snapshot she had written, *Mr. Quincy confronts his 78th birthday party, May 14, 1954....*

She had always thought of and addressed him as Mr. Quincy. What an odd but sweet Puritan.

Alice Porter, ever a shrewd observer, had remarked after meeting him, "He's crazy about you, Helen. That adoring look. Is he rich?" Helen had been annoyed.

When Mr. Quincy died following a stroke in August, 1954, she had been stunned to learn he had bequeathed his entire estate to her....

Ben North, caught in muscular pose, was adjusting the jib of his canting boat while Louise clutched the cowling with an expression of distaste. On the back Helen had scrawled *Westward ho from Montauk Aug. '56. . . .*

Ben and Louise had moved from Attica to New York shortly before Mr. Quincy died. Helen's complicated affairs after she became his land-rich but land-poor heiress composed one of the first cases Ben had handled as a new partner in the New York firm.

He could not understand why Helen was so stunned by her good fortune. "Who did you think the old man would leave it to?" Doubtless it had been naïve of her never to think beyond the acres she had been purchasing gradually. In any event, Ben had guided her affairs wisely through the labyrinth of tax settlements; the decisions as to land sales—which parcels, how much, when to sell; the complications of reinvestments in securities and tax-exempt municipal bonds. She had ceased to be a writer and became a business woman in those years. . . .

Here were Alice and Bill in someone's garden. No date, no place, no distinct recollection. . . .

"But if you had married him," Alice had said, "you might have worked out a better tax situation as his wife." *Him* was, of course, Mr. Quincy. Helen did not know how Alice had learned of her inheritance—certainly not from close-mouthed Ben. But Alice had a way of finding out or divining nearly everything of importance.

However, perhaps because Alice was very shrewd, there were some things she never would understand. As the wife of the nation's most successful politician she understood ceaseless effort, constant compromise, the theory that every transaction involved a measure of satisfaction to each of two parties. But Alice never would comprehend the quixotic: how, for example, a stubborn old man who did not really care much about money took joy in fighting the big real estate manipulators for the benefit of a woman who had given him nothing but a few pleasant words. Helen could almost hear Alice saying it: "But she *must* have done *something* for him!" And Helen had been too wise ever to insist to Alice that she had not. . . .

Here was Louise in Kodachrome, wearing a mink coat and looking forlorn against a piney hillside. Idaho was the place, 1969 the year, and Louise had penned her message: *It was final today. Glad it's over. Went for a walk with young Mrs. Stilley and she snapped my picture.* . . .

Louise, as ever, sought sympathy, little knowing that she often roused in others only a sense of the pathetic. For years there had been no evidence to Helen that Louise and Ben loved each other. When, however, Ben had moved out and asked for a divorce, Louise had tried to make it seem the crushing tragedy of the century.

Alice at once had informed Helen who the woman was. Must there always be another woman or man? "Well, Helen, I don't know whether there *must*, but there always *is*. And, much as I like Louise, I have a lot of sympathy for Ben. Her name is Rita Reid," Alice said. "She's just a secretary in the office. Young, of course. Bill remembers her. He says she's very pretty and comes from Scranton. I don't know how he remembers things like that—somebody coming from *Scranton!* . . ."

Helen pushed away the box of photographs and sipped her coffee. Somewhere in the garden a bird was singing jubilantly.

Last night, as on previous occasions, she had found Rita Reid North a delightful woman—beautiful, intelligent, deeply devoted to Ben and having a lively sense of humor.

She heard Jim speak to Janice, and then he came into the sun room.

"Jim, what kind of bird is that singing out there?"

"Some sort of wood warbler. Very weak and unmusical."

"But jubilant," Helen said. "May I look at those cuff links again?"

He went to fetch them as Janice set a glass of orange juice at his place.

"Janice," Helen said, "have you thought it over? Do you want more money? Fewer responsibilities?"

"No, Mrs. Carlton. That new girl will work out fine. You couldn't have treated me better. But my mind is set on going home, I'm weary to my bones with Washington, have been for a long time."

"You have three years before you'll collect Social Security. And I imagine they'll refuse payments to those who default on paying their taxes. Have you thought over *that* matter too?"

"I have, Mrs. Carlton, I imagine they'll *threaten*. But they're always threatening something or other. My savings will take care of me in Hennington. I've got the house, you know. I want to keep some bees and raise a garden and just *set* and watch the foliage change across the cove. Down home you don't need such a lot of possessions. I feel free there."

Possessions would be the death of all of them. Houses, land, boats, trinkets, gadgets, money, stocks, bonds, titles, positions, all possessing one instead of being possessed. Ben had been talking about it yesterday in pointing out the greatly declining market value of Helen's investments and suggesting options she might take. She was not as rich as she used to be, and there was nothing on the economic horizon to indicate that past values would return. It made one pause and think about the rash protests of people like Janice Jones and Joe McCurdy.

Drawing the box to her again, she delved deep into the accumulation of pictures. Near the bottom were the beginnings of this fragmentary pictorial history of her life. Here was a picture of the Chevrolet agency in Greenleaf.

"Here they are, Aunt Helen." Jim put the cuff links on the table.

"Look at this." Helen held up a picture. "It's the cast of a play all of us were in away back when. That's my Jim there at the left. He was the stage manager. There's your father, and your mother."

"She used to be pretty," Jim said. "Hey, Pop had quite a roguish leer in those days."

"And that's Bill Porter."

"Old President William P.? He looked happier then than now."

"This man." Helen pointed. "Jim, have you ever seen him?"

Jim studied him briefly. "Not that I know of."

"His name was Eugene Schofield. Yesterday you met Joseph McCurdy. Does Joe McCurdy look anything like Gene Schofield?"

"Not the slightest, Aunt Helen. McCurdy is fat and this guy thin. McCurdy has a beard, but he doesn't. There's something else. Schofield stands and looks very tense, but McCurdy struck me as thoroughly relaxed. I know what your friend Mrs. Stetson said on the plane last night, but . . ."

Fay Stetson had become most excited after she examined one of the cuff links carefully. A jeweler's mark on the back indicated, she insisted, that they were the links she had had made for Gene Schofield more than twenty years ago. She even remembered the jewelry shop on Tenth Street where she had bought them. And this morning she would go there with Helen, if the shop still existed. . . .

To Jim's relief the line was busy when he telephoned

Louise after breakfast. He was going first to the Geographic, then to the Smithsonian, and later he would call his mother.

"I'll drop you at the Geographic," Helen said. "I'll take the links and pick up Fay. Maybe it's a fool's errand, but she's as curious about this thing as I am. Jim, please have dinner with me here tonight. I want to talk to you about your next project."

When she stopped at the National Geographic building on Sixteenth Street, Jim swung out with his knapsack. There seemed no end to the differences of the generations: the knapsack, for example. It was the sensible way to carry his undeveloped films and other oddments, yet his most sensible father, when Jim's age, would not have gone around with a knapsack for love or money. What a wonderfully unselfconscious generation was this new one!

As she turned left on K Street she saw Senator Harold Garamond on the southeast corner waving futilely at taxis. She stopped and beckoned him. "Harold, where are you bound?"

"About the nation's business, I hope. How are you, Helen? I just came from breakfast with constituents at the Statler and——"

"And the Statler has no taxis at this hour and so you crossed the street. I'll take you to the Hill."

"Thanks." He climbed in. "I'm already late for committee."

Helen stopped for a traffic light at Twelfth Street behind a Buick. On its rear window was a sticker which read:

DON'T PAY TILL YOU HAVE A SAY

"Where do they come from?" she said. "Are there organizations that give them away?"

"I understand some of the building trade locals are

supplying them to members from slush funds. College groups are turning them out too. And you can buy them in the slop shops that cater to every fad. Davey, our ten-year-old, has been collecting them. He had three plastered on our picture window to greet me the other night when I came home from serving the country. Took me nearly twenty minutes to scrape them off with a razor blade. But it's a genuine thing, Helen. You should read my mail. It's nationwide, but seems to be strongest in the Northeast Corridor."

"You don't go along with the theory of conspiracy?"

"Definitely not!" Senator Garamond spoke almost vehemently. "It's as genuine as the Colonies protest against the Crown taxes before the Revolution. I talked with the President about it on Monday morning. I wish the Administration could understand it. Blake King does. He sees there must be a total reassessment of our national values and spending. His realization of it could take him into the White House next year. Tell me something, Helen. You're close to Bill and Alice. *Look* listed you as one of the twenty people who have most influence at the White House and——"

"But you were on that list too, Harold. In my case it was simply American journalism at work. They put together nineteen more or less plausible names, then realized none was a woman. So they put down me. They forget about Alice. If they'd listed her, it would have been accurate. But not me. Not once since Bill became President has he asked my opinion about anything political—and only once have I offered him an opinion."

"About what?"

"A few months after he was inaugurated, I said to him, 'Bill, stop the goddamn war.' He was quite startled. Not by my opinion, I guess, but because I don't think he ever heard me swear before. He said, 'I want to, Helen.' I said, 'Then do it!' And then he went into all the buts about—well, you know."

"I wish, Helen, you'd do it again. I wish you would tell him he has to take sober, thoughtful cognizance of this protest—publicly. You know his way of ignoring protests. Generally he's been politically astute about that. But this time it's different. The economy is really sick and this revolt is its most dangerous symptom. Don't you agree?"

"Yes, I do. But does anyone, including Internal Revenue, really know how widespread the thing is? Maybe it's not as bad as the journalists are blowing it up to be. Maybe the computers finally have failed us. You know yourself how hopeless it is to get full, solid information on seemingly simple things in the vast complexity of federal government. Look at our weapons systems. The General Accounting Office candidly admits it can't even find out how many weapons systems we have nor even how many tens of billions they're costing above the original estimates."

"There," Senator Garamond said, "in military spending, you've hit the basic cause of the sick economy. And it's the basic cause of the tax revolt. Last night I finished drafting a speech I'm going to send to Bill. I've never done such a thing before, and of course he didn't ask for it. But it's the approach I think he must take. A firm but friendly admonition to the delinquents to pay up. But an equally firm promise to cut military spending and take other steps toward curbing inflation. It's what he must do."

"Must, Harold?"

"Yes, if he's going to be reelected. The tide is turning, as it turned four years ago. This time I'm convinced the majority of voters want a friendly hero in the White House."

"Then maybe they want Blake King. Your speech draft sounds like one he would deliver."

"Exactly!" Senator Garamond smiled. "It's the only way for Bill to checkmate the King."

"Maybe so," Helen replied, "but it sounds totally out of character for Bill. In the town where he grew up there were a few things you simply did not do. One was that you never failed to pay your taxes. That was as great a sin as making a pass at the minister's wife."

"But that was long ago and far away, Helen. The world has changed more since we were young than it had in the preceding five centuries. And we have changed with it if we have survived at all. We are totally different people than we were thirty-five years ago."

They had come to the Senate Office Building, and Helen braked slowly to a halt.

"Helen, I'm asking you a favor. After my speech is typed today and a messenger takes it to Sixteen hundred, I'm going to have him drop off a copy at your house. I wish you'd read it. And if you find it makes sense, I wish you'd take it on yourself to see Bill and tell him so. Thanks for the lift."

Helen, thoughtful, drove along Pennsylvania Avenue. *We are totally different people than we were thirty-five years ago.* Harold Garamond, despite a fondness for rhetoric, was one of the most astute men in government. Of course she would read the proposed speech with interest. But he was wrong about her having influence with Bill. Or did he think that because she never had expressed an opinion to the President it might be effective if she did now?

Fay was ready when Helen arrived at her home. "I know we're acting crazy, Helen, but I can't get the thing off my mind. Of course, even though they were the same links, Gene might have pawned them and Joe McCurdy have bought them somewhere."

"Was Gene a beau of yours, Fay?"

Fay grimaced. "You might say so. At first I thought I loved him. At the end I hated him. I could have *killed* him!"

Helen glanced at her. "Do you still feel the same?"

"No. I can't feel the same about him or anyone or anything after twenty years. I'm just—curious."

"I know. This morning I gave a lift to Senator Harold Garamond. He said something interesting. He said, 'We are totally different people than we were thirty-five years ago.'"

"That," said Fay, "is the first intelligent thing I've heard a Senator say in at least thirty-five years."

The shop was still on Tenth Street where Fay remembered it as being. With mounting excitement they showed the links to the aged proprietor.

He studied them carefully and said at last:

"This is my mark. These are my work. I seem to remember making them years ago to a design specified by a young woman. I never made any others like them, and I've never seen any that are the same."

Jim North left the National Geographic shortly before noon and strode down Sixteenth Street with his half-emptied knapsack on his back. He had left his negatives to be developed in the Geographic photo lab and had had a pleasant conversation with the editor who would transform his effusions about the Abuña country into satisfactory language. As he cut across Lafayette Park among the greedy pigeons and the federal workers eating paper-bag lunches on benches, he was thinking about writing: the writers he admired, his wish to emulate them, his failures thus far. Across Pennsylvania Avenue the White House seemed to glow in pristine spring light. Porter's pride, and Penny's prison. Or was it Penny's pride, and her father's prison? He had been away too long to know, and he did not care.

Midway across East Executive Avenue, where pilgrims were lined patiently waiting to view the wonders of the White House East Wing, he heard the call of a red-bellied woodpecker—a rattling sound, low, sharp, and hoarse. It turned him on, as nothing had since his return to his native country—and it turned him off his eastward trend to the Smithsonian and toward the godly green of the Ellipse, where signs warned KEEP OFF THE GRASS. Seeing and thinking green, he forgot about the red of traffic on South Executive Place behind the White House grounds. He dodged a Volkswagen, heard brakes, leaped safely onto mother green. And then a female voice cried shrilly:

"Jim!"

Turning, he said, "Well, I'll be damned."

Out of a Cadillac-like limousine sprang old Miss Penelope Porter. No longer young, incredibly matured except for the gamin grin.

"Jim doll!"

"Well, I'll be damned," he said again. "How are ya, Penny?" When she reached him, he pecked her cheek.

"Oh, Jim!" She gazed up at him. "I thought—"

"Yeah. Well, I'm back. You're looking comely. Here comes your boy friend."

The ubiquitous Secret Service agent had sprung out of the car too and come up behind her, his walkie-talkie clapped on. Talk, talk, talk. Now all points hear this: The President's daughter has departed from schedule.

Penny looked around. "Oh, *him.* Pete, don't look so

alarmed! This is Jim North. Jim, do you remember Pete Harkness?"

Old dead-eye gave him the hard-pan, and Jim said, "Oh, sure. I think you helped hustle me out of Madison Square Garden a long time ago."

"Where are you going?" Penny asked him. "What are you doing?"

"I'm walking to the Smithsonian, Penny. And you?"

"It doesn't matter. Get in the car."

"I don't want to. It's nice to see you again."

"Are you staying with your mother?"

"No. I spent the night at Aunt Helen's. Mother doesn't know yet I'm here. Every time I call her, busy, busy. Would appreciate your not mentioning to your mother that you saw me till I can contact my mother. Very hush-hush errand here. CIA stuff. Yes, Penny, you're as pretty as always."

"And you're as full of bull as always. I'll walk to the Smithsonian with you."

"Don't break up the schedule. You must have a library to dedicate or a ship to launch."

"I'm going to a place I don't want to go to and don't have to. I *hate* golf."

"Then why try to play it?"

"I'll go with you." She turned to Pete Harkness. "Pete, just once would you make it free time?"

"Sorry, Miss Porter. You want me to get fired?"

Jim started across the Ellipse, and Penny said, "The signs say——"

"So they do, Penny. But today this grass is for walking on."

She came with him, saying, "This past year I've gotten interested in birds. Hear that cardinal?"

He did, and then, hearing a pair of mocking birds, he asked her what they were.

"Mated mocking birds nest-building." She went on about the starlings, which were such a nuisance, until he caught a nasal-like gargle from the heights of an oak, and halted to look. "Know what that is?" She didn't. "A fish crow. They don't caw like regular crows. They sound as if they had a fish bone caught in their throat. There he is." He pointed. "See him?" She did not, so he aimed her gaze by gently placing one hand on her chin and the other on the back of her sun-warmed head.

"I see him!" she cried, and the old crow, gargling, flapped off toward the Tidal Basin.

Behind them Pete Harkness murmured into his talkie, "We're midway of the Ellipse going south," and Jim wondered what could be worse than to be a President's child.

They went on through sunlight and tree shadows. The quartering breeze bore the scent of magnolia blossoms, and the grass was good and springy to the feet. When they came out on Constitution Avenue near Seventeenth, Jim felt no haste to get to the Smithsonian. The limousine had circled and was waiting on the Avenue while on Seventeenth another Service car had halted and an agent armed with walkie-talkie was climbing out. They were surrounded. But there was no point in fighting it, there was nothing you could do about it.

On the corner a vendor was plying the lunch trade under a gay umbrella which shaded his cart. "Want a hot dog, Penny? We could go over to the Reflecting Pool and eat 'em."

"Great! Sauerkraut on mine."

He wrapped paper napkins around four hot dogs with sauerkraut and put them along with two cans of Coke into his knapsack. Then, glancing at Pete Harkness and the other agent, who were standing back at prescribed distances and angles, he recognized their human expressions: they were hungry. Buying more dogs and Cokes, he took them to Harkness, who looked surprised and expressed thanks. Suddenly two girls recognized Penny and began to squeal. There was just time for Jim to grasp her by a hand and race the traffic light across the Avenue, leaving the agents stranded and anxious.

"Maybe we can duck 'em."

"Impossible," Penny said. "Well, it can be done, but they're nice guys and they worry so."

Not far from the foot of the Pool they found a shady spot where they sat on the grass and began to eat. The agents went to earth at a respectful distance, diminished to nothing by the wide blue sky and the magnificent perspective of the Lincoln Memorial and Washington Monument which seemed far off. Penny wanted to know everything about his trip. She was easy to talk to because she was truly interested and questioned him intelligently.

As he went on about his adventures he became increasingly aware that she had grown into a beautiful woman. Her beauty resided chiefly in her dark eyes, which held a hint of sadness to him. In the midst of a description of shooting a jungle rapids, he broke off and asked:

"Do you really like it, Penny?"

His lack of transition did not trouble her. "It's pretty interesting. You see a lot and do a lot."

"Is it true you're engaged to Señor George Farquar?"

"Who?"

"Señor George Farquar. I read in a Spanish-language paper in Santiago that you were engaged to him." He had not read it; he had never heard of said Farquar nor been in Santiago. But it seemed a delicate way of finding out some things about her.

[143]

"George Farquar!" She smiled. "Never heard of him. The guy to whom I'm most often romantically linked, as they say in the fan magazines, is Teddy Evans."

"Old Flap-head Evans who lived in Leverett House and went on to Yale Law?"

"I never heard anybody call Teddy Flap-head. He's a very nice guy. He's dated me a few times and been my escort at——"

"Old Flap-head! I'll be darned."

"Why do you keep calling him Flap-head?"

"Everybody did. He never stopped talking. Talk-talk-talk."

"Well, he's a good conversationalist."

"Flap-flap-flap. Talk-talk-talk. That's most interesting, Penny, most interesting indeed."

She frowned at him. "I didn't say I have any real interest in him. But he's a nice boy, a serious, hard-working student. Social life in Washington isn't the easiest thing in the world. I mean you have to be nice to people and you know that a lot of them are nice to you because— Well, Teddy is just a natural good friend."

"But such an incessant talker. The last time we had a little clash over something—I can't even remember what —old Flap-head Evans and some of his buddies, having decided to take law and order into their own hands—well, it became necessary for some of us to evict *them*. And as we carried out Evans, bearing him high over our heads like a writhing sapling, his jaws never stopped flapping. 'You guys will live to regret this, you guys will live to regret this, you guys—' "

She was looking at him with such a pained expression that he felt unhappy. "Well, those days are gone forever and I don't miss them. He *is* a decent guy, Penny, and I don't remember anybody but me ever calling him Flap-head."

A smile banished the pained expression. "Tell me who George Farquar is supposed to be."

"I don't know. I just made him up. I've never even been in Santiago."

Her look of wonder evaporated into laughter. "Jim, there are some amazing things about you, but the best is that you're absolutely crazy!"

Glancing at his wristwatch, he saw it was nearly half-past one. "Miss Penny, thanks for a happy picnic. My man at the Smithsonian should be back from lunch by the time I get there." He swung to his feet.

She remained still, arms clasped about her knees, looking up at him curiously. "How long will you be in Washington?"

"I don't know."

"Where are you going then?"

"I'm not sure yet."

"You want to ride to the Smithsonian?"

"No, I want to walk."

"Come on then." She got to her feet gracefully.

Avoiding the Avenue, Jim took them by the route of the Mall, past signs which warned that this tender spring grass was not to be enjoyed. The agents plodded after them with disapproving expressions while down the Avenue a limousine crept watchfully like a Mafia prowler. Near the crest of the Monument rise there was a clear view east to the Capitol, west to the Memorial, south to Virginia, endowing Washington with a sense of splendor. A sparrow hawk came freewheeling from the north on a thermal draft, and Jim had a feeling of spaciousness and freedom about this country such as the old chauvinist hymns used to proclaim.

Penny said, "You mean you have no idea what you're going to do next?"

"Well, with any luck at all I hope to be on the shores of the Arctic by June."

He told her about it as they went on across Fourteenth Street and down the Mall.

When they came to the Smithsonian, where the black limousine waited to gather her in, he was thinking about the innumerable traps that were set for the unwary traveler.

Extending his hand and leaning down to kiss her forehead in benediction, he said, "Penny, it's been fun. Take care." But then, stricken by an incredible feeling of imminent loneliness, he said, "What are you doing afterwards?"

"After what?"

"After I've seen this guy here."

"Nothing, Jim."

"I'll tell you what. I'm having dinner with Aunt Helen at her house. You come too. Maybe afterwards we can go someplace and listen to some music, maybe go hear Charlie Bird."

"Great! I'll wait for you."

"I may be a couple of hours."

"I don't care. I don't want to go home and change and all that. I'm comfortable. We'll ride out to Aunt Helen's together. You take your time. I'll go in the Smithsonian and look around. I haven't been here since I was about four or something. I wonder if they still have that kooky little airplane Lindbergh flew across the Atlantic hanging by wires in there. . . ."

Watching him go off, Penny had a sensation of sinking into the pavement. *With any luck at all I hope to be on the shores of the Arctic by June.* Oh the utter, casual freedom and magnificence in that statement! And there

[146]

was no one with whom she could share it, no one who would understand and cherish it as she did.

Pete Harkness' sensitive Basset eyes questioned her.

"You'd better call for relief," she told him. "Your day hasn't half begun."

He tried to smile. "As Rudy Vallee used to sing before you were born, Miss Penny, your time is my time. But I hope you're not thinking of going into the Smithsonian."

"Why not?"

"It's a totally insecured area. It's jammed with tourists. Ed and I simply can't handle it."

"Pete, what do you mean by insecured? This is the Smithsonian *Institution*, fount of learning in our nation's *capital*. First I want to make a call."

Stepping into the limousine, she phoned the residential quarters and asked to speak to her mother.

"Mother, the most wonderful thing has happened!"

"You made a hole in one," Alice said.

"No, I never even got there. I ran into Jim North and we had a picnic by the Reflecting Pool and then we walked to the Smithsonian."

"Dear heaven! How is the birdwatcher?"

Penny felt herself flushing. "Okay, Mother, okay. Jim is just *fine!* I called to tell you I'm *not* going to be back for that three-o'clock fitting, and I *won't* be home for dinner, and I'm *not* going to that concert. Jim and I are having dinner at Aunt Helen's and then we're going out somewhere."

"All right, Penny." Alice spoke mildly. "I think that's fine. Have a good time. I talked to Louise earlier today and she didn't mention Jim's being in town."

"He got in last night. He's staying with Aunt Helen while he tends to business at the Geographic and places. He tried to reach his mother, but the line was busy. If you talk to Aunt Louise again, would you please not mention about Jim until he has a chance to— Understand?"

"Of course, Penny. I won't mention it at the concert tonight unless Louise does."

"Mother, I want to quote something Jim said that I think is just magnificent. I have to tell somebody. Could you possibly understand it? The utter, casual freedom of it. He's planning a tremendous expedition and he said— listen—'With any luck at all I hope to be on the shores of the Arctic by June.' Isn't that wonderful?"

"Yes, Penny." Alice Porter sounded sad somehow. "It really is wonderful. I understand exactly what you mean. I used to have thoughts like that when I was Jim's age. But I never had his confidence that they would come to pass— as I'm sure this will for him. Where are you now?"

"Waiting for him at the Smithsonian."

"Not inside!"

"No, I'm in the car."

"Penny, that would be too much for Pete to handle. Don't under any circumstances go inside the Smithsonian. . . ."

Penny was waiting patiently in the limousine when Jim finally came out.

Helen took Fay to the Jockey Club for a leisurely lunch.

"Then you're agreeable," she asked her, "to my telling Jack Hochstein at the White House about this? And I want to tell Ben North too since he's involved with Mr. X."

"It's perfectly okay with me," Fay said. "Just for old times' sake I wouldn't mind seeing Gene nailed to the mast. On the other hand, I have a sneaking admiration for Joe McCurdy—if he's an authentic rebel who's fed up with the direction of government and has had the guts to join in a revolt. Helen, have you ever thought of not paying your taxes?"

"I'm constitutionally incapable of it," Helen said. "It would be a hopeless fight and there's too much to lose."

Fay sighed. "I know. The money I inherited from my family and Denton seems to grow less all the time. So there's no sense in throwing all of it away. But I'll bet both Hochstein and North laugh at you. The trouble with lawyers is that they always want solid evidence. They don't appreciate the intuitive."

"Then intuitively you feel that McCurdy is Gene?"

"I'm convinced of it," said Fay.

When Helen returned home she phoned Hochstein's office and learned he was out of town. Then she called Ben's office and was told he had not yet returned from court. At both places she left a message that it was urgent her call be returned as soon as possible.

Janice brought her a sealed envelope which a messenger from Harold Garamond's office had delivered. It reminded her of the White House and the fact she had agreed to go to a concert of the Boston Symphony that evening with Alice, Louise, and Penny. She telephoned Alice's secretary.

"Oh, Mrs. Carlton, Mrs. Porter is right here and I think she wants to say hello."

"Hello," Alice said.

"Hello," Helen said. "Alice, I just can't make that concert tonight."

"I know," Alice said, "and I know something else I'll bet you don't know yet yourself. Penny is coming to your house for dinner."

"Grand!"

"I hope so. She ran into young Jim and he invited her."

"Wonderful! Alice, I hope you understand about me and the concert."

"This seems to be my afternoon for understanding," Alice said. "Sure I do. You're as unmusical as I, but I've ducked too many concerts. And I read in a magazine last month that I'm very musical. Louise will go with me. You might drop a hint to Jim. Tell him to call his mother around eight. She'll be leaving her apartment about half-past seven."

Omniscient though Alice seemed to be, how could she know Jim was not eager to see his mother? Helen said, "I'm not sure how well your understanding is working this afternoon, but your intuition is going great."

"I feel sorry for her," Alice said.

Helen declined to comment on Louise, but she decided impulsively that she had something to report. "My intuition has been at work too, Alice. It's a day of crazy impulses for me. I want to ask you a question. Do you believe Gene Schofield is dead?"

Alice said slowly, "Why do you ask that?"

"Well, do you think he's dead?"

After a while, "I doubt it. I hadn't thought about it, but since you ask—Gene was healthy and loved life. Unless he loved it too well, I doubt he's departed it. Now *why* do you ask?"

"Something has come into my possession, something I'm positive belonged to Gene."

"Helen, what are you talking about? You can be utterly maddening when you get into one of these esoteric moods. *What* has come into your possession?"

Helen told her.

Alice was silent for a long time. Then, "I think maybe you're onto something. I'm going to tell Bill."

"He'll laugh at us. The trouble with Bill is he's a

lawyer. It's the trouble with Ben and Hochy. This is the perfect story for lawyers to laugh at."

"Maybe he will and maybe he won't," Alice said. "I have always felt that wherever Gene was he was Bill's enemy. I'm going to tell Bill about this. . . ."

Helen read carefully the copy of the speech Harold Garamond had written. It was a good one, though it sounded more like Blake King than William Porter. It was, in effect, the initial plank of a platform on which Bill might run for reelection as a sort of hero to some people who had thus far opposed him. A long time ago, Helen recalled, George Santayana had written that for a man to survive in a democracy he must be something of a saint and something of a hero. Well, Bill had been something of a saint in his survival of the slings and arrows of outrageous politics. Why should he not also try to be something of a hero? She liked Harold's approach to the problem of the tax revolt: placing it within the context of the unhealthy economy; pointing out the efforts of the Administration to bring about greater economic strength; proposing some drastic changes in the directions of government spending; asking delinquents to pay up and shoulder the rightful responsibilities of their citizenship. There was a solidity, a magnanimity about it that made Helen think of Lincoln. Curiously, while the speech sounded at odds with the Administration as viewed by opponents, it was not at odds with the subtle changes of thought that Helen had observed developing in Bill Porter. Harold had said this morning: *We are totally different people than we were thirty-five years ago.* How fully did Bill reflect that fact?

She sat at her desk, pen poised over paper, pondering how to express her endorsement of Harold's speech in a note to Bill.

When Ben returned to Pine Street from Federal Court that Thursday afternoon, Chris Marlowe rushed at him in the main-floor lobby. He looked pallid, wretched, and he was trying to say something.

"Marlowe, are you ill?"

He uttered a gasping sound. "I think so. Don't go upstairs, Mr. North. The reception room is full of reporters and photographers."

Ben looked at him with wonder.

"Here." Marlowe thrust a copy of the *Post* at him, its front-page headline awesomely large and funereally black.

IS PRESIDENT PORTER
JOE MCCURDY'S LAWYER?

Ben put his briefcase on the floor and began to read the story.

The Joe McCurdy of mythic fame is an actual person, a New Yorker bruised by the dollar crunch, whose tax problems are being soothed by President Porter's own law firm.

Joe, who is Joseph P. McCurdy of 35 East 36th Street in Manhattan and one of Madison Avenue's most renowned advertising writers, revealed the entire amazing saga to the *Post* today. As McCurdy himself suggests, the first chapter might be entitled "How the Federal Government Can Drive You Broke on Fifty Grand a Year."

Marlowe seemed actually to be swaying, and Ben said, "You need a shot of booze, but I guess coffee will have to do. Come on." He led the way into the coffee shop off the lobby and sat in a booth in a corner.

The *Post* story continued onto pages two and three where there were photos of McCurdy grinning with Falstaffian glee. A long sidebar with a chart of living costs showed how easy it had been for him to go broke on fifty grand. The lead story, recounting substantially what McCurdy had told Ben at their meeting, came to a hinge:

A spokesman for Burton, North, McGinnis, and Mosely, the prominent Wall Street law firm of which President Porter was a partner, confirmed today that McCurdy had retained its services in his tax battle with the federal government. . . .

Ben frowned. "Now here. Who confirmed this to the *Post?*"

Marlowe's hand shook as he lowered his cup of coffee. Ben suddenly and irrelevantly was glad to be in his late fifties instead of his early thirties. So much was behind you in the fifties, so many harrowing and once seemingly fatal incidents; when you reached your fifties you realized that the only fatal incident still possible was death itself. Irrelevantly, too, Ben remembered the time a kamikaze dealt the *Enoch* her mortal wound off Okinawa: the concussion had hurled him off the bridge, and there had been one horrible second when he had been suspended flat in air and known that if he fell on the steel sheeting of the forties battery he would be cut in two; but he had not fallen on the sheeting. If there was any profit for a man to have engaged in war it consisted in his realizing that nothing ever could be as bad again. Yet youngish Marlowe here, uncontaminated by military service, obviously felt he was in a hell of a fatal fix.

"I never mentioned it, Mr. North, I'd forgotten about it. I mean I don't think I ever even knew it."

"You'd forgotten about what, Marlowe?"

"I assume you're referring to the sentence that mentions—uh—your former association with President Porter."

Ben read on dourly.

North is now the senior partner of the firm. It is generally forgotten that long before North and Porter were associated in law practice North ran Porter's notorious slush fund, the revelation of which almost ended his political career. . . .

Oh *that* again! Ben liked to believe *that* had been forgotten in the mists of public memory. However, more disappointing to him than a fresh report of the ancient canard was Marlowe's tension and confusion. Bright young men were forever disappointing him: he had counted heavily on Marlowe, who, it developed, squirmed too much in the clinches.

"I wasn't referring to that, Marlowe." He read the

sentence that had prompted his question. "Who told the *Post* McCurdy is a client of ours?"

"I've traced that down." Marlowe sipped coffee hurriedly. "A *Post* reporter phoned while you were in court, and Miss Thomas handled it properly. The reporter asked her if McCurdy was a client, and she said she didn't know anything about it, you would have to answer the question. Then I got a call and thought it was J. P. Westcott——"

"You *thought?* Did a man identify himself as Westcott?"

"A woman, apparently his secretary, said J. P. Westcott wanted to talk to me, and then Westcott came on."

"Did he say to you, 'This is Jim Westcott'? Did you recognize his voice?"

"No, he didn't say that. I haven't talked to him enough to be sure, but—I— He said, 'Decent of you people to take on Joe McCurdy's case. Understand Ben North conferred with him yesterday.' I said yes, but you didn't think he had much of a case, and I wasn't sure"—Marlowe's tone became defensive—"well, I didn't know how you planned to dispose of McCurdy, Mr. North. Anyway, I told the man who, it now is obvious, must have been a *Post* reporter that he'd have to talk to you about it. Now I see McCurdy must have coached the reporter on how to go about it."

"Yes." Ben took a tablet of yellow ruled paper from his briefcase, uncapped his old-fashioned fountain pen, and wrote slowly:

Burton, North, McGinnis, and Mosely never has and never will represent the individual purporting to be Joseph P. McCurdy. He came to our office yesterday, claiming income tax difficulties, and we dismissed him because we felt he has no case worthy of representation. It must be pointed out further that President Porter severed all associations with Burton, North, McGinnis, and Mosely four years ago and has never since that time communicated with the firm on any matter relating to its affairs.

Signing his name, he turned the pad around so that Marlowe could read what he had written.

Marlowe looked up inquiringly. "The individual *purporting* to be Joseph P. McCurdy?"

"Yes. That's casting shadow of doubt on opponent. I'm sure McCurdy is McCurdy. But do you know him personally, Marlowe? Have you seen his birth certificate? Anyone who reads that statement intelligently might wonder if *we* wonder if the individual is not some nut who has assumed the name of McCurdy—and so, wondering, and so forth. Take this up to Miss Thomas, have her type it and Xerox forty copies. I'll come up in ten minutes, meet the gentlemen of the press, and hand out the copies. Have Miss Lefkowitz record the questions and answers."

"You want to *face* them?"

"Why not? Am I guilty of something? Hurry it up, Marlowe."

Ben ordered a fresh cup of coffee and lighted a cigarette. He tried not to think about his mistrust of the so-called profession of journalism and its lip service to "the truth." In his experience most pragmatic newsmen adapted their craft to a common human failing: people enjoyed bad news about anyone or anything as long as it did not affect them personally. But it was difficult for Ben not to brood while he waited.

When he stepped off the elevator into the reception room, someone said, "There he is!" and there was moderate bedlam. A trigger-happy photographer took careless aim and popped a bulb, causing two other members of that most hysterical profession to pop cameras too in their eternal anxiety over missing something that another got.

Ben stilled them. He always had been deliberate in manner, and with age and experience he had developed a commanding presence. He gave each reporter a copy of the statement, and before he had handed out the last one, a *Post* reporter demanded:

"You don't deny you've consulted with McCurdy?"

"If you'll read the statement," Ben replied, "you will see that the firm does not represent McCurdy. You're consulting me now. Does that mean I represent you?"

The *Times* had a more intelligent question: "You say here 'the individual purporting to be McCurdy.' Do you question his identity?"

"I never saw the man before," Ben said. "He was sent here by a reputable client of the firm, so I assume he is who he claims to be. At the same time there's been so much hysteria recently over the McCurdy myth that anyone with that name might take it on himself, for purposes of publicity, to——"

"Do you think," asked the *Daily News*, "that he came here because it's the President's law firm?"

"It is not the President's law firm, sir. It——"

"I know. I mean, do you think he thought——"

"I have no idea what he thinks. You'll have to ask him about that."

But the *Daily News* reporter, having conceived of an angle, pursued it tenaciously:

"Mr. North, are you still on good terms with President Porter?"

Ben tried to make his smile agreeable. "Yes, of course."

"Well, back when he was first elected there was talk of his appointing you—maybe to the Cabinet, and then later there was mention of your going to the bench. But both times that old thing came up——"

"I have no interest in government service," Ben said. "Gentlemen, you came here to question me about the relationship of this firm to Mr. McCurdy. I think I have stated clearly that there is none. Now I have to get back to work, and I assume you do too."

Silent but watchful, they made room for him to pass on to his office, then all milled to the elevator.

As he passed Miss Thomas, she said, "I put a list of the important things on your desk. Your wife called." She had finally learned not to refer to Mrs. North since there were two Mrs. Norths. "She reminded you she's going to the Brittons' at half-past five and will meet you there."

It was now twenty minutes past five. Feeling very tired suddenly, Ben went into the washroom and looked at his reflection in the mirror. His puss could stand a touch of electric razor before cocktails at the Brittons', but he would not bother. Amend his recent thought about the glory of the late fifties; at twenty minutes past five on an afternoon like this every man should feel a youngish thirty. He was ready to call it quits with this Thursday, but the day must go on to his standing in a crowded Park Avenue penthouse and yakking about nothing. Putting on his hat at an angle that defied his age, he folded Miss Thomas's list of the day's vital statistics into a pocket and left. As he came out on Pine Street, he saw with surprise an empty taxi creeping past. Whistling shrilly, he sprang toward it and barely beat another bounding citizen to the kill.

"What a hell of a place to be trapped at this hour," the driver said. "But the city's just one big trap anyway."

Ben liked New York. At least he liked it better than Attica. Henry Burton, with whom he had worked on an intricate corporate merger in Attica, had not had much trouble in wooing him to his firm. Long ago he had passed the New York bar examination; the prospect of more money, more interesting cases, and the mere fact of being in New York had made it easy for him to come to a decision.

Louise had protested, of course. Increasingly she had protested anything that offered challenge or change. But, having protested, she went along in her reluctant fashion. In time she accepted living in New York with fairly good grace. To Ben's mind, however, she did not seek fulfillment in the resources of the city. She was not in step with the theater. She never crossed the threshold of an art gallery. She rarely read a book. She continued to subscribe to the Attica *Chronicle* and thought it a more interesting newspaper than the New York *Times*. Occasionally she went to a concert with Alma Burton, but only because she felt it politic. She played bridge, she watched television, she went shopping, and she fussed over Jim's exposure to life and ideas as he progressed or regressed at various private schools—all being things she probably could have done more comfortably in Attica. After Ben bought the house on Long Island, she showed interest in it because it took her away from the city. But she never did share his enthusiasm for sailing, which was the chief reason for having the place and the only real fun one could have around there.

However, Ben always tried to temper his judgments of Louise with judgments of himself. When they moved to New York he had looked forward to seeing a lot of theater and interesting himself in art, which always had attracted him and about which he was largely ignorant. Before long, however, he discovered that either the New York theater or his enjoyment of it was limited. And he simply could not find the time to browse through the uptown galleries.

There never seemed to be enough time to do anything except work at his practice.

His progress with the firm was rapid and satisfying. Henry Burton became his peer rather than his mentor—and one day he realized that Henry and he had become the best of friends. There was great satisfaction in that, as in the perpetual learning process implicit in the intelligent practice of corporate law. The steady expenditure of skill and effort brought rewards of increasing money. But there was not the satisfaction in money that he once had anticipated. There were, in counterpoint to his sense of accomplishment, vague and curious dissatisfactions.

Occasionally he had a hankering for public service—to lift his head above the grass and look around the landscape. He felt he would enjoy and excel at a federal judgeship. Whenever his thoughts wandered in that direction, however, he knew it was impossible. His name bore a stigma as a result of the misinterpretation of the Porter fund that closed doors to him forever. The thing was gone but not forgotten; it was forgotten but not gone. Of course, friends like Henry and many politicians everywhere remembered it, sympathized with him, and resented the stigma. All was well as long as he kept his head in the grass, but if he tried to raise up to view the landscape, the enemies of William Paisley Porter would shoot him down.

At first, after the episode, he had been hurt, angry. But he understood Bill's predicament and his resulting viewpoint. It was something to be ignored—and, naturally, Ben North was the one to be ignored publicly. However, Bill comprehended politics so thoroughly that he well knew the nature of debt. He knew what he owed Ben for having launched him on the sea of politics, but he realized he could not repay him without running a chance of sinking the ship. Ben understood this, and Bill knew that he did. It left them with a personal social relationship, abetted by

Alice and Louise, that both tried to make as pleasant as possible.

When Bill made his first unsuccessful bid for the Presidency, Ben had wanted to help him, for he approved of Bill's party and principles. He believed Bill had grown and had a grasp of government his ambitious, personable opponent lacked. Ben understood, however, that he must avoid the limelight as one of Bill's supporters.

With growing dismay he observed Bill's effort to run the Presidential campaign on his own, as if it were a century ago and he could, like Lincoln, bear all the problems in his stovepipe hat. Ben urged him to delegate more organizational authority, but to no avail. In order to win the race, Bill needed the active support of the General. Ben urged him to seek it. Why was Bill reluctant to do so? Maybe it was because of the sort of pride you could hear on the lips of every failed man in Greenleaf: *I wanted to do it on my own*. In any event, the General's aid was too little and too late.

Bill, defeated, began law practice in Attica.

"Why not ask him to join the law firm here?" asked Louise. "Alice would love to get out of Attica and come to New York."

"He hasn't practiced in a long time," Ben replied. "When he has convinced himself he's through with politics, he might like to try practicing in New York."

"He's out of politics," Louise said.

But he was not. He ran for the Senate, and was defeated. Then, as if to underscore the fact he was through with politics forever, he called together the reporters who had covered his campaign and angrily accused them of having been prejudiced against him and having caused his defeat.

As Henry Burton put it: "He couldn't have ended a political career with more finality if he'd shot a policeman."

Then Henry mused. "But there's a volcano in Porter. A lot of thunder and fire. And he carries a great deal of weight with a large number of people. Whatever organization attracts him will make a profitable bargain for itself."

The next day, when Henry and Ben were lunching at the Hunt, Henry said suddenly: "I've thought of a way Porter can pay off his debt to you: join our firm."

Ben said, "If there was a debt, which I don't feel there is——"

"It doesn't matter how you feel," Henry said. "It's how Porter feels. And I judge him as a man very much aware of debts."

"How would his joining us repay some debt to me?"

Henry's eyelids narrowed, as they frequently did when he thought about money. "If you could arrange it, Ben— and I think only you could— To my knowledge at least two other firms are angling for him. But if you could manage it, it would mean tremendous prestige and increments to us. I will tell you now it would mean fifty thousand more a year to you. Why not call him this afternoon? That campaign must have cost him plenty. He must be nearly broke and skulking around out there in Attica licking his wounds. Guarantee him a hundred and fifty for the first year and—you know—a piece of things. Go to two hundred if necessary." Henry leaned toward him. "Unless you don't want him on the premises. I can understand how you might not. If you don't want him around, let's forget the whole thing."

"Why should I not want him around?"

"Frankenstein's monster. From all I've heard, he's a creature of your own creation. And it must sometimes gall you the way things got out of hand."

"It doesn't gall me," Ben said. "I'll call him this afternoon."

Bill called him back that evening at home and accepted the offer after talking it over with Alice.

As Ben stepped into the Brittons' Park Avenue apartment about six o'clock that Thursday, Jack Britton cried:

"Here he is—Joe McCurdy's counselor!"

"Oh, sure, Jack. But read the *Times* tomorrow morning."

Rita came to him quickly, her expression one of curious concern, and they kissed. Obviously she had learned of the *Post* story since she arrived; Jack Britton had made sure that it was something for everyone to chew on along with the canapés. Last night Ben had told her about his conference with McCurdy, the amusing myth that had become an irritating reality.

"Have a Scotch," Jack said. "What are you up to with McCurdy?"

Ben greeted Agnes Britton and got a Dewar's on rocks at the bar while Jack pursued him with questions. "What's the story?"

"Fiction," Ben said. "A front-page fictional on a dull news day."

Jack Britton and he were acquaintances who sometimes masqueraded as friends. Jack had a law practice uptown specializing in divorce and kindred traumas; he had, in fact, handled Ben's severing from Louise most helpfully.

Somewhat laboriously Ben explained the facts to Jack, Agnes, and several others who yearned to know the inside dope on the phenomenal Joseph P. McCurdy. Rita hovered close to Ben; it was unlike her to hover at parties unless she knew something did not please him.

Well, this party did not please him. At least his pretense of pleasure at being here bugged him. Presumably he was capable enough at the social con game so that only Rita sensed his displeasure. He had come because he had thought she wanted to: their generation gap must never become a generation barricade.

Fortunately, however, there was no barricade—not yet, and, God willing, never. Soon after half-past six Rita said to him in the hearing of the Brittons:

"Charity arrived this afternoon."

"Oh?" He looked at his watch.

All of their acquaintances had heard of Rita's Aunt Charity from Scranton, though none had met her. Was she rich or poor, stable or eccentric? She did not drink, so there was no point in inviting her to parties. She traveled by bus, and sometimes the Norths were unavailable for social engagements because they had to go to Scranton to visit her. She was a creation of Rita's, and Ben enjoyed the fiction hugely.

When they reached the street he asked her where she wanted to go for dinner. "Richelieu's?"

"No, somebody who was at the Brittons' is liable to go there."

They took a taxi to Leopold's, a quiet and plain Italian restaurant on Third Avenue where they never were in danger of running into anyone they knew.

Ben said, "All I seem to want to do any more is cut and run."

"Why not?" she said. "We have so much wasted time to recover."

Today all the major news media have canned obituary material on William Paisley Porter ready to be released at whatever future time he releases his presently healthy hold on life. All of the stories, scripts, and film clips pay some attention to the men who helped to shape his career. Interestingly, none mentions Ben North. Possibly more interesting, however, is the fact that none mentions how William Porter affected other lives and careers. Perhaps that is because of the mannered nature of obituaries, in which the subject, passive at last forever, seems acted upon rather than acting.

In any event, Ben's life might have been different without Bill, as Bill's would have been different without Ben. For example, Bill and Alice would have been amazed to know the curious and subtle ways whereby they unwittingly had helped to set the scene for Ben's divorce from Louise.

At first after the Porters arrived in New York, the Norths acted as their mentors. But it didn't last long. Ben knew it would not. Their years in the political wars had made Bill and Alice resilient, shrewd, knowledgeable. They adapted themselves blithely to life in New York and quickly were sought out by influential men and their women who cared nothing about the Norths.

Bill was an excellent, hard-working lawyer who apparently had abandoned politics forever. He understood his role as a partner in the firm: he must attract prosperous clients. And he was most successful at it. Before long he began turning over to other partners clients to whom he could not devote enough attention. That, of course, was agreeable to Ben and Henry, for it was one of the implicit conditions of Bill's partnership.

When the firm announced that Bill was becoming a partner, the news media took polite interest. The *Times*, with its elephantine memory, recalled Bill's and Ben's previous association, but it did not belabor the fact. It was reported—and passed over. Even William Porter's former enemies no longer cared much what he did, since he obviously was through with politics.

Yet was he? Ben was perhaps the first to wonder. Bill was still greatly concerned about the welfare of the Party. He was nearly always willing, if not eager, to go to one place or another to speak in behalf of one of its candidates. Its candidate for the Presidency a couple of years after the Porters moved to New York was an inept troglodyte whom Ben, staunch Party man though he was, could not tolerate (and so he voted for the other candidate, who turned out to be equally troglodytal after his election to the Presidency). But Bill valiantly supported his Party's man.

"Just a final reflex," was the way Henry described Bill's action to Ben. "Now *that* is over. Now Bill can get back to the practice of law."

Ben continued to wonder, however, as Bill's travels increased in range. There was no denying what he did in behalf of the Party was also reflected in behalf of the firm. But was it also done in behalf of William Paisley Porter's political renaissance?

Ben asked Alice about it.

"I really don't know," she said. "I'm happy here in New York, and so is Bill. Living and working here has given him a sense of—confidence that he never had before."

That was true. For the first time since Ben had known him, Bill did not seem to be seeking the approval of others. Instead, others now sought *his* approval. The circumstances of his law practice and his status as a middle-aged yet at the same time elder statesman in the decimated and faltering Party had changed his manner from hastiness to that of benign deliberateness.

Alice said, "Some time ago I read a nasty article about me by someone who never really *talked* to me. The writer said I felt I was married to a political career—not a man.

That simply is not true. I'm married to a man who makes me happiest when he is happiest."

Ben, meditating on Alice's remark in the ensuing days, wished that Louise felt similarly about him. It was difficult not to constantly compare those good friends, Alice and Louise. Both had strong senses of loyalty; perhaps it was their instinctive fealty to a remembered simpler way of life in the long ago that maintained their friendship. Louise, alas, did not compare favorably with Alice. On that afternoon in Greenleaf, long since past, had Ben been attracted to the wrong girl?

Alice tried, to the best of her capacity, to adapt to change. But Louise resented change. Alice succeeded in keeping herself slender, attractive, and actively interested in numerous things. But Louise regressed steadily in her half-hearted battle with weight and slothfulness.

For many years after the painful episode of the Porter fund Ben had felt that Alice did not like him. But as time passed in New York, he believed she was his friend—if for no other reason than that she knew he was a devoted friend of Bill's. Maybe, however, there was another reason: did she sense that Louise was failing him?

Whereas Louise succumbed easily to the battle with increasing age, Ben struggled against it. Ignoring the psychological factors, it came down to a physical matter. He resisted excesses of food and drink. He tried to keep his weight down, not because he feared disease and death but because the less he weighed the better he felt and the more alert was his mind. His sexual relationship with Louise, while not dead, was dying. She continued to convey to him her conviction that sex was a dirty thing; their coupling was like that of a caboose to a freight car for a dull downhill glide. He tried to purge himself of resentment at the Racquet Club by playing squash and pounding a bag.

One spring Sunday afternoon, when it had become

apparent to everyone that Bill would make another bid for the Presidency, Alice phoned Louise and invited them to join in a novel outing: a bicycle ride in Central Park. They went, Louise wearing something that made her look like a maiden schoolteacher in the English provinces.

They rode the prescribed course, laughing, having fun among the numerous cyclists, until they rounded a curve toward Fifth Avenue. Three beleathered youths swept by them, slowed, and let them pass. Then the three came past again in file. At the time, Bill happened to be in the lead and Ben at the rear of their foursome. As the last rider came abreast of Bill, he deliberately swerved his bicycle against Bill's front wheel and sent him sprawling to the ground. Then he stopped and cried, "Porter, you're a ——"

Everyone halted, stunned by the sight of Bill trying to get to his feet and the sound of the youth's obscene invective. Ben dropped his bicycle and walked to the youth. With a swift one-two, he drove his left fist into the solar plexus and cut him over backward with his right to the chin.

His instinctive violence left him with a sense of shock. Not in thirty years had he slugged anybody. And now, presumably, he would have to try to slug two more. But the friends of the crazy youth, after they helped him to his feet, had no more stomach for combat than Ben did.

The four turned in their rented bicycles and walked silently to the Porters' apartment.

There Alice finally said, "Neatly done, Ben."

"Uh—thanks," Bill told him. "But—well—"

"You all right?" asked Ben.

"Not a scratch. Just—uh—slight shock, I guess. Let's have a drink."

Ben said, "Make mine a double for double shock. At

myself as much as that crazy kid. What a reaction! Supposing I did that sometime in federal court?"

Louise finally released herself in a tirade against the young. She went on and on tiresomely, and neither Ben nor Alice could turn her off. From castigating the young in general she switched specifically to Jim: her concern about him, the bad influences to which he was subjected.

"Louise, knock it off," Ben interjected. "You sound worse than his mother. You sound like his *grandmother*. Except I think his grandmother would be more tolerant."

Their ensuing quarrel, sudden and angry, came as yet another shock to Ben. Realizing at last that Bill and Alice were looking at them with wonder and alarm, he got to his feet.

"Alice—Bill, I apologize. I have to shove along."

"Where are you going?" demanded Louise.

"I have an appointment with Crimmins."

"Crimmins? Crimmins? Who is Crimmins?"

"A client, Louise. A *client!*"

There happened to be a client named Crimmins, but Ben did not have an appointment with him. He did not know where he was going as he strode east in the mellow afternoon. He knew only that he did not want to go home for a long time.

Beyond Madison Avenue his pace slowed and he stopped before an art gallery which advertised a showing of David Levine's caricatures. The name Levine meant nothing to him, but the style of one of his drawings in the window was appealing and vaguely familiar. He went in.

Before long he felt his perspective returning as he stood smiling in the midst of Levine's wonderful world of the famous and the would-be. As he mused at a drawing of André Malraux, he became aware of someone looking at him. Turning, he confronted the blue-eyed gaze of Rita

Reid, surely the most beautiful young woman who ever had ɔeen employed by the firm.

"Miss Reid! What are you doing here?" The inanity of his remark struck him, and he added, "Or, as you might say, what am I doing here?"

She was not cursed by the eager, hopeful smile that young secretaries cast him in his passage through the offices and corridors of the firm. She said, "I like David Levine's drawings."

"Well, so do I," he replied, at the same time trying to place Levine and glancing about for the beau who must have escorted her to the showing. But no young man was in evidence.

She looked at him with frank curiosity, and he realized it must have something to do with the turtleneck sweater and loud sports jacket he had put on for cycling. After all, she never had seen him wear anything but an uptight Pine Street suit.

He said, "This one of Malraux is good. And look how he uses the gargoyle."

"That's not a gargoyle, Mr. North. It's a griffin."

"Griffin? Griffin?" He had the painful recollection of Louise crying, *Crimmins? Crimmins?* "I've heard of a griffin, but I can't for the life of me remember what it is."

"A mythic decorative type, half lion, half eagle. Originally Greek, I guess. Heraldry took it over. It appears on buildings in Paris."

"Where? I've been in Paris lots of times but never noticed one."

"I don't know where. I've never been in France. I've only heard that's so. I guess Levine uses it here as a Gaullist symbol. Isn't it wonderful the way he draws the griffin all wilted and sad, the way Malraux looks himself? Have you read *Man's Fate?*"

"No." Ben knew that Malraux was a politician and

[170]

functionary close to De Gaulle who once had been a significant writer; he guessed that *Man's Fate* had been one of his books.

"I haven't read it either," she said. "It's one of a lot of books I'm always meaning to read. Have you seen Mr. Porter?"

"As a matter of fact, I just came from seeing him."

"I don't mean that. I mean—"

His obtuseness was so akin to Louise's that he felt unnerved. "Stupid of me! Let's look at Levine's Bill."

She led the way. Her miniskirt revealed lovely legs. He had observed them before in the Pine Street corridors, but never so concentratedly.

Well, here was William Paisley Porter, executed by Levine. But it could have been so much more cruel. It did not represent merely the facile manipulation of facial topography such as the ordinary political cartoonist employed.

"Marvelous!"

She said, "I thought you might not like it. Why do you?"

"There's an acute projection of Bill's personality: his anguish, and his wistfulness over his anguish."

Rita Reid finally smiled at him. She stepped back and looked him up and down as if he might really be a person worth knowing. . . .

The climax of Bill's successful bid for the Presidency coincided with that of Ben's unsuccessful efforts to remain emotionally attached to Louise.

Throughout the campaign Ben remained far in the background. He contributed money and raised funds among the wealthy, but he did not sit on any committee and no one sought his advice on any aspect of the campaign. Nevertheless, he observed Bill's public appearances as closely as possible. The image of the candidate that emerged to Ben seemed too polished-diamond smooth.

"Maybe my rural roots are showing," he remarked to Louise, "but I like my candidate a little more prickly, a bit less studied. Instead of neatly brushed hair I like the wind to blow a little hair into his eyes. Just once I wish Bill would appear someplace without a tie on."

Louise reacted angrily. "Ever since he first started running for office years ago you've been picking at the way he does things. Once you thought he was too rough, and now you think he's too smooth. In these days when personal sloppiness seems to be a virtue you ought to be glad to have a candidate who looks and acts—refined."

Louise herself bustled with activity during the campaign. She was, among other things, a member of a committee of women who were doing something to try to help the Party cause in one of its strongest bastions, the Manhattan Upper East Side. Once Ben came upon her and other women seated at small tables in a vacant store. All wore hats and did not seem to be busy. Ben wanted to tell her, "For God's sake, Louise, take your hat off." But he was careful not to.

Several in the firm took leaves of absence to work for Bill's campaign. Among them were a few youthful secretaries whom Ben, perhaps uncharitably, suspected of seeking relief from tedium rather than of being zealous Porterphiles. Rita was not one of them.

Ben never saw her outside the office, but there he went out of his way to be friendly. When Henry Burton's secretary became gravely ill and the assistant secretary quit after Henry roared at her, Ben recommended Rita. Henry was delighted with her: "Best damn bright and patient girl who's come this way in years."

Ben gathered, though he was not sure how, that Rita would not vote for William Porter. Henry went him one better. He came grinning into Ben's office one day and said, "I did an Edwardian thing this morning just for the hell of it. I said to Rita, 'Of course you're voting for Bill Porter.' And she looked me straight in the eye and said, 'No, sir.' She was for what's his name, who didn't even make it onto the opposition ticket. I'm going to give that girl a raise for looking me in the eye."

Smiling, Ben asked, "As a matter of fact, Henry, who are you going to vote for?"

"William Paisley Porter, of course. I'm thoroughly familiar with my age, my place, and how my bread is buttered."

How my bread is buttered! Of course, Ben too would —and did—vote for Porter. But there was a moment of anger when he thought he might not.

The climax of Bill's campaign was a grand rally in Madison Square Garden. Tickets were provided to all of the faithful and their friends.

Not until the day of the rally did Ben learn that Louise was going to a dinner to which he had not been invited. And then he discovered that they would not be seated together at the rally; she would be close to the heavenly throne while he would be in a remote choir of angels. Perhaps it was the result of careless oversight, perhaps of careful planning. Though burned, he took care not to burst into flame.

He arrived in the Garden corridors in time to see Jim ejected from Penny Porter's party. In vain he struggled through the milling throng to reach his side; Jim disappeared, and Ben could not find him. Furious, he strode from the Garden, for he could not bear to rally round William Paisley Porter just then.

He had no wish to go home; recently home was about the last place he wanted to be. And he never had learned to kill time satisfactorily in a bar. There remained only one place to go, the place where there was always something to accomplish: the office.

When he stepped off the elevator he heard a typewriter, and as he went down the corridor a woman asked: "Who's there?"

"Ben North." He looked into Henry's office. "Miss Reid, what are you doing here?" And then he remembered having said that at the art gallery.

"I'm finishing up a brief for Mr. Burton. He's giving me a long weekend because my mother is having an operation in Scranton. I thought you'd be at the Garden rally, Mr. North."

"So did I." Ben sank into a chair and told her about Jim being thrown out. "I'll vote for Bill, of course, but I didn't feel like attending tonight. I understand you're not voting for him."

"That's right. Maybe I won't vote at all because I don't have a favorite candidate in the race. I'd like to have a President who gave me a feeling of hope for the future and made me feel that I personally could do something active about that future. Feeling that way, Mr. North, I just *can't*, in all good conscience, vote for Mr. Porter." She hesitated. "Everybody around here seems to be for him. Is that disloyalty on my part? Do you think I should leave the firm?"

Almost vehemently Ben replied, "No! I hope this is still a free country, and life isn't worth much without a sense of freedom." Then he found himself thinking, *And my life won't be worth much till I'm free of Louise.*

Coming out of Leopold's after dinner, these few years later, Ben asked Rita, "Want to walk?"

"Sure."

On Lexington Avenue a newspaper dealer was laying out the bulldog edition of the next morning's *Daily News*. Its headline read:

JOE MCCURDY IS REAL;
HAS HE A PORTER DEAL?

"Damn it," Ben said. He bought a copy and asked, "Got a *Times?*"

"Not yet."

Folding the newspaper under an arm and walking on with Rita, he said, "Damn it, I had such a good time at dinner I forgot all about McCurdy. I even forgot I practice law."

When they reached home he tossed the *Daily News* on a table and took off his jacket. The sight of the folded sheet of paper in an inner pocket reminded him he had not looked at Miss Thomas's memorandum of calls. Only Helen's call puzzled him. Was something amiss with Jim?

Finding her Washington number in the personal directory book on his library desk, he dialed it.

"Helen, Miss Thomas said— Everything okay?"

"Just fine, Ben. Jim brought Penny Porter here to dinner and now they've gone out on the town someplace."

"Oh?" His tone expressed regret.

Helen, realizing it, asked, "Are you sorry?"

"I don't dislike Penny," Ben replied slowly. "She's a sweet and tractable child. But she's solid Establishment. And Jim has separated himself from that. I like the direction he's traveling because he's happy with it. But it's a direction Penny cannot go. It's so easy for the young to make confused compass readings and imagine they can actually go in two directions at once."

"I understand." Helen paused. "Well, I didn't call to

report on Jim's social life. I want to ask you something. You're going to laugh and think I'm crazy. Nevertheless— Ben, when you met Joe McCurdy yesterday, did he remotely remind you of Gene Schofield?"

Ben did not laugh or think her crazy. He simply weighed her question and finally replied, "No, Helen, not at all. Why?"

She told him.

He had been standing while talking with her, but now he sat down slowly. "Your evidence is very slim, Helen. But it's interesting. Do you draw any conclusions from your theory? I mean, if by some improbable chance McCurdy should be Gene, what would be his motive? If a man wants to disappear and assume a new identity, why should he run the risk of spoiling it all?"

"I don't know. Maybe some motive of vengeance against Bill. A few minutes ago I talked to Jack Hochstein at the White House and told him what I wondered about. His reaction is like yours. He's curious. He asked a favor of you. Will you call him? He'll be in his office till after eleven. And I have his phone number here. . . ."

Ben strolled to the living room where Rita was reading the *Daily News*. He rarely asked her opinion on business matters, and she looked surprised that he did now.

"What's your hesitation, Ben?"

"I'm not really sure. Except that I want to keep the firm completely out of this thing."

"The firm?" Rita asked. "Or yourself?"

Hochstein came on the phone at once. Ben, taking the initiative, said the firm did not represent McCurdy. "I'm sure the *Times* and the news services will carry my statement and clear the air of *that*."

"Just journalistic fluff," Hochstein said. "The President understands it. He's sort of an expert at it from long experience. He says you'll handle it ably. But now I have a favor to ask. The Bureau can't get McCurdy's fingerprints. And we *have* to have 'em."

"*Have* to? Do you think McCurdy is Gene Schofield?"

"No, of course not. But we feel we have to establish who McCurdy is—or is not. Can you coax him back to your office tomorrow in order to cooperate with the Bureau? They'll explain to you the technicalities of how they can get the prints."

"My God," Ben said, "I just got through telling the press we do *not* represent him. If I get him to the office he'll bounce back with a revelation to the newsmen that I'm a damn liar."

"It doesn't really matter." Hochstein's tone was cheerful. "That'll pass over. Everybody understands. We *have* to establish McCurdy's identity, and we haven't been able to."

"Isn't that your problem, Mr. Hochstein?"

"Yes, it is," Hochstein said. "I understand that. All I can appeal to is your friendship with President Porter."

Late in the afternoon the siege began to wear on Hannah McCurdy. Or perhaps it was the recording of Johnny Cash ballads, blasting from the hi-fi on a third replay, that made her restless. Wooo!—Wooo!—Wooo!— Oh those lonesome railroad tracks, a trail of freedom through a hostile land! The music drowned the clat of Joe's typewriter when she went to the workroom and looked in at him.

Sensing, as nearly always, how she felt, he said, "I've had it for the day." The telephone extension on his desk rang, and he answered: "This is Joe McCurdy. I warn you that this telephone is being tapped."

"Mr. McCurdy, this is Fallothwaite the butcher. I don't care who's listening in——"

"Beware, butcher Fallothwaite." McCurdy grinned. "Anything you might say will be held against you."

"I don't give a damn. We're all for you, Joe. I know at least six of my customers that haven't paid their taxes either."

"But you have, Irving. Insert that in the record. Big Brother is listening. Announce your name, rank, and serial number, and explain you're clean as a hound's tooth."

Fallothwaite complied. Then: "I called about Mrs. McCurdy's order for mutton chops. The mutton didn't come in today."

"Unfortunately, Fallothwaite, Mrs. McCurdy has gone, disappeared, fled the coop." He winked at Hananh.

"Gone where?"

"I don't know. But Big Brother will track her down, poor soul, and persecute her for having dared in her sweet innocence to sign a form 1040A in connubial partnership with the villain McCurdy. Fallothwaite, there are still hungry children here. Forget the mutton chops. Send us a three-to-four-pound sirloin, about an inch and a half thick. And have Harold deliver it."

After he hung up, Hannah said, "I'm glad he didn't have mutton. We may be eating plenty of that. I didn't think about it when I ordered."

McCurdy got up from his desk. "Let's hold a council of war. You make the martinis."

"Do we still have to keep the hi-fi so loud?"

"Yes. From above or below or from Twenty-four A next door, Big Brother no doubt is trying to bore in with one of his sensitive antennae. The hi-fi drowns out anything we say. If you're tired of Johnny Cash, try—well, you like Engelbert Humperdinck."

"The kids are having such a wonderful time," Hannah said. "And you're so brave. I must try to be brave too."

They sat cross-legged on the floor in the center of the living room, a custom Hannah had convinced them was healthful after she had abandoned her flirtation with yoga. McCurdy, knees creaking at every shifting of his broad beam, sat opposite her, enjoying the visible feast of her

[179]

lovely thighs. Peter, facing Patricia, dragged on his Coke before his father had time to lift his martini and say:

"God bless us every one."

"*And you know that I love you*," sang Engelbert Humperdinck on the hi-fi.

"And you know," said McCurdy, "that I'm proud of all of you for what you've done today."

"Can we cut school again tomorrow?" asked Pete.

"Yes," said McCurdy.

The phone rang, and McCurdy, not disposed to unwind his stiff limbs, said, "Answer it, Pat. You know what to say."

Patricia, graceful child, rose from crossed legs without touching hands to the floor and went to the living room extension. "This is Joe McCurdy's daughter, Patricia. I warn you that this telephone is being tapped. . . . Well, I think he's busy. . . ." She covered the mouthpiece and said, "Pop, it's the manager of the Ed Sullivan Show. Will you appear on it Sunday night?"

McCurdy leisurely lighted a cigarette and savored a sense of euphoria. The moment required a memorable statement. Then he thought of one: "How much?"

Pat said, "He says how much?" She covered the phone. "The man says thirty-five hundred."

McCurdy inhaled deeply and coughed. "Four thousand."

"Pop says four thousand," Pat said. After listening for a while, she said, "He really wants to talk to you, Pop."

McCurdy got stiffly onto all fours and then staggered to his feet. Asking the man his number and saying he would call in five minutes, he checked the Sullivan office number in his TV directory book. The number was correct, so he called back, and they quickly agreed on four thousand dollars for a ten-minute spot.

Settling himself stiffly on the floor again, McCurdy said, "Well, we started a council of war here before we were rudely interrupted. Let's see where we're at. While I carried the attack this morning through the *Post*, Hank established our line of strategic retreat. You moved the car from the garage to that twenty-four-hour place on East Thiry-second near Third?"

"Yes," Hannah said. "Oh Mac, let's pull out tonight. Your first notice was in the mail today, and you say it won't take them a week to put a padlock on the door. Let's go now!"

"Yeah, let's," said Pete. "I can't wait to become a Canadian and start raising sheep."

"I'm ready," Patricia said. "The high country of British Columbia! Wow!"

McCurdy and Hannah had made the transaction in the previous September on a trip to Toronto where they transferred their savings of nearly thirty-five thousand into a Canadian bank. The favorable exchange rate had given them a couple of thousand more in Canadian money. In Toronto they had completed the deal with the man to whom a friend had guided McCurdy: title to nine hundred acres of upland grazing land and a habitable house in exchange for five thousand cash and a mortgage guaranteed by the Canadian bank. It did not matter that they had not seen the land; McCurdy trusted the man and the bank that took the mortgage. It did not matter that he never had raised sheep; he was sick to death of writing copy, of living in New York, of federal, state, and local governments that he found repressive. Hank felt as deeply about it as he. For all her years of civil protests and good works she had nothing to show but that mark on her behind made by a policeman in Bryant Park. Canada was now the land of freedom and opportunity that the United States had once meant to be. In Canada Pete never would be drafted into military service; they would breathe pure air, live beside unpolluted water, and not be taxed to death by a benign Canadian government that respected one's individual rights. Besides, ever since McCurdy had known Hannah she had wanted to go to the country and raise sheep. If they could learn the tricks of making money and surviving in New York, they surely could adjust themselves to the ways of sheep and cruel winter weather.

McCurdy, meditating on these matters and the wish of his family to go now, hesitated. He sipped his martini and said, "Courage, *mes enfants*. We're in rather deep to pull out too hastily. For instance, we're now into four thousand of Mr. Sullivan's dollars on Sunday evening."

Last September when they had bought the ranch in British Columbia he had not foreseen the incredible torrent of events. He had helped Cy Benson write "The Ballad of Joe McCurdy" in joyful protest against the monstrous behemoth on whose back rode William Paisley Porter. When the song caught on, he had been more astonished than anyone. But as the myth grew, he raptly absorbed himself in it, for the myth was vastly more powerful and compelling than ever he had been as a man. He began to believe that from the myth he might shape a telling pattern of events. It was why he had wormed his way into Ben North's office. He had intended to do *something*, though he had not been sure precisely what. But now, curiously, he was deeply afraid.

The door bell rang, and he started. Going to the door, he made out Harold through the peephole. He opened the door a bit and passed out a fifty-cent tip to Harold in exchange for a paper bag.

Harold said, "Mr. McCurdy, I want to say how much we all admire what you're doing."

"Well, bless you, Harold. Now pay your taxes, accept your draft number, and keep on smiling at Uncle Samuel. How are things in the lobby?"

"Crowded. NBC just brought a sound truck. They hear you're coming out."

"Not for a long time." McCurdy closed the door.

Hank asked suddenly, "What is that about the truth making you free?"

"As I remember, from the Gospel according to John," said McCurdy, ever happy to pontificate. " 'And ye shall know the truth, and the truth shall make you free.' "

"What the heck does that mean?" asked Pete.

Long ago, after Joseph Patrick McCurdy had begun to answer want ads in the New York *Times*, he arrived one afternoon in the reception room of the advertising firm of Street, Blazer, Kaufman. Maybe because nothing had been working out right, he tried his notion of an English accent with the receptionist:

"I say, you're looking for somebody to work in the mail room?"

The receptionist directed him to the office of the new personnel director, Miss Clements. When he stepped into her office, Miss Clements was reaching for a looseleaf notebook on an upper shelf. Her beautiful body was stretched upward, like Venus with arms recovered and toga released. Lust assailed McCurdy, who had been celibate for a long time. He sank, uninvited, into a chair as Miss Clements turned and revealed a face as lovely as her body.

Maintaining his false accent, perhaps because he was convinced Venus never would go to bed with an ordinary American, he stammered, "You're looking for somebody to work in the mail room?"

There was no way of knowing what Venus thought. She did not say anything as she handed him a form to fill out.

Name: Joseph Patrick McCurdy. Social Security Number: He fished out his card and wrote down the number. Age: Twenty-four. Address: He wrote the number of his furnished room on Hudson Street. Birthplace: Needing one that would match the accent that had begun to fascinate him, he wrote Close Under Hill, Kent, England. Citizenship: Naturalized American, of course. Education: Harrow, and Magdalen College, Oxford. Military service: Lieutenant, Welsh Guards. Languages: French, German, Swahili. Most recent employment: Instructor in Swahili at the University of California, Santa Barbara. Desired salary: One hundred dollars per week.

He passed the form to Miss Clements and beamed at her. She read it without expression and finally spoke:

"Mr. McCurdy, the starting salary in the mail room is forty a week."

"Oh, I say!" He looked crestfallen. "A bit of a pinch, you know. But is there opportunity of advancement? A foot in the door? I want to write advertising copy, but a chap must start someplace."

She continued to study his application form. "Mr. McCurdy, why did you stop teaching Swahili at Santa Barbara?"

"Never really started. Had a year's contract in order to get naturalization and all that. But do you know, not a soul at Santa Barbara signed up for Swahili. But as we used to say in Keen-ya, *Shakista tagor, tagora shista.*"

Miss Clements stared at him. "What does that mean?"

McCurdy shrugged. "What will be, will be. In effect that's what it means."

"Mr. McCurdy, in the mail room you sort mail, and

then you carry it to the proper desk, and there you pick up other mail and bring it back to the mail room. Don't you think that's rather limiting work for one of your attainments?"

McCurdy shrugged once more. "As I said, Miss Clements, *Shakista tagor, tagora shista.* Foot in the door?"

"More likely ass in the street," said Miss Clements. "The bright youth you would be replacing was sent to Bellevue with delirium tremens. But you *can* read English...."

McCurdy, trailing his accent gaily through the offices of Street, Blazer, Kaufman while taking every possible opportunity to smile and talk at an indifferent Miss Clements, finally was summoned to her office a month later.

"I have a question, McCurdy. When you applied here did you know that Mr. Kaufman is an Anglophile?"

"I thought he was a Jew," McCurdy replied.

"Is that an anti-Semitic remark?"

"That's just a factual remark, Miss Clements. What about Mr. Kaufman?"

"Watch it, McCurdy, your accent is slipping. Well, hearing your accent, Mr. Kaufman asked to see your application form. He's intrigued by it and would like you to make an appointment with his secretary. By the way, he speaks Swahili."

Ass in the street, McCurdy thought bleakly. But it turned out that Miss Clements was only putting him on. Though Kaufman did not speak Swahili, he recognized the Harrow tie McCurdy had bought at Abercrombie's.

His impetuous adoption of an English accent and the happenstance that Kaufman was an Anglophile represented the first bit of luck McCurdy had had in a long time. Kaufman offered him Opportunity by putting him in the copy department where he sharpened pencils and was a general nuisance. Before long, however, he planted his feet in the advertising ooze by pleasing the firm's smallest client, an African airline, with some nonsense copy related to the spirit of *Beau Geste* rather than the social realities of Africa.

McCurdy's longing for Miss Clements did not wane with the passage of time. He learned from the young studs about the agency that no one had been able to make out with her; they had abandoned her as frigid and turned their attentions to warmer prospects. He learned, too, that she had a secret vice: every Tuesday evening she served as an unpaid teacher of composition at an experimental black school in Harlem. Though he never had preoccupied himself with the social problems of the Negro, it was easy for him to learn the name of the school and obtain a voluntary assignment—on Tuesday evenings—without consulting Miss Clements.

Her amazement was tremendous when she came upon him at the school. Suddenly her manner toward him changed: he was the most interesting person she knew.

In those days long past, when blacks were still Negroes, Joseph Patrick McCurdy began teaching one of the first courses in the history of the black peoples offered anywhere. He did not do it with any deep feeling for his subject; indeed, he found most of the students in his class dull, belligerent youngsters. He started the course because it was such an obvious way to attract their interest and make him the most popular teacher in the school. Besides, it was an easy subject to teach: there were such scant scholarly resources on the history of the black peoples in Africa and America that McCurdy often substituted fiction for fact. Within a few weeks his classes overflowed with eager students enchanted by his thrilling accounts of how the white race had screwed the black.

No one was more enthralled with what he was doing than Hannah Clements.

She lived in a small apartment on West 110th Street, and it became McCurdy's habit to accompany her home through the hazards of Harlem at night. Until he arrived on the scene, convoying Hannah Clements home had been the pleasure of one of her students, a handsome black named George Kane. The arrangement had shocked McCurdy.

The first time he took Hannah home, George went with them. When they arrived at her converted brownstone, she said, "I'm out of Cokes tonight, but there's ginger ale."

McCurdy, realizing it was George's custom to go to Hannah's apartment, felt deeply disturbed as they went up the stairs. George, sensing how he felt, was silent and ill at ease as Hannah went into her kitchenette for ginger ale and cookies. McCurdy watched him through narrowed lids: the handsome, lustful black trying to keep his gaze off the desirable white woman. Hannah had remarked once to McCurdy that she *loved* Negroes. How far might love go?

She said, "Joe, I've told you about George. He shows more aptitude for writing than any of my students."

McCurdy asked, "How do you make your living?"

George could not meet his gaze. "I'm a porter in the garment district."

"He's working at a really exciting novel about a Negro family in Georgia."

"Autobiographical?" asked McCurdy.

George nodded.

"But so far," Hannah said, "neither one of us has been able to think of a good title for it."

McCurdy remembered a story he had heard somewhere. "Are there any trumpets in it?"

"No."

"Are there any drums?"

"No."

"Then why not call it 'No Trumpets, No Drums' ?"

Hannah laughed heartily, but George's effort at a smile only made his expression more grim. A few minutes later he left.

McCurdy and Hannah began to have lunch together, a sandwich and coffee at one or another of the counter feedbins near their office. To McCurdy, Hannah had progressed from something to behold to someone to be with. She drew him, she quartered him, she hung him. As never before in his life, he committed his emotions to her.

He asked her to a movie he thought she might enjoy, and they went late on a Saturday afternoon. Afterwards he took her to dinner at a tourist-trap restaurant off Times Square where she said she would like an old-fashioned. He ordered Seven-Up for himself.

"Joe, I've never seen you have a drink. Are you off it?"

"Yes. I don't handle it well."

It was true he had not had a drink in a long time. Possibly it was the only true thing he had told her about himself.

Before he left her that night he asked her to a play on the next Friday evening.

"I'd like to," she said, "but I promised George I'd go to a gathering of a club he belongs to. It's whites and Negroes mixed. It sounds interesting."

In the following week McCurdy did not go near her office and he cut his Tuesday evening class. He was engaged in a mighty struggle with himself.

On that Friday evening he did not know whether he had won or lost when, shortly after six o'clock, he sat down on the front steps of the brownstone where Hannah lived. In his right fist he held a tightly rolled copy of the *Saturday Evening Post*.

Around half-past six George came along the street, sharply dressed, face and shoes shining. Seeing McCurdy seated on the steps, he halted, and they stared at each other.

McCurdy said, "George, Hannah has changed her mind. She doesn't want to go out with you. And she thinks it would be a good idea if you dropped out of her class."

George continued to stare, not into his eyes, but at the magazine in his fist. Did he know that a tightly rolled magazine was as potent a weapon as a steel rod? You could smash a man's balls with it, or drive it two inches into his belly or throat. But how did it compare as a weapon against a knife? Perhaps, however, the knife in the ribs would come later.

George did not say anything. He turned suddenly and walked away.

McCurdy, assailed by a thirst such as he never had known, went down the street to a liquor store and bought a fifth of Scotch. Then he returned and buzzed Hannah's apartment.

"George?"

"Mmmm."

When she opened her door to him, she looked dismayed. "Joe! I thought—"

"I met George on the steps. I told him you didn't want to go out with him. May I come in?"

She stepped back.

"May I pour us a drink? Just one, I promise. It took a lot of guts for me to do what I just did, and I don't have much guts. Can we have one drink?"

They did not speak until they were seated on the sofa, drink in hand, looking at each other. Then she said, "Joe, who are you?"

"A bum."

"I know you lost your phony accent awfully fast, but that doesn't make you a bum. Who are you?"

"I love you, Hannah."

"But you know all about me, and I don't know a thing about you."

"I'm a bum and I love you."

Taking his untasted drink from his hand, she carried it with her to the kitchenette and poured both down the drain. Coming back, she sat down on the sofa again and took his right hand in both of hers.

"Joe, tell me about you."

A faint tapping brought McCurdy wide awake from fitful sleep. Where were they boring from now? Hannah was awake too. She gathered him to her, as on that night long ago on West 110th Street.

The telephone rang on the bedside table, and she said, "Don't answer it."

His fear made him tremble and he wished he could hide forever in the protective warmth of her body. But he said, "I must," and lifted the phone.

"This is Joe McCurdy. I warn you that this telephone is being tapped."

There was momentary silence, then a voice: "Mr. McCurdy, this is Christopher Marlowe at Burton, North, McGinnis, and Mosely. We've had some second thoughts about your case. You've put the firm in an embarrassing position with that loose talk to the *Post*."

McCurdy snapped on the light and planted his feet on the floor. "Did you call me in the middle of the night to berate me about that? What second thoughts have you and Mr. North had, Mr. Marlowe?"

"Have you received a notice yet from Internal Revenue?"

"Yes. There was one in the mail today."

"Well, could I take a look at it? Could you bring it to my office at ten in the morning? And I suppose it would be asking too much of you not to inform your friends in the press."

McCurdy spoke slowly. "Let me get this straight. You are going to represent me?"

"I didn't say that. That's a matter for Mr. North to decide. But some facts have come to our attention that make me want to discuss something further with you."

"What sort of facts?"

"I can't discuss them on the phone. Certainly not a tapped phone. Can you leave your apartment without— uh—being observed?"

"That's a hell of a question to ask on a tapped phone, Mr. Marlowe. But since Big Brother is listening in and presumably will cooperate, let me put it this way. The reporters have the death watch on McCurdy. But late in the lobster trick—let's say at six A.M. in the morning— McCurdy will take the elevator down from his castle and I trust Big Brother to have shied the death watch off somewhere. I won't squeal to the newsmen, you have my word for it. And I'll be at your office. Okay?"

"Okay," Marlowe said.

He cradled the telephone and looked around at Hannah, who was sitting up. She said, "They're going to take your case? You said Wednesday you thought they would."

"That's what I thought then," McCurdy said. "I thought Ben North would come around because I thought he had no more use for Porter than I do. But after he issued that statement, I changed my mind. And now he's

[191]

going to try to do something I never expected of him. Frame me."

Hannah gripped him by an arm. "Then don't go down there, darling."

"I'm going," McCurdy said, "but I'm not ready to sit still yet for framing. And when a frame is finally hung, we'll see who's in the center of the picture."

Ben arrived at his office early on Friday morning. By ten o'clock he counted the butts of six cigarettes in his ashtray. A few minutes later, when Miss Thomas signaled him, he was smoking a seventh and staring blankly at the wall.

"Mr. Marlowe and Mr. McCurdy are in the east conference room, Mr. North."

He walked slowly down the corridor, opened the conference room door, and stopped dead. McCurdy sat facing Marlowe with his back to the door and his hands resting on the table. He wore thin white cotton gloves.

Ben said, "Why did you do it, Gene?"

McCurdy started and looked around at him. "Who are you talking to, Mr. North?"

"I'm talking to Gene Schofield from Greenleaf!"

11

I was raised in Methodist parsonages by devout parents. Ceasing to believe in God when I was twelve years old, I ever afterwards was ripe for regeneration. . . .

With these words the writer began a strange story.

Gene Schofield saw enemies of the Republic almost everywhere in the days when he was legislative assistant to William Porter, first in the House and then in the Senate. Bill Porter saw them too. Together they were members of a loyal band of public servants who were determined to destroy the communist infection and purify the American bloodstream.

When Gene began investigative work for Bill in situations that led to the Jerome Butler case, he was told by members of the loyal band that the communist menace lurked chiefly among homosexuals and those known as "intellectuals" or "eastern establishment." Gene was pleased to hear this, for homosexuality always moved him to righteous indignation and so-called intellectual people roused his suspicion that they scorned him as an inferior. So he assumed the task of rooting out and destroying the enemies of the Republic with a crusader's passion.

His tenacious efforts in helping Bill pursue the Butler case brought him the wholehearted respect of the loyal band. For the first time in his life he had a sense of security, a feeling that a large group of strong men accepted him as their peer.

Though much in the company of others at work and socially, Gene was basically concerned with himself. He served Bill with the appearance of total loyalty, but his first loyalty was to his own interests. Highly ambitious to make money and attain position, he nevertheless was uncertain in what direction ambition might take him. Probably into the administrative branch of federal government, he thought; higher up in the tree were fine-feathered nests which he would occupy comfortably someday. So he was always on the lookout for targets of opportunity: someone to impress, some favor to be done now that would be remembered later.

Similarly he was always on the lookout for targets of opportunity in women, for he prided himself in being strongly sexed, a great lover. Actually he never fell in love with anyone—except Helen, who was one of the few women he could not get to bed. Maybe it was partly why he thought he loved her, for, once he had played a sexual game or two with a woman, he found himself growing bored with her and looking around for another.

Such was his experience with Martha Dennison, a pretty young woman from Attica whom an important politician recommended for a job in Washington. Gene had no trouble in placing her in Commerce.

Martha being attractive, it was time for a game of what Gene called tit for tat. He invited her to his apartment on Maryland Avenue for what she expected to be a cocktail party, but where she found herself the only guest. Gene, sizing up Martha as a naïve midlander, tried a ploy that usually was not necessary in Washington. While plying her with drinks, he carried on about the loneliness of bachelorhood and his wish to marry and settle down. After a time he hinted broadly that he had fallen in love with her. After further time, he went to the bathroom. When he returned, Martha had fled.

The next day he telephoned her and asked, in deeply injured tone, why she had run out on him.

"Oh, Gene!" She sounded short of breath. "The way things were going I didn't know *what* might happen. I—I didn't trust myself."

Smiling, he made a date to take her to dinner that very evening.

He arrived at her small apartment early, before she had finished dressing. Letting him in, she fled to the bedroom in her robe with a flustered cry that she would hurry.

He hesitated only a moment, then pushed open the bedroom door and said, "Can I help you?"

"Oh, Gene!" Such a swirl of underthings and shocked modesty to try to cover her charming body.

He said a crazy thing: "Let me de-Marthatize you with a Eugenic regeneration."

Holding a slip to her, she gaped at him.

"I mean, we're going to get married, but right now let's screw."

"Yeah." Her little girl's tone became as tough as a whore's. "I've heard that line once before. And all I ever got was a nasty deflowering on the back seat of an Oldsmobile before the guy disappeared. And worried myself near crazy because I was two months late."

"Then, Martha, there's something to finish and

something to begin." He took the flimsy slip from her hands. "No worry because I brought along a pack of Trojans."

He got them both undressed and her upon the bed where she said, "Tell me that you love me."

"I love you."

"And tell me when we're going to be married."

"As soon as I finish this investigation."

But she would not tolerate anything more oral than words. "What's the matter with you?" she cried. "You queer or something?"

He failed to de-Marthatize her and failed to enjoy a personal Eugenic regeneration; it was like taking a cold bath in his socks.

He took care not to see her again. . . .

After Bill was elected to the Senate and managed to have himself appointed to an important investigative committee, he called Gene into a closed-door session. The subject was Senator Ormandy, a member of the opposition. Did the Senator have subversive connections with dangerous sources in East Germany? Was he a part of a new and most mysterious conspiracy?

"We have to be very careful in this situation," Bill said. "We can't go off half-cocked. We have to assimilate all the evidence before we're ready to make a case. The Bureau knows something about this that has it worried. But it has to be very careful. After all, this is not our administration. You'll have plenty of cooperation in time. But you start carrying the ball."

Even with the cooperation of friends in the loyal band, it took Gene a while to find a path into the maze. Finally he was introduced to one of Senator Ormandy's secretaries, Fay Warner, at a cocktail party at the Mayflower. She was a comely, blond young woman so reserved in manner that Gene thought he never would get through to her. A dossier prepared by the loyal band on all of Senator Ormandy's employes had informed him of her background: distinguished old Philadelphia family; wealthy; a graduate of Smith who had gone to work for the Senator two years previously after graduation.

Suddenly—and he never could remember what he said that touched her off—she began to talk to him in a low tone. She was talking about winter plants, the cultivation and preservation of cyclamen, Jerusalem-cherry, false holly, Christmas begonia. Her mellifluous voice fascinated him despite the eastern accent he had come to view with vague suspicion. Her ripe young body fascinated him too, though he knew he would have to proceed with utmost caution in that direction. She was no Congressional tramp; he sensed barriers in her that could not be easily surmounted.

He took her to dinner at Harvey's. She liked to drink; they had two martinis and would have had a third if Gene had not wanted to keep his mind clear. He ventured a remark that he thought might shock her: "One martini, two at most, three under the table, four under the host."

Fay Warner looked at him with surprise, then laughed uneasily, and he switched to the safe subject of problems involved in living in Washington.

She said, "We have an old house off Pennsylvania in the southeast. It's not a fashionable district, but it's quiet and we like it."

"We?"

"My brother and I. He's a bachelor. He has a civilian job at the Pentagon."

"Oh? What branch?"

"Army G-2. I guess it's very hush-hush. He never says a word about it."

"Oh. Maybe I've met him. When Senator Porter was in the House I had some business with a guy named Warner at the Pentagon. But I can't remember his first name. Was it Martin?"

"My brother's name is Paxton."

"Oh. Well, I don't know him."

After dinner he said he would take her home. He sat close beside her in the taxi, his thigh pressed against hers; she did not move away from him, as he had expected she would. Thus encouraged, he squeezed her hand and said, "It was fun having dinner with you. I *like* you, Fay."

"I enjoyed it too, Gene." When they reached her house, she did not invite him in, saying, "Paxton has company this evening."

After Gene returned to his apartment, he phoned his contact in the loyal band and said, "Your dossier on her is incomplete. She has a brother, Paxton, single, who's a civilian specialist with Army G-2 at the Pentagon. They live together in the southeast."

"We know that, Gene," the voice replied. "We just wanted to hear confirmation from you that you're on the job. You may be onto a big one here, and it may take you a while."

Matters proceeded even more slowly than Gene had anticipated. Obviously Fay liked him, which was surprising, for she seemed different from the kind of women who took a quick fancy to him. He wanted to meet her brother, but she frustrated his every attempt. What was the key that would unlock her door? Social life and meeting people did not enchant her. Money meant little to her because she had a lot. She did not seem susceptible to vanity.

One evening after a party at the Statler when he said he would take her home, she replied that she had something to finish at the office. She did not object when he said he would go with her and wait.

She had drunk quite a lot at the party; her face was flushed, her fingers slow as she sat at her typewriter. If he encouraged her drinking, would that eventually win her complete confidence? He prowled the offices restlessly while she typed on slowly. The stacks of locked filing cabinets fascinated him. Burglary of the files might solve the Ormandy case, but burglary seemed impossible in the Senate Office Building.

Gene studied carefully the designations of contents on various drawers until he came to one lettered *Porno*.

"What's porno?" he called to Fay. "Pornography? Does your Senator collect it?"

"Of course not. But he's on that subcommittee investigating it and they have to store the stuff someplace."

He went into her office. "I haven't seen any pornography in years. Let me take a look."

She stared at him. "No. It's confidential material."

"But I'll bet everybody in the office has studied it thoroughly. Including you."

She shook her head. "No, I haven't. I don't *want* to. I've never wanted to look at junk like that. I think it—it must disturb one."

He went to the reception room in search of a magazine to read, and soon Fay called to him. "I unlocked that drawer for you if you want to take a look, but I think it's a—an immature thing to do."

Slowly Gene thumbed through photographs which showed two females and two males in a congress of fellatio, pederasty, and coition, orifices exposed generously to the camera, expressions reflecting passion.

"Wow!" He took the pictures into her office. "Look at these!"

She stopped typing and closed her eyes. "I don't want to."

He had a sudden sense of dominance over her. "Pornography isn't supposed to affect women—only men. Pornography is supposed to be anything that gives a man an erection."

"All right." She opened her eyes and got to her feet unsteadily. Her hand, slowing his as he leafed the pictures, grew damp. She began to breathe quickly and leaned against him.

Perhaps it was her stimulation, perhaps the pictures that roused him.

"It's pornography all right." He sounded breathless. "You can see the proof."

She gazed trancelike at the bulging of his trousers. Her voice came almost incoherently: "You said this stuff doesn't affect women, but it does. I knew it would."

"Then let's lock it up."

"No!" Her right hand stayed his and with her left she timidly traced his bulging.

"Does the Senator have a couch in his office?"

She shrank from him. "I don't do that. I'm a virgin and going to stay one. There's been too much—trouble in my family. I'm afraid of getting pregnant—or getting a disease." But then she reached out and touched him curiously again.

Never had he known a woman to become so excited at sight of his manhood. He said, "You're not a virgin."

"But I am. You can find out for yourself."

She was. After they had spent themselves in twisting, frantic onanism against the filing cabinets, Fay wept quietly. Gene, remembering his deflowering a girl who had cried like this afterwards and refused ever to see him again, was alarmed.

"I'm sorry. You're so wonderful I got carried away

and went too far. But you're all right. I mean you're still —you know."

She stopped crying as suddenly as she had begun. "I think we didn't go far enough. You're the first man I ever saw and felt. I imagined, but I didn't know. I didn't *want* to know."

He found that incredible. "My God, you must have. I mean—well, you have a brother and——"

"What an awful thing to say! Pax and I have the sweetest, rarest relationship that ever existed between a brother and sister. Now take me home."

He cursed himself for having spoiled everything. But to his relief she did not dismiss him when she got out of the taxi; instead, she invited him inside for the first time.

It was a household of expensive furnishings and dim lamps. Someone stirred in the living room.

"Pax? Has Colonel Morgan left?"

"He couldn't come tonight." A blond, handsome young man stepped into the hall, and Fay introduced him. "How are you, Gene?"

It had been a long time since Gene had met such an engaging man. While Fay went for a bottle of champagne, Paxton showed him his collection of rare chess sets in the library. There was a lighthearted enthusiasm for living about him that was almost childlike and made Gene feel old and crass and dull. It was a quality Fay displayed too when at ease at home.

As the days passed, Gene had a growing and altogether pleasurable sense of unreality about his relationship with Fay. It was as if he had discovered a happy adolescence such as he had not in fact enjoyed as a youth. At the same time his discovery involved an invasion of Fay Warner's life, a conscious corrupting of her innocence for the sheer pleasure of corrupting rather than toward the end that had started him on this curious mission.

He had, indeed, almost forgotten the mission when one of the watchers and listeners of the loyal band reminded him:

"You're forgetting you're supposed to get into Senator Ormandy's file drawers, not Fay Warner's lace drawers."

So they were being observed. Was suspicion focusing on him too? Increasingly he feared that he was being watched, for he knew there was a great deal of watching and listening in Washington. Sometimes he dreamed of hidden cameras and microphones and would awaken sweating.

Yet increasingly, too, Fay obsessed him—as he obsessed her. Or perhaps it was the erotic games they played that obsessed both. At first he was the teacher, she the most apt pupil he ever had known. But after a time both became children experimenting together—children because their love games lacked adult fulfillment. He gave up striving for the prize she withheld from him. Vaguely he even saw it her way: to lose her virginity would be to lose the carefree gaiety of childhood.

Always on the fringe of their consciousness was the shadowy, benign presence of Paxton. No one could have seen less—or cared less what they did. Gene believed Pax was a homosexual. But he put aside his belief in his great fondness for him and Fay and this strange liaison that obsessed him.

He realized his work as Bill's assistant was suffering. But he could not bring himself to try to go on with his original purpose until he was thoroughly convinced he was being followed and closely observed.

At last, trying to put it casually, he told Fay he had heard indirectly that there were suspicions about Senator Ormandy's dealings behind the Iron Curtain.

She was angry. "That's ridiculous. There isn't a more

honest and loyal American anywhere. All he's been trying to do is help the families of some of his constituents who are stuck in East Germany and are trying to get out. It's very complicated. He has to deal through sources in Switzerland. The State Department knows all about it and is helping him."

But, alas, most sources in the State Department were suspect to the loyal band.

"You're supposed to have a lot of influence," Fay told him. "Have them take the finger off Senator Ormandy."

"Let me take a look at the correspondence so I have the evidence to present to—*them*."

"No!"

But she relented, and a few nights later they spent three hours together going through the correspondence files. What he read convinced him that Senator Ormandy was innocent of any wrongdoing.

The next day he told Bill so in a closed-door session. But then he realized Bill did not believe him. His consternation turned to anger as Bill began to lecture:

"How far have you really carried your investigation? Are you being taken in? Frankly, Gene, I've been increasingly annoyed with you lately. You're drinking and chasing around too much. Most of the time you don't seem to care whether school keeps or not. . . ."

A couple of evenings later Fay presented him with a gift—a handsome pair of cuff links which had been made to her specifications. The red herring motif was intended as their private joke: the President had characterized the hunt for communists in government as a red herring to divert attention from more important national matters. So much for suspicions about the honest, patriotic Senator Ormandy.

Gene accepted the joke at first, perhaps because the cuff links were so handsome. But on reflection he saw the abandonment of his old principles as like abandoning the helm of a ship in a storm and accepting destruction.

Ceasing to believe in God when I was twelve years old, I ever afterwards was ripe for regeneration. . . .

He tried. He curbed his drinking, avoided Fay, and tried to devote himself to his job. For the first time in months he found himself thinking of Helen. He would become a whole man, and she was the woman to make him so. He would recover the virtues of the midlands— marriage, children, sobriety, hard work.

But then came the evening when Helen said marriage to him was unthinkable. After he left her apartment he went to the Warners' house.

Paxton let him in. He had been crying. It was incredible; Gene could not remember when he had seen a man with eyes red and swollen from tears.

"Pax, what's wrong?"

"What's right, Gene?"

He followed Paxton into the living room where Fay looked at him curiously. A book was opened in her lap. "I was positive you wouldn't be back. But sit down and listen, if you're capable of any pleasure except the sexual."

Gene sank down on a sofa next to Paxton, who ran a hand across his eyes and said, "Read that octave again, Fay."

Fay said to Gene, "We are reading from something entitled 'Atalanta in Calydon.' Do you know the author?"

Gene looked at her dumbly.

"His name was Algernon Charles Swinburne and he lived in the good-bad century called the nineteenth. He was a genius confused in his sexual life. Listen to this—

> 'For winter's rains and ruins are over,
> And all the season of snows and sins;

The days dividing lover and lover,
    The light that loses, the night that wins;
And time remembered is grief forgotten,
    And frosts are slain and flowers begotten,
And in green underwood and cover
    Blossom by blossom the spring begins.' "

Fay read for nearly an hour from Swinburne, the
Rosettis, and, surprisingly, the country-store common sense
of Ralph Waldo Emerson. Gene was not bored for a
moment; he listened raptly, and at the same time he con-
templated his impoverishment of mind and emotion. And
then Paxton, seeming as serene as always, went to bed.

Gene asked Fay what had been troubling him.

"The end of an affair."

"Who was she?" As soon as he said it he realized the
stupidity of the question.

Fay looked at him with surprise and scorn. "You
can't be that dumb. Pax's lover was named Dan. He decided, as he put it to Pax, to try to reorient himself with
his wife and two children."

"My God!"

"What are you my God-ing about, country boy? What
does God have to do with it? Where did you get your
illusions about what's right or wrong, round or square,
straight or crooked? Where did you get your illusions about
yourself?"

"Well—but, you know, a married man with children."

"You know, you know"—her scorn surged—"so he's
Colonel Dan Morgan, an American hero's name and a
hero by his own battlefield right. Assigned to G-2. Does
that mean rats are undermining the bulwark of the Republic? No! It only means there are sad, mixed-up stories
wherever you turn."

"Colonel Dan Morgan!" Somehow the name seemed the most shocking thing of all to Gene.

Fay's expression changed and she leaned toward him. "I got carried away. Nobody knows anything. You forget that name. If you ever repeat it, I—I'll kill you!"

Gene left at once, deeply disturbed, and walked home. Under the rules of the loyal band, he possessed information he should report immediately. Morgan and Pax, serving at the highest level of military intelligence, were deeply involved in the national security. It was axiomatic to all watchdogs that homosexuals were security risks, and when one security risk had a secret relationship with another there existed the threat of a spy ring conspiring against the Republic. So it was Gene's duty as a loyal citizen to report the matter tomorrow.

But he did not, perhaps because he had a horrible dream of Pax chained to a flaming stake, crying piteously, his face contorted torturedly.

He decided to pretend that neither the Warners nor a security risk existed. With all his might he tried to act like the virtuous American his parents had raised him to be. But it was to no avail. For Bill and others in the loyal band had lost faith in him, and he could not do anything right in their eyes. Bill was his enemy—and Gene hated him. Alice and Helen were his enemies too. If a conspiracy existed in Washington it was against *him*.

Three days before Gene's thirty-third birthday he was walking along a corridor of the Senate Office Building when he saw Fay coming toward him. She was half running, and she was crying. He wished he could shrink into a wall of the corridor, but there was no place to hide. As she passed, she sobbed and mouthed an obscenity at him.

That afternoon he read a headline in the final edition of the *Star*:

The story reported that Paxton Warner III, a civilian specialist in military intelligence who had been released from his job two days previously, had returned to his office to pick up some personal belongings and there had hanged himself with a bit of rope suspended from a ventilator duct. . . .

So they had caught him. And they must know that Gene Schofield had let him go. But Fay did not know he had let Pax go, and an eternity of explanations never would convince her that he had.

The next morning's office mail brought him an unsigned note:

Ralph Waldo Emerson sends you this word through Paxton Warner:
He who has a thousand friends has not a friend to spare, And he who has one enemy will meet him everywhere.

That morning Senator William Paisley Porter, who was having one of his irascible days, bawled him out for something or other he had failed to do. For fully ten minutes Gene sat at his desk in a turmoil of rage and despair, then put on his coat and left the Senate Office Building. He never went back.

It was a day of wind and rain, and the view from the western steps of the Capitol afforded only the Mall fading into murk. Yet Gene stood in the rain for a long time and stared west as if seeing something. What he saw after a while was that he had no living friend or relative; he did not love Fay. He hated his job and Washington, for he

[207]

could not go unrecognized here; there was no place to hide.

Leaning into the wind, he walked downtown to the bank where he had a checking account. The balance proved to be three hundred and eighty-seven dollars, his sole financial assets. Pocketing the cash, he went to a bar and had three ryes, drinking them slowly, until he came to a conclusion that pleased him: he never would drink again. Then he walked home.

When he entered his apartment, the telephone was ringing. He did not answer it. For the rest of the afternoon he pawed through his belongings, selecting and rejecting until he began to realize he possessed little of value to him, so little that he could put it all in one suitcase. The phone rang occasionally, but he did not answer. And each time he did not, he felt greatly pleased, as if putting distance between himself and a pursuing enemy.

Gradually he realized he was waiting for something, though he knew not what. At last he understood what it was: darkness. No one must see him leave. For he was going someplace, though he did not yet know where.

His rent was paid until the end of the month, but he decided to leave a cryptic note for his landlord, who was named Mars.

Mr. Mars—
Called away. Will not return. Dispose of my stuff any way you want to.
Eugene Schofield

When it was dark he lugged his suitcase to Union Station. There a new thought occurred to him. He always had been a coward, he never had had the courage to face up to anything unless he could look down at it. But instead of sneaking away from Washington in the darkness, he would have a final confrontation with Bill Porter. Checking his bag, he took a taxi to the Porters' house and paid the driver to wait for him.

Bill listened with startled wonder while he delivered his little speech. He and Bill always had dealt in corn, and apparently they must be corny to the very end.

Bill, glowering, said, "You're fired!"

And Gene, grinning gleefully, replied, "You can't fire me because I've already quit!"

Then, intoxicated with a feeling of happiness, he returned to Union Station and got his suitcase. He did not believe he really knew where he was going as he approached a ticket window.

But all railroad lines end in New York.

In early morning the train slowed to a halt in Trenton. Gene stared through the coach window at a dimly lighted and rainswept platform, trying to ignore the garrulous old man who had boarded at Thirtieth Street in Philadelphia and taken the seat beside his. Through the rain he made out an election campaign poster which had been pasted on a pillar.

JOSEPH P. MCCURDY
FOR FREEHOLDER

Suddenly he laughed sharply, happily.

"What's the matter?" asked the old man. "What do you see?"

"That sign," he said. "Somebody with the same name as mine ran for freeholder here."

There has long been current a journalistic cliché that approximately one million Americans disappear annually. Another cliché holds that detection and law enforcement agencies find at least ninety-five percent of those who disappear. Gene Schofield, having been a Congressional investigator, was familiar with the reports and wondered about their accuracy. What were the chances of his succeeding in becoming another person?

On his first morning in New York he found a furnished room and the right to share an unclean bathroom for ten dollars a week on Hudson Street. At first he oscillated between a fear that he was being followed and joy at no longer being a person he had come to dislike.

His fear subsided, however, once he realized that no one would pursue him because no one cared what became of him. The assumption of a new identity was an absorbing process, involving being born again and growing to maturity within a few reflective days. He always had looked younger than his years, so why should he not be a carefree twenty-two instead of a burdened thirty-three?

The first test of his identity came when he went to the Social Security Administration in Manhattan and told a receptionist he wished to apply for a card. She gave him a form and told him to fill it out. At first glance the questions looked easy. He knew the names of his new parents, of course, and even had worked up a little fantasy about them: his father, Donald McCurdy, had been a captain in the Merchant Marine who went down with his ship in a typhoon off Madagascar; his mother, born Genevieve Cook, had remarried an Alaskan bush pilot and been killed in a plane crash near Point Barrow. Very romantic, exciting people, totally unlike the parents of Eugene Schofield. He had chosen to be born in Los Angeles because the rapid expansion of that city might have led to a confusion of municipal records.

But then he came to the next-to-last question on the form, and his forehead grew damp. Had he ever had a

Social Security card? There was no space for explanations; there were simply boxes to be checked. "Yes" would lead to a possibly fatal investigation. "No" might lead to dangerous questioning about his age. But his enemy, the former sharp interrogator of the investigating committees, offered him a shrewd tip: the most difficult witness always was one who claimed not to know. So he checked the box that said "Don't know."

When he took his form to an interviewer, she glanced over it and said, "Your card will be mailed to you in about ten days."

Faceless people deserved an eyeless government.

When the card arrived in the mail he was elated. Now he had official sanction of the fact that Joseph Patrick McCurdy had been born and come to the prime of young manhood. Future documents would be easy to obtain. He knew of a racketeering office in Washington where for a few dollars one could obtain the most authentic-looking birth certificates, baptismal certificates, divorce decrees— anything you wished except a passport or Social Security card.

His first job was as a pickup man and dishwasher in a Fourteenth Street cafeteria. It had the advantage of being nighttime employment which enabled him to hunt for a worthwhile job during the day. What career did young Joe McCurdy wish to pursue? He hunted signposts in the *Times* classified ads. Gene Schofield might have made a pretty good salesman, but it was a life that Joe McCurdy scorned. He set his sights on advertising because he felt he had creative talent and it seemed an attainable goal. He had just about despaired of achieving it, however, when he finally went to Street, Blazer, Kaufman.

At last, Joseph P. McCurdy was twenty-three years old, gainfully employed, a registered voter of Manhattan in the party which Eugene Schofield and William Porter had always opposed. He did not have a draft card, but he did not look young enough to carry one, so no one ever asked him about it.

There was, however, more convincing proof of his existence than the documents and experience he accumulated. He was deeply in love. He believed that life would not truly come to him unless Hannah Clements became his wife.

Maybe he really was born on the evening he confronted George Kane on the steps outside Hannah's door, holding in his right hand the tightly rolled copy of the *Saturday Evening Post* like a scepter of the sovereignty he finally had won over his doubts and fears.

"Joe," Hannah had said, "tell me about you."

He did, ignoring not a single detail he could remember. When he had finished he realized it sounded like the most improbable story ever told.

But she said, "I believe you. For the first time since I met you, I believe everything you say. I remember reading about Porter and Schofield and all those bastards. I hate them. But I think I'm in love with Joe McCurdy."

12

"*I'm talking to Gene Schofield from Greenleaf!*"

When Ben North uttered the words, McCurdy's heart began to knock. But he managed to reply calmly:

"What are you talking about, Mr. North? Who is Gene Schofield? Where is Greenleaf?"

"Why are you wearing gloves, Gene?"

"The name is Joseph P. McCurdy. I put them on this morning because I have psoriasis, a recurrent infection. Why do my gloves bother you? Because of the meaningless form Mr. Marlowe just handed me? It's gummed. It's fingerprint paper. I came here in good faith. You really are Establishment. Big Brother wants my fingerprints, and so you're cooperating with him. I doubt if you've handled any civil rights cases in your years of remunerative practice. But you must know it's my right not to be printed. I haven't broken any criminal law. You Establishment people love to talk ethics. But how ethical are you really?"

Ben made a wide turn around the table and halted, staring at him.

McCurdy, having observed the slightly opened table drawer in front of the chair where Marlowe had told him to sit, pulled the drawer all the way out and saw a small, delicate microphone wired to a spool. He held up the microphone and smiled at Ben.

Ben came swiftly around the table and snatched the device out of the drawer. Ripping its wire apart, he threw the pieces on the floor and glared at Marlowe.

"This I didn't know about! Did you?"

"Yes, sir."

"Get the hell out of this room!"

Marlowe, pale, hurried out.

Pacing slowly around the table, Ben sat down facing McCurdy in the chair where Marlowe had been seated.

McCurdy asked, "Is tape-recording any worse than fingerprinting?"

"Yes." Ben lighted a cigarette and put his pack within McCurdy's reach. "Prints are admissible evidence. Tapes are not."

"Before you go any further, Mr. North, may I suggest something. Pull open the drawer in front of you and see if there's anything in it."

Ben opened the drawer, and his expression turned from surprise to anger as he took out a recording device. Tearing it apart, he tossed the pieces into a corner of the conference room.

"This is a law office, not a branch of the FBI!" His voice was husky with rage. "You have been wronged. How can it be set right? Do you want to go?" He hesitated for several seconds. "Do you want me to represent you in this —this thing in which you really have no case at all?"

McCurdy took his time in lighting a cigarette, wishing to still the racing of his foolish heart. "Why did you call me Gene Schofield?"

"Just a bluff. No strong cards in my hand."

"Why did you offer to represent me?"

"A quixotic offer. But you know why. Let me ask you a question. Why did you come to this firm in the first place?"

McCurdy grinned. "I'm quixotic too." He hesitated. There was not enough time really to think. And yet there never had been. You rode with your instincts and trusted to luck.

He said, "I was raised in Methodist parsonages by devout parents. Ceasing to believe in God when I was twelve years old, I ever afterwards was ripe for regeneration. That's the way I begin the autobiography I'm writing. Maybe I'll call it 'A Tale of Two Men.' Do I sound crazy?"

Ben stared at him.

"Okay, if you're going to represent me, I have to tell you everything. I used to be Gene Schofield. How did you know, Ben?"

Reaching for an ashtray, Ben moved it agitatedly. "I never would have guessed it. All that weight, the beard. Even your voice has changed."

"But why did you bluff?"

"When I saw you wearing gloves I began to wonder. But the basis for suspicion were those cuff links you loaned Jim. He flew to Washington with Helen, and a friend of hers they met on the plane recognized them. Apparently she gave them to you."

"My God!" McCurdy shook his head in wonder. "Fay Warner, after all these years!"

"No, that wasn't the name. The name Helen mentioned on the phone was Fay Stetson."

"So she got married! I thought she never would. The one thing I know is that she hates me." McCurdy reflected for a moment. "It wouldn't have happened if I'd thrown away those links. But they had—significance to me. I liked to wear them on certain occasions when— Well, coming here to see you on Wednesday was one of those occasions. And it meant a lot to me to give them to Jim. I *like* him, Ben. How's Louise?"

"We're divorced. She's living in Washington."

"So you were ripe for regeneration too. Maybe you should write your autobiography under the same title as mine."

"No danger of that, Gene."

"Ben, my name is Joe. Gene Schofield is dead. Who else besides you did Helen tell?"

"A Presidential adviser she knows who apparently is riding herd on this tax revolt. And I wouldn't be surprised if she told Alice Porter since they're such close friends. And if Alice heard about it, I'm sure Bill did too. But Gene—Joe—what happened? What made you decide to— form a new identity?"

"It's a longer story than you have time to listen to."

"I have time." Ben phoned Miss Thomas and told her he was not to be disturbed for the rest of the morning.

After McCurdy had finished his story, Ben said, "So your wife knows all about it."

"Of course. I wish you knew Hank. She's the most remarkable woman who ever lived. Without her, Joe Mc-Curdy never would have been born and lived happily. There are no secrets, no double-dealing between us—except one. She thinks I have a much more original wit than I really do. The only trace of the bastard Schofield left in me is the way I steal other people's thoughts and phrases and pretend they're mine. You might say that's the advertising business. But it's really Schofield."

Ben smiled. "And your children? Do you plan to tell them someday?"

"They know. They know Papa is not infallible. They

[216]

know that good man Jesus was about the best Jew who ever lived—and nothing else. They know there is no Santa Claus and the stork did not bring the babies. They're good, wise, resilient kids."

"Remarkable."

"But they have a remarkable mother," McCurdy said.

"And she goes all the way with you on this thing?"

"Yes. She's getting a bit tense—as I am. Big Brother can really wear on your nerves when he begins to take a bead on you. But Hank hates him as much as I. She sees Bill Porter and his Administration for what it is, with no reminders from me about times past with Bill. She has an acute ear for pious mouthings that are just double-talk to all but the gullible—who naturally compose the majority of citizens. She sees that Porter acts *cynically*, that he's nothing more than the cleverest, most self-seeking politician who ever made it into the White House. When I finally got to you, Ben, I thought you'd see it that way too. It's why I tried so hard to get to you."

"No, I don't see it that way—uh—Joe. I think Bill is wholeheartedly devoted to the welfare of the country——"

"And its number-one citizen, William Paisley Porter. Wholeheartedly but half-assedly. On the old Wasp theory that what's good for W. P. Porter is good for the country. I thought for sure you secretly felt the same. Has he ever been anything but cynical with you? Using you—and dropping you. Using your firm—and dropping it."

Ben said, "But you forget something. I acted cynically too, for the benefit of myself and the firm, when I got him to come here. He delivered—and left, as I once delivered for him—and left. Speaking of man's cynical acts, Joe, how much do you have stashed away in secret accounts?"

McCurdy opened his mouth, but no words came. He found a cigarette on which to close his lips. Lighting it, he said, "The truth, the whole truth, and nothing but the truth, so help me Hannah." Then he described the financing of the family's escape to a sheep ranch in British Columbia.

Ben said, "Without wishing to indulge in pious mouthings, I'd say there is some cynicism in McCurdy's heart too. It was not that you could not pay, but that you did not want to. Once the 'Ballad of Joe McCurdy' caught on and you found yourself taken up in this high drama of protest, how did you plan to shape it? I mean what was— or is—to be the conclusion?"

McCurdy suddenly felt far older than his fifty-five years, too weary to stir in his chair. At last he said, "I'm trying to tell you the whole truth, and there's something else I forgot to mention. Hank has about seventeen hundred more under an assumed name at the Bowery Savings Bank."

Ben shrugged. "So, as the commercial jingle goes, it pays to save at the Bowery. Is that the end of the drama?"

"Another thing." McCurdy brightened. "I'm appearing on the Ed Sullivan Show Sunday evening. I'm getting four thousand for that."

"On which I'm sure the government will immediately slap a well-publicized lien."

"My God, I never thought of that!"

"But no doubt Internal Revenue has. Joe, you're only one mind against hundreds—to say nothing of the computers."

"I've been thinking"—actually the thought occurred to him at that very instant—"the Sullivan Show is where I'll make the big revelation. You know he has a fifty-million audience. I'll reveal the whole story."

Ben raised his brows. "Like how you're really President Porter's former aide Eugene Schofield?"

"Yes!"

"It certainly would be good publicity for your autobiography. Do you have a publisher?"

"Not yet. Nobody's read it but Hank. It's about two-thirds finished. But it's a natural. I'll bet I can get a twenty-thousand advance on it."

"And you should get a magazine sale from it," Ben said.

His dry tone made McCurdy frown. "You're putting me on."

"You're putting yourself on. Like President Porter and nearly everybody else these days you're talking about nothing but money, money. You still haven't told me the proposed end of the drama. Is it because you don't know what it is yourself? You tell me that the only people who know you used to be Gene Schofield are your wife and children. You hate Gene Schofield. Your identity as Joe McCurdy is the most precious thing you have—so precious that you insist I call you Joe. And you'd blow that for five minutes of self-exposure before fifty million people? To what end? As soon as you revealed who you once were, you'd destroy the myth of Joe McCurdy—and with it the credibility of your protest. As Joe McCurdy you seem invincible to many people. As a disaffected employee Bill Porter once fired you're totally partisan—and vulnerable."

McCurdy twisted his legs about. "I don't know what to do!" Then he leaned forward. "But I do see you're wholly for me."

"I'm for you because I agreed to represent you. And I agreed to represent you because you were done an injustice in this office by an overzealous government act that chills my spine."

"Ben, what would you do?"

"Have you thought of paying your taxes?"

"No!" McCurdy slammed both gloved fists on the table. "Surrender to them now? I'd be a laughingstock!"

Ben spoke mildly. "I don't think you would. You have a ready-made audience Sunday night on Mr. Sullivan's picture tube. You could end the drama with dignity and feeling. Describe how you have been hounded, say you've had it, and are digging up the money to pay your taxes. I think you've been trying to dramatize the omnipotence of government and the impotence of the individual. All right, you have dramatized it. Curtain."

It was a way, McCurdy thought.

Ben said, "Let me call in Muttonhead Marlowe, if he hasn't run off to enlist in the FBI. Don't reveal anything while he's here. I want to see your file and how much you owe."

Marlowe came as cautiously as one entering a cage of lions.

"Chris"—Ben smiled pleasantly—"I want to look into Mr. McCurdy's folder. Thanks." Opening it, he asked, "What's new in the *Post* today? How are all the old and new crises?"

Marlowe, sounding hurt, said, "The White House announced something. The President is going on television and radio at nine on Sunday evening to discuss the tax revolt."

McCurdy began to pant. "Right after the Ed Sullivan Show!"

"Yes," Marlowe said. "He wouldn't want to antagonize people by preempting the Sullivan Show."

Ben, scribbling notes on a yellow pad as he scanned McCurdy's folder, said, "Watch it, Marlowe. You sound like a member of the opposition."

"Mr. North!" Marlowe cried. "I want to tell you something. I *am!* I think it's time I left this firm!"

Ben looked up at him. "You want to take an early lunch? Help yourself."

Marlowe strode out and slammed the door behind him.

"There's hope for that boy yet," Ben said. "He slammed the door. I used to slam doors all the time."

"Nine o'clock!" McCurdy exclaimed. "The President is trying to top me!"

Ben put down his pen, took off his glasses, and ran a hand across his eyes. "I know we're all paranoid, but—Joe, being fifty-five years old, do you ever have trouble in getting away with pretending you're forty-four?"

"Hank doesn't think so."

"That's all that matters." Ben put on his glasses. "Let me finish my arithmetic." At last he said, "Federal, state, and city, with overtime, you owe around six thousand."

"I won't pay it!"

"But you're going to *think* about paying it. I suppose I must make some kind of statement to the press about the fact I now represent you. Did reporters follow you here today?"

"No. Big Brother helped because he planned to frame me here. The tap man must have passed the word I was coming out at six. So the Feds sent any watching reporters off on a wild-goose chase. I was tailed through cafeterias where I drank coffee and read the papers."

"I suppose," Ben said, "they're giving the same treatment to a few chosen others around the country who didn't pay. Now here are my telephone numbers at the office and the unlisted one at home. Give me yours. I expect to hear from you before long, Joe. When you call me just say, 'I've made up my mind.' Then I'll know you've decided to finish this up in the wisest way. I'll come to your apartment with the forms for you to sign."

McCurdy grimaced. "Suppose, by some remote possibility, I decided to pay. How am I going to get the money out of that Canadian savings account on a Friday afternoon?"

"When I bring you the federal, state and city returns, each will include the proper check written on this firm."

McCurdy stared at him. "You'd do that?"

"Of course."

"Why?"

"Maybe because I know you'd pay it back."

"I will—I would."

Ben went with him to the elevator where they shook hands and Ben said, "Keep your gloves on, Joe."

As he returned to his office Ben mulled over the saga of Gene Schofield Joseph McCurdy. He believed all he had heard, believed it so thoroughly that he had no trouble in thinking of that transformed person as Joe McCurdy. Fleetingly he wished there was some friend from the old days with whom he could share the extraordinary story. But, having become McCurdy's counselor, he never would.

He was certain now that McCurdy would pay up and bow out. If he did, he faced nothing more than a slight fine. His incredible story revealed certain things: he had neither conspired with nor counseled others not to pay their taxes. Rather he had joined in a ballad. Even those taped recordings, in which he had gleefully participated a couple of times with others, had simply held government up to ridicule while never urging revolt against it. Like a steer gamboling on the farthest range and happily enjoying the daisies, McCurdy had not visualized the stockyard slaughter at the end of the journey.

It must be the same with most who had refused to pay their taxes—loners all, people in whom hope had been overwhelmed by despair and anger. The country might be destroyed someday not by nuclear war but by inordinate love of the almighty dollar. So much wasted time, so much misdirected effort. It was witnessed specifically in the auto-biography of Gene Schofield Joseph McCurdy—a work begun with the prospect of making money, but to be abandoned in dread of the prospect of loss of identity, that thing infinitely more precious than the dollar.

Ben's own transformation today from friend of government to friend of McCurdy had occurred in angry haste, but he did not regret it. He had been a reluctant friend of the government in its case, and many might think he sliced the ethical too thin in his differentiating between snooping for fingerprints and snooping for a recording of what the subject said. But he found basis for it in the workings of so-called justice.

Now he must square his change of mind with the damned news media. His composition of a brief statement was not easy.

Burton, North, McGinnis, and Mosely announced yesterday that it did not represent Joseph P. McCurdy. Following further consultation with Mr. McCurdy to-day, the firm has decided that it will serve him as legal counsel. For the present this decision will not be explicated.

He signed it, smiling at that fine-feathered legal verb "explicated" and trying not to think of all the questions the statement would raise with newsmen. ("But if you didn't represent him, why were you consulting with him?") Then he gave it to Miss Thomas for distribution and told her he was unavailable to reporters.

His desk was laden with neat stacks of work, but he found it hard to concentrate as his thoughts wandered to the strange lives and times of Joe McCurdy.

About half-past two Miss Thomas told him there was

a call from Jonathan Hochstein at the White House.

"Mr. North, Jack Hochstein here. I'm seeing the President in a little while, and I wonder how the McCurdy thing went."

"Well, Mr. Hochstein, it didn't go at all. I thought once of phoning you, but I can't hold you personally responsible for what happened. Some zealous son of a bitch bugged my office."

"Your office!"

"A conference room of my office."

Hochstein swore.

"So it turns out the firm is now representing Mr. McCurdy."

Hochstein uttered a moaning sound. "Was it necessary to go that far?"

"I thought so. Have you ever had your office bugged while consulting someone who wants to be a client?"

"The President will be upset by your decision."

"Frankly," Ben replied, "I couldn't care less how he feels about it."

Saying it gave him a sense of satisfaction, as if it were something he had wanted to express for a long time. Despite his frequent protests to the contrary, did he harbor resentment of Bill? Where, indeed, could resentment lie more cherished and guarded than within a tightly buttoned Wasp bosom?

Hochstein, hanging up, realized he would have to give the President unpleasant news when he wanted to present nothing but marshaled conclusions.

At precisely three o'clock a secretary phoned and said the President would see him in the Oval Office.

It was raining in Washington at that hour, gently,

persistently. In the Oval Office, however, there was a glow of warm pastel light, as if sun shone eternally on the stacked flags.

"Jack"—the President looked up from his desk—"have you read the proposed speech Harold Garamond sent me?"

"Yes, sir."

"What do you think of it?"

"I think the Senator would make a very effective speech-writer for Senator Blake King."

"Helen Carlton doesn't agree with you. Harold had her read it and she sent me an enthusiastic note. This is the first time in all the years we've known each other that Helen has ever offered me her opinion on anything—political."

So her opinion bore weight with him. It was a gloomy thought to Hochstein.

"Helen seems to have become quite exercised about the tax thing," the President continued. "Alice told me a curious story at breakfast this morning. Helen thinks the great McCurdy might really be an assistant I fired years ago named Gene Schofield. Sounds pretty wild to me. But I'll bet Helen has told you too."

"Yes. And it's being checked out." Hochstein hesitated. "They haven't been able to get McCurdy's fingerprints. So last night I phoned Ben North in New York and he agreed to cooperate with us—reluctantly. But something happened. I talked to him a while ago. They bugged his office. So now he's representing McCurdy."

"They *bugged* Ben's office?"

"Yes. I think he has—uh—overreacted, but . . ."

The President swore.

"I agree," Hochstein said. "But they have to get the prints. We have to establish whether McCurdy has a criminal record or——"

"Well, did they get the prints?"

Hochstein winced. "I don't know yet. I didn't ask North. I—uh—frankly, I *forgot* to ask him. Which shows, I guess, that I'm getting unnerved along with a lot of other people about this crazy revolt."

"Unnerved." President Porter spoke reflectively. "It's unlike Ben ever to be so. But he must have been to take on this McCurdy character as a client." Tipping his fingers together, he stared for a long time at the portrait of Washington. "Well, Jack, I've read your proposed draft of the talk I'll deliver Sunday evening. It's a good one."

Hochstein leaned forward intently. Did he mean it was substantially what he would say on Sunday?

"It's a good one if I take the hard line," the President continued measuredly. "And Harold's is a good one if I take a softer line."

Oh God, another of those waiting and wondering periods! Did President Porter always wait until the very last minute to make up his mind about something vital? Or had he already decided but was remaining secretive about it?

"I'm going to stay here this weekend and work at my talk. I hope you haven't any personal plans, for I'd like you here too, passing me all important information."

"I'll be here," Hochstein said.

"Naturally there are many more vital issues involved than McCurdy. But if anything significant about him is uncovered, let me know at once."

After McCurdy left Ben's office he strode along Pine Street, relieved and pleased.

You've been trying to dramatize the omnipotence of government and the impotence of the individual. All right, you have dramatized it. Curtain.

He would do it! The check from the Ed Sullivan Show would almost pay the delinquent taxes. And "A Tale of Two Men," like many nobler works of art, would remain unfinished. What except the euphoria of being a McCurdy who could challenge a Porter in the White House had made him undertake writing it? Ben had been right when he said that his identity as Joseph P. McCurdy was the most precious thing he possessed.

Smiling happily, McCurdy came to Broadway. The traffic light was changing as he started across the street, but he scampered on. Like every gamboling citizen of Fun City, he had learned to take his chances.

The cop seemed to come from nowhere. Suddenly he was at McCurdy's side, saying, "Hold it!"

McCurdy grinned at him. "Well, I made it without creating a traffic jam."

But the cop did not smile. He said, "We're cracking down on jaywalkers." His face had no more character than a side of meat; he was just a faceless cop.

McCurdy, alarmed suddenly, said, "Okay, then give me the ticket."

"We aren't giving tickets," the cop said, "we're taking 'em in."

McCurdy's legs felt like Jell-O and his voice left him. People were jaywalking across Pine Street, but no one was taking them in. All over Manhattan thousands of people were racing lights, but only one was being taken in. If they didn't get him in the financial district, they'd get him on Murray Hill. And if they missed him there, they would catch him somewhere else. There was no fathoming how they managed it once they put themselves out to pull him in. The picture had been framed, and in the center was not Joe McCurdy but Gene Schofield.

His glance darted about, seeking an escape, and then he saw a patrol car at the curb and two cops coming from it. His hands fluttered helplessly as he started to turn away.

Hands seized him roughly and a voice, sounding angry and distant, said, "Resisting, eh? Frisk him. . . ."

The charge at the precinct was resisting arrest. Or maybe it was assaulting an officer. Everything had become vague to McCurdy.

Finally a voice came through to him, a voice as persuasive as an evangelist's, and the words sounded the most hypocritical he ever had heard:

"Now listen to what I say. I'm telling you what are your legal rights. You don't need to give any information except your name and address. . . . Okay, fingerprint him and put him in a cell."

McCurdy curled his gloved hands and clenched them tightly.

"*Print* him!"

13

It was almost midnight when Ben led the way from Night Court through a corridor that reeked of sweat and stale apples. McCurdy, eyes filled with tears, came behind him.

Rita, waiting behind the wheel of the car, unlocked the door, and Ben said, "Joe, this is my wife, Rita—Joe McCurdy. Climb in the back. Rita, you drive."

"You say you phoned Hannah?" McCurdy's voice was choked.

"Yes. She and the kids are okay and waiting for you."

"That goddamn judge with his phony lecture about losing my temper on the street. I *didn't!* I told you I *didn't!* It was a total frame-up. Was the judge in on the plot too?"

"No. Just be glad he let you go. I thought he was rather sympathetic. He felt he had to say something, and when a judge feels he has to say something all he knows to do is give a pious lecture. He released you, dismissed the charges. Maybe he cheats on his income tax returns too."

Rita asked, "Were reporters there?"

"No. I understand they usually don't bother to cover

Night Court unless tipped off about a hot case. And the police aren't tipping off on this one."

McCurdy said, "The cop who testified I resisted arrest — He *lied!* You could see it on his face he was lying."

"Yes, Joe, you and I could see it."

"And they won!" McCurdy cried. "They got the fingerprints, and by this time— They ripped my gloves to shreds and my hands are so sore I can hardly move them."

Rita glanced curiously at Ben, but she did not speak. This was law as he never had practiced it; fleetingly he wondered if ever again he would care about the outcome of a corporate merger case when the really significant action lay between omnipotent government and the impotent individual. Well, government had won again, and Joe McCurdy had lost his identity.

"We'll drop you at your home," Ben told him, "and in the morning you and I had better get together and figure what next."

"What next?" McCurdy's tone was bitter. "I decided that as soon as they printed me. We—Hannah, the kids, and I—are getting out of this country and never coming back. I'll send you the tax money, but we're *going!* Before morning."

"I understand how you feel, Joe, but you're moving too fast. They're still—" Ben hesitated, reluctant to utter banal words about being followed. Maybe, however, the words expressed accurately the banality of the age.

McCurdy looked through the rear window. "Mrs. North, isn't that car following us?"

"I don't know," Rita said. "I can't tell."

"Circle around the next block and you'll know."

Rita circled the block while McCurdy and Ben looked back. It was true that a Chevrolet station wagon was following them.

"You see what I mean," Ben said. "If you try to run now, you'll be followed all the way and maybe— Dear God, what's come over this country?"

"Say it." McCurdy's tone was more cheerful. "Stopped at the border."

"Yes."

"But not if they don't know where we're headed. Not if we can get out of this damn city without their knowing it. And we can if you'll help. Will you?"

"Of course, if that's what you really want to do."

"Then do what I tell you. I want you to go to our apartment. Stop at that phone booth on the next corner, Mrs. North. I'll phone Hannah and tell her you're coming to see her and to do what you say. . . ."

When McCurdy went to the phone booth, Rita said dryly, "And I'd always thought you had the dullest law practice in town."

Rita turned left at Thirty-fourth Street, then south on Second Avenue. The Chevrolet station wagon followed them. When she stopped in front of Campbell's Bar and Grill, it stopped too.

"Thanks, Ben." McCurdy rested a hand on his shoulder. "Thank you, Mrs. North. Ben, tell her the whole story when you have a chance. So long."

McCurdy climbed out, and Ben watched a man leave the station wagon and follow him into Campbell's. As Rita circled east and north, the station wagon came after them. She stopped near McCurdy's apartment house and said, "I'll pick you up here later—I hope."

When Ben stepped into the lobby, four young men looked at him curiously and the doorman asked, "Can I help you, sir?"

[231]

"I'm going to the McCurdy apartment, Twenty-four B."

"They're not seeing anybody."

"But I'm expected. I'm Mr. McCurdy's attorney. The name is North."

Three young men came to him while the fourth, an agent presumably, watched him alertly.

"I'm from the *Times*, Mr. North—"

"AP, Mr. North—"

"The *Daily News*. McCurdy isn't up there, we understand. Where is he?"

"I'll have something to say about that in half an hour or so," Ben replied. "I'll answer your questions in the lobby after I've talked to Mrs. McCurdy." He turned to the doorman. "Please ring her and tell her I'm coming up."

Ben's tension grew almost unbearably as the automatic elevator ascended, surely more slowly than any in the city. If the government had placed a corridor watch on the McCurdy apartment, the plan was hopeless—they would have to try something even more farfetched. The elevator door opened, and he stepped into a carpeted hallway. It was empty. He saw that, like every recently built high-rise, the building had two enclosed fire exits. Going first to one and then the other, he opened the doors. There was no sign of anyone. Then he went to the door of 24B, rang the bell, and stepped back so that he could be clearly observed through the peephole. Its faint light became clouded and he said, "Mrs. McCurdy, I'm Ben North."

When he stepped inside he confronted a woman who, he knew at once, possessed extraordinary strength. It was implicit in her face, her body. She dispelled his lingering doubts about her part in the mad birth of Joe McCurdy.

"I'm Hannah McCurdy, Mr. North. Where's Joe?"

He touched a finger to his lips, and suddenly was

amused by his conspiratorial role. As McCurdy had directed him to do, he pointed to the television set. Hannah turned it on loud to a movie perhaps thirty years old: penitentiary prisoners were beating spoons on dishes in protest of something. On a sofa beyond the television set, Pete and Patricia McCurdy bore the expectant expressions of children seeing something destroyed and something new begin.

"Joe was fingerprinted, Mrs. McCurdy, after a phony arrest. By this time he must have been identified in Washington as Gene Schofield. He's free, and my wife and I left him at a place on Second Avenue he knows well."

"Campbell's?"

"Yes. He was followed in there. He knew he would be. He's going to order a drink at the bar and then go to the men's room. But he knows his way out a back door. So he'll shake off the man following him. He'll meet you and the children at the garage where you parked your car."

"We're leaving for Canada?"

"Yes."

The children grinned at each other.

"But how can we get out of the building without being seen and followed?"

"There's one risky chance." He took from a pocket the key which McCurdy had given him and handed it to her. "Joe asked me to pass this along to you. He got it from one of the porters a couple of days ago. It's to the sub-basement door which opens on the areaway."

"Yea!" exclaimed Pete, slapping both hands on the sofa.

"My wife is waiting in our car for you on Thirty-sixth Street." He described the car and told her its license number. "She'll take you to the garage where Joe will be waiting. He specified one thing. Don't take any luggage.

Just jewelry, coats, and important papers. And he asked you to bring his manuscript. You must be very careful when you come out the door and the areaway. I'll be in the lobby talking to reporters and I hope I can attract curious agents."

"Decoy," Pete said.

Ben smiled at him. "Son, you know your melodrama. But so does your father." He turned to Hannah. "Something occurs to me that didn't to Joe. I don't know how you both are fixed for cash, but I have plenty. Here's three hundred. One other thing. You'll lose everything in this apartment since Joe says you're never coming back. The state or federal government will levy it—whichever gets to it first, I presume. Is there anything of great personal value I can try to salvage and send to you?"

Hannah McCurdy shook her head slowly. "No—and that seems odd. But Joe told me about going through this same thing once a long time ago. Nothing matters now except him and Pat and Pete."

"Then get your things together quickly, Mrs. McCurdy."

She swung to her feet, gazing at him. "Joe trusted you, Mr. North. Now I see he was right. You're too decent ever to have been a friend of William Porter's."

"Times change. Maybe Bill Porter realizes it—and maybe he doesn't. Now get your things."

When she and the children returned to the living room, she carried only her purse and a large manila envelope. Telling her to leave the television set on loud and come out in a moment, he went into the corridor. It was empty. After checking the exit stairways again, he pressed the Down button as Hannah McCurdy and her children came out quietly. There were tears in her eyes, but she was trying to smile.

Everything seemed to be taking an agonizing length

of time. Ben expected an agent to appear from someplace at any moment and accompany them silently. Yet luck seemed to hold, for one of the two elevators finally arrived—and no one was in it. They stepped into it and Hannah pressed the sub-basement button. None of them spoke as they tensely watched the descending floor level numbers light up. At last the door opened on a dimly lighted sub-basement corridor. Ben held the door while Hannah McCurdy gripped his hand for a moment, and then she and the children were gone without a word.

He ascended two flights in the elevator and stepped into the lobby.

"There he is!"

A score of men milled about; NBC had a TV camera set up; photographers and radio reporters jostled for advantageous spots. Had the scene drawn all of the agents working on the stake-out?

"I'll make a general statement before answering questions. . . . Some overly zealous federal agents planted hidden microphones in my office today before I began to confer with Joseph P. McCurdy. . . . After Mr. McCurdy left my office he was arrested by members of the New York police force on a jaywalking charge which was blown up to a resisting arrest charge—falsely, I maintain. Mr. McCurdy has just been freed. . . . Without discussing the merits of his tax case, I feel he is being persecuted unmercifully. . . ."

"Where is he now, Mr. North?"

"I don't know. But I presume that the agents who have been hounding him for days know where he is."

At last the questioning ended, and he went out. Hurrying down Thirty-sixth Street, he saw his car at the curb. It appeared to be in the same spot where he had left it with Rita. She rolled down the window and looked up at him.

"What happened?" he demanded. "Didn't they come out of the building?"

"Of course they did. I took them to the garage. Joe McCurdy was waiting there. And then they drove away. No one followed them."

At that hour in Washington, Fay Stetson asked Helen for the second time within a few minutes, "You really think Hochstein will drop around?"

"I'm positive. He promised, and he doesn't break promises."

Fay had gone to the theater with Helen and then returned home with her in the hope of hearing what Hochstein had learned about the mystery of Joe McCurdy. Hochstein would stop by after he left the White House around midnight, Helen had said.

Once upon a time Fay would have delighted in exposing and humiliating Gene Schofield in any way possible. But that had been years ago under circumstances she wished to forget. Whether or not Gene had established a new identity, she certainly had succeeded in doing so. If she once had been as ill in her way as Paxton had been in his, she now was well. Perhaps analysis had helped her, but dear Denton with his gentle ways had been of greater help. Their son had lived only eight days, but from his conception, birth, brief life, and death Fay Warner Stetson had emerged as a whole woman.

Why wish anything less for anyone else, including Gene? In truth, she wished him only well. Especially she wished the rebel Joe McCurdy well because he had had the insanity to stand up against the insanity of the times. Last night and today she had become deeply disturbed over what she had done.

She said it aloud now, "I wish I could learn to keep my big fat mouth shut."

Helen looked at her curiously. "You regret tracing the cuff links?"

"I regret it so much, Helen, that I hope I've led the Administration on a wild-goose chase."

"Why?"

"Well, for one thing I'm not greatly fond of this Administration. But there's something else. You said it yesterday in quoting Senator Garamond. We aren't what we were, and why shouldn't we have the right to our new identities? But curiosity made me do it."

The bell chimed, and Dave let in Hochstein.

"Hochy!" Helen started toward him, then introduced Fay. "*Tell* us! The suspense is killing us."

Hochstein poured himself a brandy. "The suspense is killing *me!*"

"Then you still don't know if McCurdy is Gene Schofield?"

"That I know." Hochstein sniffed his brandy. "That has been established. He is. They have the same fingerprints."

"Oh damn!" Fay's tone rose in a wail.

Hochstein looked around at her, and Helen sank into a chair.

"You've told Bill?"

"Naturally."

"And Ben knows?"

"I'm not telling him. But he's a smart lawyer, and I imagine he's found out by some means or other."

"Mr. Hochstein"—Fay spoke unsteadily—"if you know that McCurdy was Gene Schofield, what is it you *don't* know? What suspense is killing you?"

Hochstein sipped his brandy. "I don't know whether

the President will use the information on Sunday evening to dissipate the myth of the invincible Joe McCurdy. I *think* he will, but——"

"You mean," Helen said, "you don't yet know in which direction he'll go?"

"That's right. And I don't think I'll know till late on Sunday."

Fay said, "It doesn't matter much what line he takes. He can't possibly be reelected President."

Hochstein sat down slowly and frowned at her. "Now what makes you say that, Mrs. Stetson?"

"Helen has told me about the direction she and Senator Garamond recommend instead of his typical hard line. But I don't think it matters. The country wants a change, and it's too late for him to make an overnight change in his attitudes and make them stick convincingly. He is what he is. And the majority of people want something different, I believe. No man could have done a better job in the routine of the Presidency than William Porter. But capable executives, good presidents of all sorts of things are a dime a dozen these days. That's not what the country wants. It wants a very human hero—a dream—an aura—pie in the sky."

Hochstein sat staring into his glass. He never did reply to her. Did his silence imply agreement?

Not long after Hochstein took Fay home, Jim North came in.

He had dropped Penny at the White House about midnight and since then had been driving around the city in the car he had borrowed from Helen. There was something he must decide, but driving had not helped him.

"Did you and Penny have a good time?" asked Helen.

[238]

"Yes." He sprawled in a chair. "And then again no. I think she had a good time, but I didn't really."

She looked at him with the worried expression of one trying to solve a problem. It was the way his mother looked at him. In fact, almost every aging person he knew cast that expression at him—except his father. The thought was related to the decision he must make. He was attracted to Penny, but repelled by her family, her way of life. So what was really so difficult about the decision?

"Thanks for loaning me your car, Aunt Helen. I certainly wasn't riding to hear Charlie Bird in a White House limousine."

"You didn't have to bring the car back tonight."

He had spent the previous night at his mother's apartment; he would bet ten to one she was sitting up even this late waiting for him, and so he was in no hurry to get back there.

"Jim, I can understand how it's not pleasant to have everyone gawking at you when you're with the President's daughter. But—" Helen paused.

"But what?"

She sighed. "Strike out the 'but.' I understand, period. By the way, Jack Hochstein just gave me some news. It turns out Joe McCurdy is Gene Schofield. His fingerprints prove it. Isn't that fascinating?"

"Frankly, Aunt Helen, I don't think it's fascinating. It just strikes me as sad. I met McCurdy. I liked him. He did a decent, generous thing when he gave me his cuff links. And for that he must be crucified?"

She went on the defensive. "I don't think he's being crucified. For one thing, he has a good lawyer. Hochy said your father is representing him."

"Pop is? Does he know McCurdy used to be Schofield?"

"We're not sure. I suppose I'd better call him in the morning and tell him. At the same time I don't like to violate the confidence of the White House."

The confidence of the White House! The restraint that accompanied power was as stifling as a death mask. His father had said once, with a measure of sorrow rather than disdain, that Helen had wanted to be a significant writer but had settled for becoming a rich and influential woman instead. So if you were going to be the compeer of Presidents, you must learn to put down your friends and guard your confidences.

Jim got to his feet. "Aunt Helen, knowing Pop as well as I do, I'll bet he's representing McCurdy for just one reason above all. He must have learned that McCurdy used to be Schofield but wants to forget he was ever anyone but Joe McCurdy. That's the one great thing about Pop. He has undying respect for the idea that people should be what they want to be."

She looked at him again with that expression of worry and puzzlement, and then he wondered if the worry and puzzlement were directed at herself.

"I'm going to head for Mother's apartment. Hope I didn't keep you up too late."

"You're going to *walk?* I'll have Dave McKenna drive you."

"I'm going to *walk*, Aunt Helen. No problem."

As he walked along the dark and deserted streets of Georgetown, he knew that indeed there remained no problem at all.

Ben and Rita had planned to spend the weekend at their house on Long Island. But that had been before the world seemed to have turned upside-down to Ben.

In the early morning hours of Saturday he was

troubled by insomnia for the first time in years. Lying awake, he decided they would not go to Long Island. They would stay here in their apartment while he waited for something. But what was it? Some word from Joe McCurdy on whether he had passed safely across the border? Some word on how President William Paisley Porter would cope with the tax revolt and present the case of Gene Schofield Joseph McCurdy?

At ten minutes after six he went to the kitchen in his pajamas. He was frying a pan of bacon when Rita appeared, hair rumpled and looking downright haggard.

"Ben, there's a question I forgot to ask you when you told me the story. Can McCurdy be extradited from Canada—if he gets there?"

"Yes, but he won't be. Because I personally am paying his tax bills if he doesn't send me the money. The interesting thing is that I never liked Gene Schofield any more than he liked himself. But I'm fond of Joe McCurdy."

They were drinking a third cup of coffee and pretending to read the *Times*. Actually, however, Ben knew that Rita, like himself, was simply killing time while waiting for something as yet unknown to happen.

Looking again at his photograph in the newspaper, he said, "My God, I look old."

"You do not. You just look handsome."

The ringing of the telephone brought him to his feet.

"Pop, did I wake you up?"

"No, old buddy. I just ate a lot of greasy bacon and am enjoying heartburn. How are things?"

"I'm at Mother's apartment. She's not up yet. You know how she always sleeps late."

"I know."

"Pop, I think I'll get out of Washington. I hate this place."

"I never was very fond of it either," Ben said.

"What are you and Rita doing this weekend?"

"Just sitting around waiting to hear from you."

"Do you both feel like going out to Long Island and taking me along?"

"Yes!"

"Pop, Aunt Helen says you're representing Joe Mc-Curdy. Do you know he used to be Gene Schofield?"

"Yes, Jim, I know. In fact, that's why I took his case."

"No kidding! I thought it might be something like that. Some slave of Porter's told Aunt Helen about it, and I wasn't sure if she'd let you know. She's a nice old gal in a lot of ways, but she gets more Establishment by the day and you really can't trust those people. I'll take the eleven-o'clock shuttle. Have to say so-long to Mother and call Aunt Helen."

"We'll pick you up at the Eastern desk at La Guardia and go on from there."

"Do you understand why I can't stay here any longer?"

"You bet I do. Run, Jim, run, just as fast as you can!"

After Ben hung up he said to Rita, "Now *that* was the call I've been waiting for."

Yet he was waiting for another. He recognized it when it came just before Rita and he left for La Guardia.

"Ben, this is Helen. Jim called me and said he's going back to New York. I have the feeling something's wrong, though I don't know what it is. Except, maybe, that he's broken Penny Porter's heart."

"Well, Helen, at least he hasn't broken her mother's heart. And he certainly hasn't broken his own."

She was silent for a time. Then, "Ben, there's something I must tell you because we're so close. The government has proved Joe McCurdy is Gene Schofield."

"Was, Helen, *was* Gene."

Again she fell silent. "Then you knew?"

"Of course. That's why I took his case. Helen, Joe McCurdy hates Gene Schofield. His identity as McCurdy means everything to him. It's water under the bridge now, but I don't see why you ever messed around with the question."

Sadly rather than angrily she said, "What you mean is that it really was none of my damn business."

"Yes, Helen, I mean something like that."

"I see what you mean, Ben." Then, ever trying to look on the brighter side of things: "Well, I'm glad I told you. And I'm glad you already knew. Now I don't feel I've violated a White House confidence. You and I are the best of friends, as my call must prove. But I wouldn't want to violate government confidence."

"Right, Helen, right. A girl can't be too careful."

14

Joe and Hannah McCurdy and their children finished
dinner about seven o'clock on Sunday evening in the
restaurant of a motel on the outskirts of Toronto. Then
they returned to their rooms and turned on the television set.

At eight o'clock they located the Toronto channel
which carried the Ed Sullivan Show and all leaned forward, watching intently. There were jokes, music, dancing,
laughter, but they waited in vain for some word as to
why Joseph P. McCurdy failed to appear.

"Well," McCurdy said as the show faded off the air,
"it's good to see they're glad to forget. That's show business. And now we're at the witching hour—the President
Porter hour. Anybody taking odds on what he'll say?"

Hannah said, "He's going to blast you, Mac. He's
going to blast everybody who has dared to protest against
his all-powerful government."

"Pa," Patricia said, "maybe he'll do what Ed Sullivan
did. Maybe, like Sullivan, he'd just as soon forget the
whole thing."

Pete shook his head. "No. It'll be the same old blah-blah-blah."

"Quiet!" ordered McCurdy. "Here we go!"

There was a dirge of music and onto the screen came an old and dreadful movie called *The Sins of Rachel Cade*.

Cursing, McCurdy lunged to the set. He twisted the channel dial frantically, but nowhere could he find the voice or image of President William Paisley Porter.

Swinging to the radio, he turned it on full blast and worked through the full spectrum of stations without catching even a whisper of the President's familiar voice.

He dashed outside, his family hurrying after him, and snapped on the car radio. "Buffalo!" he bawled. "We got Buffalo yesterday! It's only a few miles from here. Where's Buffalo?" He could not find it.

Flinging himself out of his car, he trotted into the motel lobby and slapped his sore hands on the reservations desk. "Listen!" he shouted at a startled clerk. "President Porter is on television and radio in a nationwide hook-up and we can't get him! What's wrong here?"

The clerk took a step back, then shrugged. "Who cares, sir? This is Canada."

ABOUT THE AUTHOR:

Charles Mercer has been a President-watcher since 1939, when he became a reporter for the Washington *Post* after graduating from Brown University. For many years he was with the Associated Press, first as a reporter, and then as a feature writer and columnist before becoming a free-lance writer. Mercer served as an army intelligence officer in the Southwest Pacific during World War II and was recalled to active duty during the Korean War. He has published many stories and articles in national magazines besides writing novels and books of nonfiction. At present he and his wife live in New York, where he is an editor with a publishing house. *Revolt in April* is his thirteenth novel.